Princess of Darkness

Jennifer L. Kelly

This is a work of fiction. All of the characters, organizations, and events portrayed in this novel are either products of the author's imagination or are used fictitiously.

Copyright © 2023 Jennifer L. Kelly
BoxerBull Books
Cleveland, Ohio
All rights reserved.
ISBN-13: 978-0-9992017-6-3

Dedication

To everyone who reads my books or has read my books—sorry for the delay on this one.

In Memoriam

Menis "Mennie" Ann—my precious first fur baby. I know you sent me Sunshine and we are both eternally grateful. Thank you for watching over us in Spirit.

Prologue

The mirror had to be lying.

Since when had the folds of her skin become as rigid as the lines of tree bark? The once youthful color of her face had faded to a whitish gray hue. Even her hair had finally lost its luster from a deep shiny green to a muddy shade of seaweed.

The tiny buds that usually ran across her forehead were wilted and brown. Even the baby's breath that usually wound around her temples and across her crown were brittle, crumbling away at the tiniest gesture.

Her fingers were clumsy as she braided her waist length hair.

But the worst part of the reflection staring back at her, wasn't the skin or the hair, or even the deep grooves that hugged the sides of her mouth.

It was the eyes that looked back at her.

Once a deep, crystalline blue, the color had turned so faint that the whites and the irises were barely distinguishable. The non-color gave the creature looking back at her a vacant, dead look.

She knotted her hair to tie off the braid and pushed back from the vanity.

She had had enough.

How long had it been? Centuries? Millennia? Long enough that she had lost all sense of time. Days seemed like years, seconds like hours. Time didn't matter when your life was merely standing still.

She moved to the window, pushing aside the gauzy white curtains.

It was dawn, but the sky was an angry bruised color. The normal pinkish-orange of the rising sun had been traded for a deep purple and dark blue.

The field surrounding her house was empty, as it usually was. The road was far enough away that cars could not be heard and were nothing but mere specks as they passed by.

Her house was in the center of the field, and the field was surrounded by a forest. A forest that was enchanted to keep passersby far, far away.

She squinted. Except for right now.

In the distance she watched as a single headlight made its way across the field.

She huffed under her breath, but continued to watch.

The motorcycle slowed down near the edge of the forest, eventually coming to a stop.

She let out a sigh of relief. It was quite annoying when they came roaring through, shaking her very foundation and knocking pictures straight off the wall. She crossed her arms and glared out the window, even though the visitors paid her no mind. They never did. It was as if they didn't even know she was there. The nerve!

The hellhound swung his leg off the motorcycle and extended his hand to the girl on the back, but she waved him off. The hellhound shrugged as the girl hopped off the back, tightening a backpack across her shoulders.

The girl was slender and tall, but not as tall as the hellhound who was broad across the shoulders and tapered at the waist. He was dressed as if it were summer and not as though it was nearing the first day of winter.

His arms were marked with tattoos, visible since he was only wearing a t-shirt.

The girl, on the other hand, was wearing a long black coat, knitted beanie, and boots that hit her mid-calf. She shifted from foot to foot as the hellhound said something to her. Whatever he said made him laugh, the whites of his teeth catching the morning light. But the girl did not laugh. Instead she shoved him in the shoulder and began to march into the woods.

The hellhound's shoulders slumped slightly, as though he had been trying to impress the girl and had failed. He gave his precious motorcycle a final glance, then trudged reluctantly after the girl.

She let the curtains fall back over the window.

There was only one girl who was accompanied by a hellhound. Hades' daughter, Victoriana. The last several months, that was the cause of the incessant shaking and rumbling of her home. Hades' child had one foot in the under realm and one foot in the above realm.

She moved to the small stairwell, taking the stairs slowly and carefully. When she first lived here, she could practically float up the stairs. But the magic was thinning and it was exhausting to use it.

At the top of the stairs was a small room. Every wall covered in books.

The ceiling was all glass giving her a 360° view of the sky.

Lightning crashed and a single bird flew across the sky, silhouetted black against the rising sun. The sun was hazy and barely visible against the ominous gray clouds. Good. She'd had enough of staring at Apollo as of late.

This was all his fault and she'd grown weary of it.

She ran her gnarled, root-like fingers along the spines of the books. Each spine had a neat, hand-written three or four digit number.

They used to all be in numeric order, but on days of great boredom she would pull them out and re-read them, often too lazy to put them back. Normally, she would eventually have a cleaning day where she'd tidy them all up, putting them back in their proper place. But she hadn't done that in a while because she felt tired and weak.

She finally found the one she was looking for in a small stack on the desk that was in the center of the room. The desk was made of her own wood and carved by her own hand. Its chair was a rich emerald leather. A gift from Hades and one of the few reasons she tolerated the constant disruptions from the under realm.

Having found the volume she wanted, she slowly lowered herself into the soft leather chair. She flipped through the book, its scent of fresh cut grass, vanilla, and musk washing over her. Her fingers found the page.

She picked up a pair of glasses—another gift from Hades—and began to read. It was through the reading that she remembered.

Today is the day. Zeus has agreed to it. I am not sure if it is the right decision, but I am not sure what choice that I have. It is not often that a human girl refuses a god. Especially a god like Apollo. Let this journal serve as a reminder. No, not a reminder, a remembrance. A remembrance of who I am and who I was. My name is Daphne. I am a mortal. I am sixteen years old. My life was normal. I love the outdoors and living with my mother in our small cottage. I am a wonderful seamstress and have a green thumb. I love animals and my horse Cayenne. But now things must change. Zeus said it is nothing that I did. Apollo fancies who Apollo fancies, whether or not the object of his affection reciprocates. He is egotistical and selfish. He said if I did not return his love, then he would take everything I love away. After Cayenne drowned with Sister upon her back—and pray tell how exactly does a horse and a girl who is an excellent swimmer drown???—I knew I could no longer do this alone. And that something had to be done. So I prayed to Zeus and he answered. We made a deal. Don't ever forget: your name is Daphne.

Her shoulders slumped and she pushed the book away. A single crystalline tear rolled down her cheek. Daphne. That had been her name. She closed her eyes remembering. She'd been young and beautiful with long blonde hair that fell to her waist and she had sky blue eyes. Her mother used to say surely she could not be her child and must be the child of Demeter or Persephone. The rest of the village could always count on Daphne for a smile and a kind word.

The first time she'd seen Apollo, he'd been strumming a lute at the fountain in the village square. Thinking him a beggar, she'd tossed some coins and a couple of flowers at his feet. Her kindness had been the beginning of her end.

Being beautiful and kind had once been her curse.

But now she understood that she had only traded one kind of curse for another.

Thunder boomed and the glass above her head rattled. But soon this curse would end once and for all.

Chapter One

Vic

The pull was irresistible.

Its blackness was as dark and deep as the bottom of the ocean. If it wasn't so frightening, it would be mesmerizing.

A high-pitched howling sound emitted from the gigantic black hole—too high for regular human ears to hear it. But Vic was not a regular human.

She tightened the rope that was encircled around her waist. The other end was tied several times around a large oak tree. Surely a tree that had been around for a century or two, and survived tornadoes and blizzards and whatever else Olympia had experienced over the years, was strong enough to keep Vic from disappearing into the gigantic black hole that now loomed before her.

"Are you sure this is a good idea?" asked Asher.

The hellhound held the end of a leather tether, the other end also wrapped around Vic's ankle.

"Of course it's not a good idea," she replied.

And it wasn't.

In fact, it was a horrible idea. One of the worst she'd ever come up with, which is why she'd asked her childhood friend Asher for help, instead of her boyfriend Callum. Cal wouldn't understand. He thought things through. He was logical and preferred to have a plan.

But this was also incredibly dangerous. And she knew that he would not approve of the idea. Neither would her father or the rest of the council. To them, they had all the time in the world. They had seen millennia of towns and people come and go, but Vic liked this town. She liked its people. So she was prepared to do anything to protect it.

"So you understand what to do?"

Asher gave her a bored look, carefully studying the intricate tattoos scrawled across his knuckles. "Blah blah. Too close. Blah blah. Pull you back."

Vic snorted.

She had known Asher since she was a child, and the hellhounds were her family's most trusted protectors. In her early teens she'd dated Asher, but he was not predictable—no hellhound was—and if Vic's life had taught her anything, it was that she needed predictability and consistency.

Nevertheless, she trusted him with her life. And her life was exactly what was on the line right now.

She rolled back her shoulders and took in a deep breath.

On the exhale, she released the tension from her shoulders, allowing them to relax. As she did so there was a sound like the snapping of sails on a ship. The bones of her shoulder blades twisted and crunched. It felt as though her body were being ripped in half.

And just as soon as the feeling had started it ended.

Her wings unfurled and she tested them, giving them a couple of fluid beats with the slightest movement of her shoulders.

She'd been working on mastering her newly found appendages. It wasn't every day that even the gods sprouted wings—at least not anymore.

Hades had concluded that they'd grown out of a necessity laced with desire. The DNA had been there—Hades had wings of his own—lying dormant for the right moment to manifest. Being the daughter of two gods, one was often endowed with certain gifts and abilities. Her affinity was for dreams. The wings seemed to be a bonus.

Considering her boyfriend, Cal, was born of the night and the sky, it seemed fitting that she should have wings with which to transverse the domain of which he was a part.

Her wings were black and leathery—resembling that of a bat's. The bat charm, a gift from her mother, hung at the base of her throat and was now a fitting symbol for what she considered her true identity. If only her teachers at Olympia High could see her now!

She flapped again and allowed her wings to lift her a few inches off the ground. She'd been practicing. Mastering the feel and movement, how the wind felt when it provided lift. How to get off the ground, and stay off the ground. How to land without breaking an arm or a leg.

The air was brisk and held the crisp scent of a promising snow. But her coat lay in a bundle over her back pack on the forest floor.

Vic tested the rope around her waist one more time, then satisfied, urged her wings to lift her higher. It was not unlike learning to walk, the feeling of being unbalanced, and the need to urge one foot in front of the other.

The tether around her ankle felt slack as she soared higher above the tree line.

Her ears clogged as she rose in altitude. She plugged her nose and blew hard until they popped and cleared.

She went a little higher and paused—treading air much like one would tread water.

At this height she could see her house and Cal's house, as well as Olympia High school, The Rooster, the town square and even the ancient tree that acted as passage between the Above World and the Below World.

She turned her attention back toward the sky. It was nearly dawn. But the sky was not bright, instead it was dark and ominous, like a bruised plum.

Vic knew it was not because of the incoming snow storm that the air seemed to promise.

She flew up and west, pushing past the low cloud cover. The vapor clung to her skin and her eyelashes, dampening her black hair. Her skin erupted in gooseflesh, but still she continued. The thin cotton of her t-shirt, clung to the small of her back.

Up ahead, there was a small opening in the cloud cover.

The howling grew louder telling her exactly what lay ahead.

Emerging on the other side of the cloud cover, the sky was bright. The sun was cresting over the horizon and it shone brilliantly on the clouds, illuminating the crystalline water droplets inside.

Vic squinted.

A black hole large enough to swallow up all of Olympia High howled angrily at the sun. At the clouds. At Vic. At Olympia. At everything.

She flew closer. The rope around her waist began to grow taught, followed by the slight jerk of the tether around her ankle. She ignored it.

The mass was mesmerizing. It was nothingness. Its blackness was so dense, it emitted nor reflected any light whatsoever. The howling sound was the result of the motion one couldn't see with the naked eye, a slow counter clockwise swirling of energy.

As she drew nearer, the mass began to pull her toward it. With the howling, Vic could easily imagine giant teeth lining the hole's edges, ready to swallow her up.

She fiddled with the belt at her waist and pulled out a flashlight. It wasn't just a regular flashlight but an infrared flashlight. Born of the Under World, her eyes were naturally equipped with photoreceptor cells, increasing her aptitude for night vision. The combo would allow her to see the unseen.

The wind from the air surrounding the hole picked up, loosening her braid and drying her damp t-shirt. There was another pull on the tether, the leather digging into her skin even through her calf-high boots.

She turned on the light and shone it into the hole. With the light she could actually see the dark green shadows that generated the counter clockwise motion. With her free hand she opened the tiny pouch at her waist and pulled out a marble. She threw it into the gaping black hole. If things were as they should be, the marble would come spewing back out. It did not come back out.

So there it was, plain as day. The proof that she needed.

At the beginning of time, the entire world was born of Chaos. In one brilliant nanosecond, the universe went from wasn't to was. And just like that the planets, the stars, all the amino acids needed to propagate life—appeared. Chaos was the Creator and he created the world from the Void.

The Void is what gave the entire Universe life.

Vic plucked another marble from her pouch. One time could be coincidence. A good researcher disproved coincidence. She tossed the marble into the gaping black hole. For a second time, a marble did not come back out

Instead, she felt it pull on her harder, as if giant hands were trying to grab at her wings and pull her closer. The rope around her waist grew tighter, digging into her flesh. She yelped and dropped the flashlight, which was immediately sucked up into the gaping black hole.

Perhaps this hadn't been the best idea, but she had to be sure.

The Echidna had said that time could be written.

Vic was no astrophysicist, but she knew that black holes altered time at a fundamental level. That they could speed up the passage of time—was it possible they could speed it up so much that it could move backwards?

The hole did not care. Backwards. Forwards. It paid no matter.

As she tried to pull away, it fought with her, pulling her in the opposite direction. She tried to turn, but she'd gotten too close. Her mind wandering and her curiosity had gotten the better of her. She had planned for this.

The rope now digging into her waist and the leather strap cutting the circulation off at her ankle had been the precautions. She knew that Asher—charged with protecting her at all costs as all hellhounds vowed to do—was digging in his heels and pulling with all of his supernatural hellhound strength to get her back to the earth.

What she hadn't anticipated was the increased hunger of the black hole. It was growing bigger and coming closer to Olympia. Soon it would suck the entire town into its gaping mouth. But why? What did it mean? And more importantly, could it be stopped?

Vic grabbed the rope around her waist, now pulled taut, and began to hand over hand climb back down it, pulling herself back to the earth. Asher's tugging prevented her feet from flipping over and being yanked in the opposite direction. Her necklace hovered around her mouth, threatening to rip away and follow the marbles and flashlight into the black nothingness. Never to return.

She released a hand and tucked the necklace safely beneath her t-shirt.

Her wings fought to gain momentum, caught in the windstorm. If she could get back under the cloud cover, she could fly easily back to Asher.

But for all her efforts, she didn't seem to be getting anywhere.

Vic heard the roar of a motorcycle. A Harley-Davidson Sportster Iron 883 to be exact. And then felt a hard tug on her leg that snapped her out of the air. She tumbled through the cloud cover, her wings trying to gain purchase.

When that failed, she wrapped them around her body like a cocoon. Tree branches tried to tug at her hair and she heard them snap as her weight crashed through the forest canopy.

The sound of the motorcycle disappeared and the tether around her ankle went slack, causing pins and needles to rush through her leg. She tried to unfurl her wings, but it was like trying to open a parachute too late.

She sensed the ground before she hit it.

But the ground was not hard as she'd anticipated.

It was kind of muscly and slightly squishy.

Asher grunted as Vic scrambled to get off him, her wings folded tightly back up into her shoulder blades as if they were never even there.

"Asher!" she hit him. "Were you trying to kill me!?"

The hellhound glared at her, his green eyes piercing in the early morning light. He rolled over and pushed himself to his knees, his butt resting on the heels of his boots.

"I'm pretty sure you were doing a good job of that on your own."

That was kind of true. He rose to his feet and used his knife to slice the leather tether from her ankle and then the rope from around her waist. She let out a long breath, like being released from a corset after hours of wear. She didn't even want to look at the markings that surrounded her waist. Immortals healed faster than mortals, but it didn't make wounds any less painful.

She noticed the other end of the tether tied to the back fender of Asher's Sportster. If he hadn't been quick thinking, she wasn't sure she was strong enough to have gotten away on her own.

"Thanks," Vic mumbled rubbing at her side.

Asher nodded. An unspoken understanding between them.

"Did you find what you wanted to find?" He handed her coat over and slung the back pack across his own shoulders, but it looked funny—like a toddler's backpack. With the tattoo sleeves and shaved head, it almost made Vic giggle. It would have if she wasn't so terrified by what she'd just experienced.

She put her arms into her coat, sighing into its warmth.

"I did. It's worse than I thought."

Asher gestured to the tether and the rope now lying on the ground.

"Obviously."

Vic picked both objects up and gripped them tightly in her fist as Asher mounted the Sportster. She slung her leg over the back, wincing at the shooting pain across her torso. Asher flipped the ignition and the bike roared back to life, once again disrupting the morning stillness. He tore across the field heading toward the main road.

What Vic didn't tell Asher was that not only was it worse than she thought, but that she also had no idea of how to stop it. The Void had entered their earth dimension. And the very thing that had brought them all into existence was now seemingly intent on destroying them.

Chapter Two

Cal

Concentrating on calculus homework was not easy when it was only two more weeks until winter break. It was even less easy when you were still wrestling with the idea that you were an immortal and that your entire life had basically been a lie.

Existential crisis.

He was only eighteen and he was already having an existential crisis.

Callum Bishop dropped his pencil and ran both hands through his brown hair. His mother—his adoptive mother—hadn't cut it for him in weeks, so it was longer than usual.

He listened to the sounds of his mother moving about the kitchen below his bedroom. His younger sisters were all still asleep. There were soft bangs and clanks as Rachel moved about heating the oven, flouring the counters, and rolling out dough. She may not be his biological mother, but Cal knew Rachel better than anyone. He knew that since the events of the Fall Festival and Apollo, and then the events before Thanksgiving Break involving Aphrodite, that his mother felt some palpable relief. There were now no more secrets between them, and it made for a freer conversation. But it still left a pang in his chest because even though there were no more secrets, there also were still no answers.

Never in a million years would he have guessed that moving to Olympia from their surfer town in California would completely turn his world inside out and upside down. It started when he'd seen Victoriana Haden—with her long black hair and piercing green eyes, she was striking. And then he witnessed her Take someone's soul. At the time he didn't know what it was that he'd just seen—a soul was a person's essence and Vic needed it in order to save her mother, Persephone's life.

It turned out that Apollo, who loved Persephone even though she was married to Hades, as in God of the Underworld Hades, had poisoned her. And with the help of Cal's own father, who happened to be the Titan Cronus. It also turned out that some of the Titans were seeking out Olympian allies in an effort to overthrow the rest of the Olympians who had established a more or less easy life blending in as normal mortals over the last few centuries.

Zeus, Hades, and Poseidon had captured Apollo and thrown him into Tartarus with the other Titans who had been placed there during the Titanmacy. Cronus had been the sole Titan to escape. And he escaped a second time and was still out there doing who knows what.

Then just when Cal was settling into the fact that he was half-mortal and half-immortal, or as Vic liked to say a Halvsie, Vic was kidnapped by Aphrodite. As in that Aphrodite. Goddess of love and all that stuff. Apparently, the mythology books left out the fact that Aphrodite was one of the few gods who were considered both a Titan and an Olympian. She had kidnapped Vic to lure Cal to her sky ship, in the hopes of throwing him into the Void.

Because apparently, Cronus wasn't even his father. Uranus was. The Primordial God of the Sky. And his mother was the Primordial Goddess of the Night, Nyx. Nyx had abandoned him as an infant, leaving him in the care of a young seamstress named Rachel. She raised him as her own and met Christopher—really Cronus—who not only sired his sisters, but was using Rachel to get to Cal in hopes of an alliance. Cronus was the Titan god of time. With Cal by his side, he'd have an ally that was a Primordial Deity. But Cal—having already fallen in love with Vic—chose to side with the Olympians.

Pythia—the Oracle of Delphi—prophesized that Cal was Air. And that's exactly what he found out his name meant. *Caelum* meant air. He was the God of Air. And if that wasn't enough, he was not a Havlsie at all, but an actual immortal.

How could anyone focus on calculus when they knew that they were going to live forever? It sure put things into a different kind of perspective.

He moved from his desk beneath the window and back to his bed. A midnight blue velveteen blanket lay across his pillow. He touched it and immediately stars, moons, and constellations appeared and began to swim across the fabric. He pulled his hand away and it stopped. He touched the cool fabric again and the objects once more appeared.

What did it mean to be the God of Air? What did it mean to be immortal? At least now he could live forever with Vic by his side. So he wouldn't be lonely. He smiled.

There was a soft knock on his door and it slowly opened.

Rachel shuffled in, her dark hair speckled with flour and still wearing her apron. She was holding a plate of cranberry orange muffins.

"I saw your light beneath the door," she smiled.

He sat up and took the plate from her. It was nearly 4:30 in the morning. Rachel woke up early because she baked goods that were sold in various shops around Olympia. The owners with shops that opened early would be stopping by soon to pick up their orders. After Rachel took his younger sisters to school, she'd then take the baby along on her deliveries to the remaining shops. She was a hard worker and a caring person. He'd been lucky that Nyx had chosen so wisely.

"Thanks."

She lingered by the door. "I know it's difficult to focus on school right now, Cal. Especially knowing what you now know. But I think Mr. Dalton will let you finish out the second semester on independent study." She knotted her hands. "I just think it's important that you earn your diploma."

Cal had no intention of not finishing high school. Vic's lessons in the Under World had been so advanced that she basically breezed through every assignment, project, and test despite her copious amounts of absences. He had lived a human life for eighteen years and he didn't know how *not* to live a human life.

"Don't worry, Mom. I plan to do just that." Rachel's shoulders softened whenever he called her Mom now. "Do you think Mr. Dalton would let my independent study be on Greek mythology?"

Rachel's smile widened. "I can't think of anyone better suited for such an undertaking. Well, except maybe Vic."

They shared a laugh and Rachel headed back down to the kitchen, closing Cal's bedroom door behind her.

He picked off a piece of muffin and chewed it thoughtfully.

It was going to be difficult concentrating the next couple of weeks. For all of Vic's huffing and puffing about wanting to stay in Olympia and lead a normal life, there was a certain almost electric buzz in the air. He could feel it and he knew that she could too. But it was another thing that he didn't quite yet know what it meant.

He glanced at the window. The sun was coming up but the sky was still dark, almost resembling a plum. There were thick clouds lit from within that promised snow. His bedroom was often warm since it was basically the attic, and he'd opened the widow to let in some of the cool, near winter air.

The roar of a motorcycle snapped him to attention. Not many people in Olympia had motorcycles. It was a small, Podunk town. All the residents knew one another more or less. And not many people would be riding a motorcycle in near freezing temperatures.

He leapt off the bed and slid his calculus book and notebook off his desk and into his backpack. He threw his scarf around his neck, grabbed his coat and shoved the rest of the muffin into his mouth. His mother needed the van for her deliveries, but his bicycle was waiting on the side of the house when he burst through the front door in a flurry of winter gear, school stuff, and his mother's call of "Have a good day!"

Cal was certain that motorcycle had been the sound of a hellhound motorcycle. Which meant one thing: Vic. He threw his leg over his bike and pedaled like mad in the direction of the manor where his girlfriend lived. His phone buzzed in his pocket with a text message.

I'm back. And ouch.

Chapter Three

Vic

It was an understatement to say that everything hurt.

After Asher dropped her off at the manor, Vic had made a beeline right past the gingerbread cookies Richard had left on the kitchen counter—fresh-baked by his wife and in cute little humanoid shapes—and straight to the bathroom.

She tossed her clothes onto the floor and stepped into the steaming hot shower.

Her waist was covered in a crisscross of rope burns that were pinkish red. The tether had left a blackish-blue bruise around her ankle that resembled a shackle.

All her muscles ached. The shower helped remove the chill that the icy cloud cover had enveloped her in, but it didn't do much to ease the chill in her mind of what she'd seen.

The Void was here. In Olympia. But why? How?

Vic turned off the shower and threw on her robe, sinking into its fluffy warmth. She kicked her clothes out of the way, and headed toward the kitchen where she helped herself to a gingerbread person.

Richard was the manor's caretaker. He was really more of a gardener, so unless there was snow to be shoveled, there was not as much for him to care take in the winter. While her father was thankful for Richard to keep an eye on Vic and make the manor presentable, Vic was more thankful for his wife and her endless baking talents.

There was a thump and shuffle outside the kitchen door, then it burst open.

Cal stumbled in, catching himself on one of the kitchen chairs. That seemed to be happening more lately. His energy was becoming chaotic and adrenaline-filled. It was a common psychological turned physiological effect after finding out one was immortal, except for Vic it had happened at about the age of six. It's as if this new knowledge fills the body with a kinetic energy it doesn't know what to do with. People think being immortal would make time pass more slowly, but really it makes it pass much faster.

No doubt Cal probably biked over twice as fast as he normally would have been able to and with no explanation of how he'd done it.

He noticed Vic standing there and his amber eyes lit up, his lips forming a lopsided smile. "Good morning."

Vic held out a cookie. "Cookie?"

But Cal shook his head. "Mom made muffins this morning."

Vic shrugged and bit off the gingerbread person's head. Milk. She grabbed a glass and some milk from the fridge.

Cal squinted as she poured. "Is that milk yellow?"

"Uh, of course. Why, what color is your milk?" She put the carafe back into the fridge—which Richard always kept well-stocked because Hades was afraid his daughter would apparently starve to death if she didn't have a plethora of demon servants at her beck and call like she did at home.

Cal shrugged out of his coat and slung it over the back of the kitchen chair.

"Um, well. If it's cow's milk it's usually white. Soy milk is kind of more off-white in comparison. Same with almond milk, I guess."

Laughter bubbled up from Vic. "Whoever heard of milking an almond?"

The thought was incredibly absurd. But Cal looked at her blankly. This was one of those awkward growing up in the Above Realm versus growing up in the Below Realm moments.

When she realized Cal wasn't actually going to answer, she replied. "It's ambrosia."

"Wait. That's a real thing?" Cal asked stepping toward her. He picked up the glass and sniffed. The smell of ambrosia was sweet and subtle, like honey mixed with vanilla bean and apricots, with some chamomile which gave it a subtle apple flavor.

"Of course it's real. You should know by now that all of mythology is real. Well, there may be some embellishments from various authors, but in general, it's real. You and I are living proof of that."

"Touché." Cal bowed slightly. Vic rubbed his hair with her hand sending it further every which way.

"Although, ambrosia doesn't make one immortal. Nothing can make someone immortal but good old-fashioned DNA. However, it does help inhibit the aging process from a cellular level. It reprograms your RNA. It's actually a highly scientific beverage."

Cal wrapped an arm around Vic's waist. "And where does the highly scientific beverage come from?"

"Unicorns. Obviously."

Cal laughed. "Obviously."

He squeezed her in a side hug and Vic winced, the vise-like sensation too soon after the incident with the rope.

"What's the matter?" Cal pushed her back so that she was arms' length away from him.

He took in her damp hair, the dark circles under her eyes. She grabbed his hand and led him into the living room which Vic had converted to a bedroom.

She was the only one in this giant manor, and she didn't feel it necessary to take up two floors of space. The first floor contained her bed, the bathroom, and the kitchen. She didn't see the need for much else. Hades more or less kept the top floor for his antique storage. It was pretty difficult for him to walk by an antique shop and not find at least one thing he couldn't live without. Her father had a taste for the finer things in life.

Cal knew something weird had been happening with the boundary between the Above World and the Below World. And he knew that Vic would be compelled to investigate it.

She flopped dramatically onto her bed, which was still unmade from the morning before. Cal sank into one of the high-backed, purple velvet chairs that were not really Vic's style, but very much what Hades thought his daughter would like.

"How'd it go?"

"Well, you know the Void is getting closer and still sucking the world in on itself. It nearly sucked me in despite all my careful planning."

Cal raised an eyebrow. "Careful planning meaning some rope from the hardware store and Asher?"

Vic scowled at him. "I survived, didn't I?" She rubbed at her rope burned waist. It still felt like she was wrapped in snakes of fire.

She sighed. "This is serious, Cal. The Void is here. In Olympia. Our home."

Cal moved to the bed and sat beside her. "I know. But what can we do?"

Vic rested her head on his shoulder. "I have no idea."

...

Usually when Vic had no idea what to do, that meant a trip to see Pythia. Cal went to school and Vic had called herself in sick—again. It was lucky she was such a good student. She aced all her tests and completed any projects in record time. Attendance was only a small percentage of her overall grade.

Her pristine turquoise F100 with white leather interior ambled down the road. Cal had let her throw his bike in the truck bed and drop him off at school, even though it was probably better for him to have rode his bike to wear off some of that energy. It was freezing out and Vic just wanted to spend a little bit more time with him.

Since the incident with Aphrodite, he was knee-deep in his studies in hopes of being granted an independent study the following semester so that he could trace his own genealogy to the Primordial deities. While Vic was obsessed with the Void and all the little changes she had been noticing in Olympia, Cal was obsessed with finding out just who he really was.

As she drove, she pointed out that the colors seemed less bright—Cal insisted it was due to winter approaching—but Vic knew it was more than that. The high-pitched howling that played in the background was a constant, lingering reminder.

She parked the truck outside the House of Snakes, an apt name for Pythia's shop which had its origins in her time at Apollo's temple, but also became the name for the society intent on restoring the seemingly natural order of things—and that had kept Cal's identity secret for nearly two decades. Instead of a society to try and get rid of him, Vic wished someone had taken the time to establish a society to protect him.

Cal was grateful and excited to know his true lineage, but Vic couldn't help but be a little bit bitter. She was happy he was immortal too—now there would be no growing old without him. But it made her angry to think that Nyx and Uranus just disposed of him into the mortal world without much consideration. Nyx had been lucky Rachel was such an amazing and kind person, even if she'd had the unfortunate luck of crossing paths with Cronus. But the gods were manipulative and deceptive—especially the older regimes—so it could have happened to any young, intelligent woman wanting to fall in love.

The shop was always open, just not always to the general public. Vic was not general public. Pythia was a longtime friend and trusted ally of Hades.

Vic placed her palm against the old wooden door with its familiar snake carving. It swung open, a small bell chiming above her head. A black cat rushed out and immediately began entwining itself in figure eights around her legs.

"Samson!" Pythia hissed from inside the shop. "You get back here you naughty thing!"

The cat looked up at Vic and blinked as if to say, "Does she really think I'll listen to anyone but myself?"

"Samson? I thought you'd already changed his name before." Samson's original name was Apollo, but after all the turmoil he caused, and Pythia's closeness with the Hadens, she'd changed his name. She said she'd changed the shop name too if it wasn't so much paperwork.

"It didn't suit him. Besides, I thought naming him after a hero was better than naming after a traitor."

Pythia appeared from the shadows.

For a small town like Olympia, Pythia was as exotic as they came. Both forearms were covered in silver, gold, and bronze bangles and each of her fingers had a ring with a different stone: turquoise, quartz, amethyst, obsidian, and others Vic couldn't even name.

Today her hair was in thick black dreads tied up with a colorful silk scarf. Normally in long skirts, today she was wearing loose wide leg pants due to the cold and a thick knitted sweater, both in cream, which contrasted nicely with her milk chocolate skin. Her red-framed glasses sat on top of her head, her eyes outlined in thick kohl eyeliner and her lips a brilliant shade of boysenberry.

She encircled Vic in a big hug.

"It's good to see you. Come, I've already got some tea brewing."

Vic followed the Oracle through the shop and to a back door. The door led to a backroom with a stairwell that led to the apartment above the shop.

As soon as Pythia opened the door, Vic was enveloped in the scent of lavender and sage. It was a relaxing, earthy aroma that she associated with Pythia since childhood. The bright yellow kettle sang from the electric stove top and Pythia shuffled over to the kitchen to set up a tea tray.

The ceiling of the Oracle's home was draped with brilliantly colored scarves and macramé plant holders, spider plants and snake plants bringing life to the small space. There was a table in the center of the living space from which Pythia did Tarot and tea leaf readings. It was a low-style table where the only way to pull up a seat was to sit on the floor, which happened to be covered with mismatched cushions and pillows.

Vic shrugged out of her jacket as Pythia brought the tea tray into the living room. Samson chose a golden yellow floor pillow, circled two times then plopped down, his tail curling up over his nose.

It seemed as good an invitation as any.

She sat and took the steaming mug of ginger mint tea that Pythia offered her. The mug was shaped like Mrs. Claus. Vic adored the mortal tradition of Christmas. Of course, her father being the God of the Under World, or as some might call him El Diablo or The Devil or Lucifer—he hated that last one, saying people could at least use his proper name and not some name from a story—one would think that Christmas would not be celebrated.

But au contraire, Persephone had raised Vic on the Pagan tradition of the Winter Festival, Yule. However, she'd also explained to her the concept of Christmas, and Vic found it much more fantastical than Yule. While the Yuletide celebration was something she felt deep inside her bones, and had occurred for millennia and was celebrated by the ancestors, Christmas had a sense of magic and whimsy that pleased her childish heart.

Pythia winked. "I thought you'd like that mug best."

"Thank you." Vic took a careful sip of tea, the ginger immediately creating a warming sensation deep in her stomach.

The table had several candles in various stages of melting on a rectangular tray. The light was dim despite the wall of windows. Outside, the clouds still promised snow.

"So, is your mother well?"

"Oh, yes, thank you. She's content to stay in the Under World a bit longer, given her previous condition. Hopefully, she will feel up to returning to the Above World in the spring—that is if there still is an Above World." Vic raised an inquisitive eyebrow.

With Pythia she usually saw your showing up and knew what you'd be seeking. But that didn't stop the pleasantries and niceties.

Pythia chuckled. "You and your father always prefer to get straight to the point."

Vic took another sip of tea and set the smiling Mrs. Claus back down. Samson purred, fast asleep, on the floor pillow beside her.

"The Void is here. In Olympia."

The Oracle set her lopsided, hand-thrown mug down. "I know, Child." She gestured to a pair of giant headphones resting on a hook on the wall. "Sometimes I have to wear those atrocious things just to get some peace. It's howling and carrying on so." She scowled at the window.

"But what does it want? Why is it here? I didn't think...is it following us?"

Vic recalled Aphrodite's sky ship full of her monstrous creature siblings being dragged into the gaping Void. That had happened in the stratosphere. Nowhere near this realm.

Nowhere near Olympia. And yet it was here. Just a few miles down the road.

"I'm…not sure."

Samson's ears perked up at that, but his eyes remained closed. It wasn't often the Oracle was unsure. However, she was directly tied to Apollo, much to her chagrin, having served him against her will as the Oracle of Delphi for nearly three-thousand years. Things like that kept you tied to someone, invisibly linked.

"My vision around it is foggy. I can't tell if it's attached to someone—you or Cal—or if it's been summoned here. But if it's been summoned that could be much worse."

"It would mean there's another traitor in Olympia." Vic snorted. "Traitors around here seem as common as lamp posts."

Pythia smiled sadly. "It does, but Victoriana, you know how old some of us are. It's a long life. Minds change. Hearts change. Alliances and allegiances shift. It's just the way of things."

Vic knew that was true, but it didn't mean that she liked it.

"It can't just suck up the entire town!"

"I don't think it wants to."

"But then what does it want?" Vic's frustration was palpable. It wasn't Pythia's fault. She was an Oracle. Well, she was The Oracle. But oracles were often known to be vague and cryptic, talking in riddles and in circles.

"The Void is an ancient thing. It's the origin of everything. Everything created from nothing. But it's not meant to destroy. At least, that was never the intention. Whoever persuaded it to behave in this way, must be very powerful."

She didn't say it out loud, but immediately her mind wandered to Cronus. But could a Titan control something as old as the Primordials? Could something like the Void even be controlled? She imagined it would be like trying to control the sun, the moon, or the stars.

"It's close. Near the entrance to the Under World, but above the cloud cover. Most mortals wouldn't notice it. Especially with all the storm clouds that seem to be hovering around."

"That's part of it. It's not meant for them to see or know it's there. They can't hear it—mortals have notoriously poor hearing." Pythia tapped a fuchsia-colored fingernail against her chin. "But why the entrance to the Under World?"

"The veil is thinner there. Maybe it was an easy way to slip in?"

Pythia nodded. "But there's more to it than that. I just don't know what." She frowned. "I'm sorry, dear, I know that you came to me for guidance, but it's as if someone has filled my third eye with cobwebs."

At the mention of cobwebs, Samson jumped up onto the table, arched his back and hissed. Then he sauntered over to Pythia and placed a paw on her shoulder.

"Oh goodness. You're right, Samson! Thank you!" She reached for the saucer of cream she'd brought over for the tea and placed it in front of him. Samson sat and meowed before taking a sip.

"Could someone fill me in on the conversation that just happened?" Vic asked, amused at Samson's insistence and even more amused at Pythia's clear understanding. Just how old was this cat?

"Samson thinks we should pay a visit to Arachne. Smart kitty." Pythia patted his head and Samson mewed happy to have been of service.

"Arachne? As in arachnids?"

"Well, yes, that is the origin of arachnids. But Arachne has been around much longer than any arthropod. You could say she's the original."

Vic recalled some of the story. Arachne was a weaver who dared to challenge the goddess Athena. Athena was one of her father's trusted advisors. She was formidable—with her leather miniskirts and the battle swords crossed at her back—she imagined that being challenged wouldn't exactly go over very well. Needless to say, it didn't. And Athena turned Arachne into a spider. So she was still a weaver, just a creepy crawly one. Her father had an interesting take on what was considered appropriate bed time stories for a young girl.

"How do we find her?"

"Well, my girl, you simply follow the cobwebs."

Chapter Four

Gal

Gal left school after last period. As he waited for the bell, he checked his messages. Vic had messaged him several times. Something about spiders and the Void and Pythia.

The messages didn't completely seem to make sense, but few things did when it came to Vic or Pythia, let alone the two of them together.

He shoved his books into his back pack. The velveteen blanket was squished into the bottom. It never left his side—it felt like a tangible reminder that the world around him was an illusion. Just like how the baby blanket looked like a plain blanket, but really was enchanted by his touch. Brought to life with its dancing moons and stars. Luckily, it never seemed to wear or soil, so he didn't have to worry about it being ruined by his rough, every day handling of it.

He slammed his locker closed and half-walked-half-ran down the hallway toward the entrance on the side of the school that faced the student parking lot.

The hallway was filled with students in heavy winter coats and hats pulled low over their brows. People called out to one another about homework assignments and the basketball team award dinner. Of course, there was a bottleneck in front of the doors he wanted to go out of. Everyone was headed in the same direction to get to their cars and trucks, and try to make it home before the sky opened up and the severe snowstorm, the weather people were promising, came to fruition.

In the kerfuffle, Cal's elbow caught on a smaller girl—probably a freshman—wielding a huge diorama so large that she could barely see over it, her gigantic puffer coat all but swallowing her whole. He stumbled forward his head brushing against the back of the guy in front of him.

Before he could catch himself, it felt like he was freefalling. He jerked backward to stand upright and the guy was gone. And so was the girl, along with everyone else. He was standing alone in the hallway. And it was dark. Eerily silent. Cal stood still, afraid to move. The silence was broken by a distant, high-pitched howl.

And then, just like that, everyone was back. The noise and return of light and full color jarring after the long seconds in the darkness.

"Hey, watch it, Bro," the guy said. Cal had pressed his palm against his back to prevent himself from falling.

"Sorry," he mumbled in apology. The guy nodded and disappeared out the door.

Cal was two steps behind him, thankful for the burst of cold, near-winter air that greeted him when he crossed the threshold.

Not wanting to block the doorway, he stepped out of the way and leaned against the building, feeling the cold brick on the back of his head.

What had just happened? Where had everyone gone?

Maybe he was stressed. Or tired. Or stressed and tired.

Or maybe something very, very bad was happening.

A horn honked snapping him out of his thoughts. Vic's truck sat at the curb.

Pythia sat in the passenger seat and rolled down the window.

"I'm afraid it's going to be a tight fit, Callum."

He smiled, relieved to see both Vic and Pythia, and leave behind whatever had just happened. Even though he knew at some point he'd have to tell them. It wasn't easy keeping secrets from Vic or the Oracle.

Pythia scooted over so that she was in the middle of the bench seat, squished between Vic and Cal. Samson was left to mind the shop. Without the summer and fall tourists, business at the House of Snakes was slow except for any regulars. If the tourists only knew the statues and crystals and tinctures they purchased were bought at a store owned by the Oracle of Delphi!

Cal had tossed his backpack in the truck bed next to his bicycle from the morning.

"So where exactly are we headed?" he asked.

Vic had the heater set to full blast, high heat. He could already feel all the moisture being sucked from his skin. His mother had packed extra muffins in his backpack that morning and now he shoved half of one into his mouth. They were pretty small muffins. He wished he had extra bottles of water. He feared that by the time they reached their destination, nothing of him would remain except a shriveled up prune.

"We're headed to see an old friend of mine," Pythia replied.

"And is this old friend…human?" Cal asked. With Pythia it was important to ask the right questions.

Vic snorted. "Define human." She reached over and turned down the heater which was blasting so much air it was almost difficult to hear.

Cal knew he wasn't likely to get a straight answer from either of his travelling companions. They drove in amiable silence, until Vic turned on the truck radio to a station of 24/7 Christmas music. It reminded Cal of the time they'd driven—at Pythia's advice—to see the Fates. He and Vic had belted out Christmas carols at the top of their lungs on the long drive to the middle of nowhere.

He hoped they wouldn't be driving for hours today. As much as he liked Pythia, her herbal scent could be a bit heady and it was giving him a headache. Not to mention Vic's fascination with the heater—granted, she was raised in Hell. What she considered hot and uncomfortable could be considerably different than what Cal considered hot and uncomfortable. The passenger window was fogged from his body heat contrasting against the crisp outside air.

Vic turned off the main road about ten miles from the high school. The houses had grown farther and farther apart. Tiny little snowflakes had started to fall. Sunset was in about three more hours and total darkness after that.

The sporadic houses turned into brown fields, cut down for the winter. Vic made another turn and they were heading steadily up hill, out of the foothills and into the mountains. Why was it that all of Pythia's friends lived at the top of a hill and in the middle of nowhere? Couldn't any of them live in town?

The old truck groaned in protest as Vic shifted gears. While the truck was pristine, it was historic. The Hadens, well, at least Hades and Vic, had a love for all the things vintage, antique, and oldfangled.

"Slow down, Victoriana. I know it's up here somewhere."

Up here somewhere? They were nowhere. Literally. They hadn't passed another car for the last forty minutes and hadn't even seen a house for the last thirty.

The road was lined on either side with a thick forest of trees. Since it was early December most, if not all, of the coniferous trees had shed their leaves, but there was a fair amount of pine trees that rounded out the forests' menacing vibe.

"Here! It's right here!" Pythia clapped her hands excitedly as if she'd just discovered a treasure.

Cal craned his neck toward Vic's window. He didn't see anything. Just forest.

Vic turned left off the narrow road and when she did, two tall, thin pine trees seemed to bow out of the way. The trees behind them followed suit and a road—more a path overgrown with time—emerged.

The truck entered and had barely made it past before the trees snapped back up to their full height, closing off the tow road from the side road. Vic glanced nervously into her rear view mirror and bit her lip. She flicked the truck's headlights on, illuminating the path ahead.

Only about five feet was visible at a time as the trees seemed content to not bow out of the way until absolutely necessary. Unfortunately, this didn't allow for them to see any curves, twists, or boulders that could be lurking in the road ahead. Compared to the evening light of the road, driving through the forest was like driving at night.

The hair on the back of his neck stood up. The forest definitely had an eerie vibe, even Pythia had grown silent. Only the sound of an instrumental version of "O Come All Ye Faithful" wafted from the truck's radio.

They moved along at about five miles per hour. It was as if the forest wanted them to get a good look. And the longer they looked, the more oddities Cal noticed. The trees bent and moved with the rigidity and grace of soldiers. Their branches were like arms extending out to one another and creating a fortress. Although it was nearing winter, there were no animals in this forest. Not a squirrel, deer, or even a single bird. That was the part that disturbed him the most.

Pythia cleared her throat. "It should, uh, just be a little ways more."

Vic shot her an uncertain look, clearly not enjoying this road trip as much as she thought she would when it was first suggested.

They crawled along for another ten minutes or so when there finally appeared an opening. It was simply an overgrown gravel circle, covered in leaves and pine needles. Exactly big enough for a car or truck. Or maybe a tent if someone was looking to sleep in the creepiest forest ever.

Hard pass.

Vic stopped the truck and put it in park.

"Are you sure this is it, Pythia?" She glanced out the windshield. "I don't see anything."

Pythia pointed off to the left. "There's a foot path there that winds a little ways up the mountain. I told you. Arachne doesn't care much for people."

Arachne? Cal immediately tried to sort through his Rolodex of Greek Mythology.

Vic got out of the truck, pulling her pom-pom beanie snuggly down over her head against the chill. Cal slid out, grabbing a flashlight out of his backpack. His mother had taught him to always be prepared. And for good reason knowing the things that she knew and that he now knew.

"Great. Doesn't like people. I'm sure this is going to go really, really well."

She let out a sigh and followed Pythia who had already started toward the footpath. Her small frame was all but drowned in a bright purple down parka with a fur trimmed hood and knee high gold snow boots trimmed out in fur. She looked more like a ski bunny then someone about to go for a hike.

How had she not been dying in the heat of the truck? Surely, he couldn't have been the only one worried about being admitted to the Olympia ER for dehydration upon their return.

There was some distance between Vic and Pythia, so Cal fell into step with Vic and cast his flashlight across the ground before them. The snow had picked up pace, falling fatter, fluffier flakes now. They caught on their lashes and lips. Vic looked up and smiled, flicked out her tongue and caught a fat snowflake. Then laughed. She looked innocent and happy—any irritations instantly gone. Cal looped his arm through hers.

"That's what I love most about you. Simple things give you so much joy. I wish more people were like that. I wish I was like that."

"You're like that. You just get wrapped up in your head sometimes. It's okay to come out and play once in a while." She nudged her shoulder against his. "Also, remember what you said about loving me because once you see where we're going, I'm not sure you'll still feel that way."

...

They followed Pythia around a bend. To their right was a wall of rock. To their left was forest, but you could see where it dropped off to the valley below.

The path was quickly becoming covered with snow and it was a real concern that when they were done with this visit the trip back to Olympia could be filled with treachery.

Cal kept waiting for a dilapidated house to come into view. Maybe a shack with boarded up windows and a mysterious light emanating from the crack beneath the door. Or maybe an old manor with shutters half falling and a picket fence with pickets missing and then lime green smoke coming out of the chimney. Which wasn't completely out of the question because Cal had been to the Under World and the flames in the Under World were lime green instead of the orangey-red of the Above World.

He was both greatly disappointed and confused when Pythia stopped in front of a span of solid rock.

They watched as Pythia rapped her knuckles against the cool, slate stone. She knocked lightly a few times as if testing it. Then satisfied, they watched as she closed her eyes and pressed her palm flat against the rock.

Cal watched in amazement as her hand slipped through the solid rock. It swallowed up her left arm to the shoulder.

She turned to look at them and winked before stepping all the way through the side of the mountain.

Vic sighed. "Well, then."

She stepped up to the rock wall and pressed her palm to its surface.

Nothing happened.

Cal stepped up beside her, pressed his palm against the rock. It felt cool beneath his fingers, but did nothing alchemical. It didn't turn to a liquid or even soften.

"Is this one of those things where, like, if we wish really hard or believe in Santa it will work?" he asked.

Vic looked at him. "I believe in Santa Claus and nothing happened. So I think it's something a little more complicated than wishing on a star."

Cal moved his palm across the rock. It was exceptionally smooth as if well-worn. The surrounding area had a lot of ridges and grooves, except this particular section. He shone the flashlight revealing tiny white flecks in the stone.

"Maybe it's..." Vic said. She tapped her knuckles on the stone moving from top to bottom. The stone gave beneath her fingers on the final tap, and her arm sunk into the rock. She reached for Cal, but it was as though someone on the other side had grabbed her sunken arm and pulled her through before her fingers could reach his.

"Greeeeat," he mumbled.

Clearly, it was the tapping that did the trick. He knew the pattern was two raps top to bottom, so he tapped a total of six times moving down the rock surface every two taps.

But the stone didn't change. It didn't soften or liquefy. His fingers didn't slip through the solid wall.

He tried again.

Still nothing.

He sighed.

The snow was coming down faster now, the elevation of the mountain and its proximity to the cloud cover giving everything an eerie luminescence.

Cal knew that the pattern was two taps high, two taps in the middle, and two taps low, but there must be something else to it. How on earth was he supposed to figure out what else it could be? He half hoped Vic would text him from the other side and let him know, but knew that was unlikely to happen if she was surrounded by solid rock.

Had Pythia and Vic just visualized the rock softening while tapping?

He tried that. Imagining the gray surface turning into a mercury like substance. Tap-tap. Tap-tap. Tap-tap.

Again nothing happened.

He felt the sensation of being watched, so he turned around, shining the flashlight into the valley below. The forest was creepy and silent. Shadows danced and something white flashed from behind a tree. It was quick, but unmistakable. It looked like the face of a skeleton. He rubbed his eyes. It didn't reappear. But the shiny white bone and the dark sunken sockets had been distinctly skeletal. Something to his left slithered across the leaves. The hair on the back of his neck prickled.

He had an idea.

He did the double tap again but this time he tapped the top to the right, the middle taps slightly to the left, and the right back toward the right, in a loose interpretation of an S or a snake.

He felt the rock yield beneath his knuckles before he finished the final tap.

The sensation was like pushing through a curtain of chainmail. It was cold and heavy. His arm slipped through and he nearly lost the flashlight as he felt warm fingers grip his hand on the other side.

Vic pulled him all the way through and into a hug. “It took you long enough!”

He hugged her back, brushing his lips across her cheek in greeting.

They were standing in a wide tunnel, its walls lined with torches that threw a lime green flame.

“Is this the Under World?”

“Don’t be silly,” Pythia said. “Hades isn’t the only one who can conjure a green flame.” She turned toward the long tunnel, its end not in sight. “Come. This is the way.”

Cal suddenly wanted to tell Vic about the skeleton face and about everyone disappearing at school, but she squeezed his hand and pulled him into a march after Pythia.

“Come. This is the way to your dooooom!”

She was clearly joking, except Cal felt that there could potentially be some truth to those words. He squeezed her fingers in return and let Vic drag him down the long, dungeon-like tunnel.

Chapter Five

Vic

Vic had to hand it to Pythia. She was pretty good with the theatrics. The whole slipping through the rock thing had been a pretty good show, but it wasn't very nice to not let Vic and Cal in on the surprise before disappearing.

When Vic had slipped through, she'd felt the Oracle's gloved fingers slip around hers and pull her through before she could tell Cal that he needed to knock in an S pattern. A snake. Or an S for spider. She had thought to text him, but her phone had no service this high up in the mountains, let alone inside a tunnel of solid rock.

She was relieved when Cal's hand had appeared through the rock wall. Pythia had stood by patiently, arms crossed and humming quietly. Cal was smart, she had known he'd figure it out, but part of her had still been scared that Pythia wouldn't have wanted to wait and he'd have been left on the other side of the wall, in that creepy forest in the snow all alone, until they'd returned.

They followed Pythia down the wide tunnel that burrowed through the mountain.

The torches flickered an eerie light, but Vic took a teensy bit of comfort in the lime green flames which reminded her of home. She wondered what her mother and father were doing. Surely by now, Asher had told them what they'd discovered about the Void.

"So who is Arachne?" Cal whispered. Pythia was several strides ahead of them.

"She was a very talented weaver who challenged Athena to a weaving contest. That's one of her affinities."

"War and weaving? What, was she, like, assigned the W's or something?"

Vic suppressed a laugh and it came out in an odd sort of hiccup.

Cal brushed his fingers across the back of her neck and to her shoulder, pulling her into him and brushing his lips across her ear. "So, how did this contest end? Having met Athena, I imagine not well?"

"Athena doesn't take well to a challenge. You've met Ares, she's essentially his war-loving counterpart."

"Except she dresses way better."

It was true. Athena's corsets, miniskirts, and intricate braided hairstyles were way cooler than Ares' Mohawk and ripped sleeve t-shirts and skinny jeans. Viking warrior princess versus misunderstood angry rocker. No contest there.

"So they each wove a tapestry," Vic continued. "Athena wove a tapestry of the gods bestowing fruit, wine, and gold onto the mortals. It was beautiful—Athena even wove her hair into it which may look blonde to you and me, but actually turns into golden thread when she uses it on her magical loom."

"Of course."

They continued to follow Pythia, rounding a slight bend to the right.

"Arachne, on the other hand, wove a tapestry of the gods pillaging and fornicating with mortals. Destroying everything for their own petty whims."

Cal nodded. This was a common theme in Greek mythology, even if all the gods that Cal had met so far had seemed relatively nice. Well, intimidating, but nice. Maybe nice wasn't the right word. Okay enough? Fair enough? Except Apollo, of course. He liked Apollo (the God, not the cat formerly known as) least of all. If at all.

"Who won?"

"Nether. Zeus flew into such a rage at Arachne's tapestry that he banned her."

"That seems like getting off a bit easy for Zeus."

"Well, that's where the story is a bit fuzzy. Some versions say she was just banned, but others say that he turned her into a spider. Like, the mother of all spiders."

"Arachne. Arachnid."

Cal's voice had that low, breathy quality to it that Vic knew meant his heartbeat had sped up.

"Let's just hope that the banned version is the true version." She gave him a small smile.

Ahead of them Pythia came to a stop. They looked up and saw that she had stopped in front of a large wooden door with identical twin iron handles. They'd arrived.

Chapter Six

Cal

Pythia gripped one of the iron handles and the door groaned in protest as she opened it. The smell of musk, dust, and earth filled his nostrils.

Not pleasant. Nor a good sign.

Vic's hand automatically brushed against her hip for the knife that was no longer there. She was a real whip with a knife. She'd given up her original, the one she'd used to Take souls for her mother's survival. Hades had eventually given her a replacement knife, but after a while she'd said it wasn't the same.

Not that Vic needed a weapon. She herself was a weapon.

Cal had watched in horror, amazement, and adoration when Vic had risen out of the wreckage of Aphrodite's ship. Her eyes had been blazing red and her wingspan was easily nine feet. Her black hair had been all wild, surrounding her head like a halo, almost as though she had been electrified. She'd been terrifying and yet never more beautiful.

It was hard to believe the girl now peering over Pythia's shoulder in curiosity—in her purple puffer jacket and knit beanie with knee high black leather farm boots—was the same girl that had looked so feral.

Cal knew that people had many sides—his own family had made that exceptionally clear. Christopher his father. Cronus the Titan. Rachel his mother. Rachel his adopted mother and protector. Pythia the Tarot card reader and Pythia the Oracle of Delphi. Even Hades—sharp-dressed and impeccable in every nuance. Hades portrayed as a devil with horns, tail, and wings. So far Cal had only seen the wings once, but he'd yet to see the former two. Or Ares the God of War and Ares the lead singer of a metal/rock/punk/whatever band.

He wondered what his other side was? Cal the normal, former surfer human mortal boy. Cal the immortal child of two Primordial deities; Cal who never should have been born. Nope. That was significantly more anti-climactic than turning into a winged devil on command.

"Hey, are you coming?" Vic's whisper cut through his thoughts.

He'd stopped walking without even realizing.

He wiped his palms across his jeans. "Yeah. Coming."

Pythia had already disappeared inside the gigantic, wooden door. He followed Vic and they entered into a large cavernous room.

The ceilings were high and arched with wooden beams for additional support. A silky white rug was rolled out not unlike the red carpet rolled out for a king or queen. The room was round, but there were three other openings which

Cal assumed led to other tunnels and caverns. More torches lined the room, casting everything in their eerie lime glow.

The white rug created a runner that came to a stop before a large…

Cal leaned into Vic. "Is that a…?"

Vic swallowed. "I think so."

It wasn't a throne. Arachne wasn't a queen. Unless she was one in her own mind. Cal knew a few girls like that back in California. They definitely thought they'd ruled the school. He was thankful Olympia High wasn't like that.

No, it wasn't a throne. Or even a sofa. Or a bed.

It was a nest.

A giant nest. Easily the size of a house. It was woven out of the same white material as the rug and had sticks, pine tree branches, broken bottles, pieces of cloth, acorns, pinecones, leaves…things that most likely had been found or left behind in the forest outside.

"Ew, gross!"

They'd come to a standstill in front of the gigantic nest, and when Vic tried to move, her boots stuck to the white fibers of the rug. They connected in strands, like when one stepped in gum.

"Oh, mind the silk fibers. They're very strong."

Vic again reached for a knife that wasn't there.

Pythia pulled a pin from her hair, and stabbed across the fibers, severing the connection.

Cal hadn't been still for as long, so he carefully moved to the rock floor before he also ended up stuck to the rug.

"Wait. Silk fibers. As in from a spider?"

"Precisely," Pythia replied, jamming the hair pin back into her pile of dreads.

"That's disgusting," Vic mumbled.

Pythia lowered her voice. "I wouldn't say that too loudly."

They eyed the nest waiting for a tarantula the size of a house to burst out of the top of the nest.

Instead, there was the sound of chittering and clicking, and hundreds of tiny black spiders came pouring out of one of the doorways off the main room in which they stood. Moving as one, they looked like a black mass—an ocean of spiders—crawling across the floor.

Cal's heart seized in his chest and Vic grabbed his arm in alarm.

The spiders continued to chitter, as if they were talking to one another, they crowded around their guests, leaving a bit of space between them, but surrounding them, so that there was no way to leave the circle unless they stepped on hundreds of spiders.

"What on earth is all the fuss about?" A voice came from the same opening from which the spiders had just emerged.

A woman appeared. "Oh, my. Guests." She didn't sound excited.

The woman was pale with long black hair. So long that it pooled around her feet as she walked—bare foot—across the room. Cal wondered how she didn't trip over it, but it seemed to swim out of her way with each step. She was also thin. The angles of her bones were easily seen beneath her skin; her cheeks were gaunt and angular. Her lips white and her eyes so dark, they were nearly black—they certainly looked black in the eerie light of the room.

She made no noise as she approached them. Her long white dress had a high lace collar and long sleeves that were also lace from her elbow to her wrist. It hit at her ankles. The way she moved and the dim light gave her a spectral appearance. Vic gripped Cal's arm harder.

Arachne stopped and raised a black arched eyebrow.

"The Oracle of Delphi. My. What have I done to deserve this pleasure?"

Her voice dripped with acid. Hadn't Pythia said they were old friends? This didn't sound like the greeting of old friends.

"Arachne. You look…" There was a long pause as Pythia searched for something to say. "Underfed."

Arachne cackled. "I can't say the same for you."

Pythia was not overweight by any means, but Cal tried to picture her in the images he'd seen in books of the Oracle of Delphi. A slender writhing woman in a gossamer-thin dress, high on the vapors coming out of the volcanic floor on which rested the Temple of Apollo. It was hard to imagine Pythia's face on the images. But she was also thousands of years old. A lot could change in thousands of years Heck, a lot could change in a single year. Even a week the way things were going. Heck, a day.

Pythia laughed off Arachne's comment. The cavernous space filling with her rich laughter.

Arachne smiled. It seemed genuine, crinkling her eyes at the corner, but because of her gauntness it still had a slightly sinister effect.

"You've brought guests." She stepped forward and the tiny spiders skittered away to accommodate her steps.

She paused in front of Vic. Vic was fairly tall, not quite as tall as Cal who was a little over six foot, but Arachne still was at least an entire head taller.

Arachne inhaled deeply and Vic squeezed Cal's arm even harder, gripping him in a vice.

"You smell of brimstone and sulfur." Cal always thought Vic smelled like her floral shampoo and maybe a small hint of incense. Like nag champa. Not like Asher who had the overpoweringly masculine scent of leather and incense. Or the other hellhound Brimstone, who had the smell of sulfur mixed with the smell of men's cologne. Cal kind of imagined Asher and Brim smelled like what Mafia men would smell like. Under World Mafia men. And Hades was like a devil version of Al Capone.

"You are Hades and Persephone's child." She turned toward Cal and he grew still as Arachne took a second deep inhale.

"Vanilla, cinnamon, and a hint of fresh wooded air."

Arachne leaned in closer and Cal felt like his heart was going to pound right through his chest. Up close, Arachne was even more intimidating. She was very thin and nearly skeletal, but there was something in her—something very old—that emanated strength.

"Human, but not. Young, but not. Interesting."

She cocked her head, her black eyes fully taking him in.

"Arachne. This is Victoriana Haden and Callum Bishop."

The woman stepped back and the tiny spiders ebbed and flowed at her feet, accommodating space so that she never stepped upon any of them.

"Old friend. Why have you come? Why have you brought them here?" Her voice sounded sad as she moved away. Her movements seemed tired.

"We need your help," Pythia replied simply.

Arachne laughed, but it was mirthless. "What help can an old spider woman give?"

She walked toward the nest and ran long fingers along its silky fibers. The tiny spiders around her chittered and began to climb up the sides of the nest covering it in black before disappearing over the rim.

"I have not had visitors in years. Decades? Centuries? The passage of time is meaningless for me here."

"Not to be curt," said Pythia. "But wasn't that the point?"

"The gods knew what I showed them was the truth! But they didn't like it!"

"No one likes their darkness on display for everyone to see," Pythia shrugged.

Arachne turned back to face them. "What is it that you want?"

"Help," Pythia repeated.

Arachne's cruel smile returned.

"Why should I help you when all these years no one has helped me?"

Vic jumped into the conversation. Her fear momentarily abandoned.

"We're here now. Help us then tell us how we can help you."

Cal waited for Pythia to object, but she just bit her bottom lip and remained silent.

"You promise me the help of Hades?"

Vic shook her head. Her braid landing over her shoulder.

"I can't promise you the help of Hades. But I can promise you my help. I may not be the God of the Under World, but I *am* the Princess of Darkness. If you will help us, I will do my best to help you. Given any conditions."

When she talked like that, Vic seemed every bit the royalty that Hades had groomed her to be. Pythia's eyes shone with pride.

Arachne appraised Vic, whose chest had puffed out slightly and her gaze was unwavering. Her intensity made Cal realize that they'd never actually explained to him why they were even here. He was not the only one keeping secrets.

"Conditions." Arachne tilted her head the other way. Her black hair fell across her face and her black eyes seemed to grow wider in her face. "You are wise, Princess of Darkness. I want my old life back."

"That is something I am not granted to give you. What do you miss from your old life? Maybe I can help you get that," Vic suggested.

A single tear rolled down Arachne's cheek. She crouched down into a small ball, wrapping her long arms around her bent knees.

Pythia grabbed both Vic and Cal by an arm and yanked them away.

Arachne began to cry, rocking herself back and forth. Her sobs caused the tiny spiders in the nest to begin to chitter again. Something black began to sprout from Arachne's curled back. At first, Cal thought it could be wings, but he soon realized that it was fur. The fur spread over her back and down her arms and legs. She unfurled and stood upright. From beneath her dress a furry leg dropped out, and then another and another. Her abdomen swelled up and then her chest and shoulders doubled in size forming her cephalothorax. The fur continued to spread, her pale skin and her white dress disappearing. It spread up her neck and over her face. Then something glistening and black popped out. Cal thought it was a boil, but then after five more appeared over Arachne's forehead and cheeks it dawned on him that they were eyes.

Spiders usually had eight eyes.

Two pinchers spread out of the top of her head like horns.

Cal gulped nervously. A furry black, seven foot spider now hovered over them.

Chapter Seven

Vic

Arachne dropped down so that she no longer towered above them on her hind legs.

"I don't understand," Vic said to Pythia. "Why did she change?"

"Her emotions. If she's angry or sad, it can trigger the transformation."

Arachne sighed. "I miss all of my old life."

"The world isn't the same, Arachne. You would come out to a very different place, Old Friend," Pythia said softly. Then turning, she whispered toward Vic and Cal. "Don't make any sudden moves. She's used to her spider form, but sometimes even she is not strong enough to override the arachnid instincts."

"I'm sorry, Arachne," Vic said taking a tentative step forward. "Your consequence seems cruel. And while I can't undo it. I'd like to make it better."

"Athena deserves the fate of the Titans! She should be cast away into Tartarus to be forgotten!"

Pythia *tsked.* "Arachne, don't be dramatic. You know that you were wrong back then and you also know that you are now more spider than human as the centuries have passed. What's done has been done. While you have experienced a curse, you have also been granted gifts and responsibilities you would not otherwise have had. Would you give those up?"

Arachne sniffled. "I suppose not."

"Good. Then stop trying to make the girl feel sorry for you, and tell her what you wish for in return so that we can get on with it."

"I wish for food. I live here alone, but the winters are difficult. My domain is the forest. The animals know that a vicious beast resides here. Over time, they've come to avoid the area. Occasionally, a loner—a wolf, a deer, or a fox—wander into the forest and I can have fresh meat. But it has become rare. I would like one kill a month brought to my door during the long winter months."

Vic glanced at Cal. He shrugged. *Why not?*

It seemed easy enough. She glanced at Pythia for the reassurance that she didn't need to consider wordplay or read between the lines. The Oracle nodded encouragingly.

"Then it is done. One kill a month from Winter Solstice to Spring Equinox."

"Then it is done, Princess of Darkness."

The spinnerets at Arachne's rear spit out silk and she used her pedipalps to quickly weave the fibers together. She held it out to Vic. It was a bracelet—like one of those string friendship bracelets that she imagined girls made for each other at sleepaway camp. She held out her wrist, the one without her favorite leather wrap bracelet, and Pythia took the bracelet from Arachne and tied it around Vic's wrist with deft fingers.

"A spider's silk is stronger than iron. Let this bracelet serve as a reminder of the agreement we have made," Arachne said. "Now, tell me, Old Friend and New Friends, why have you come?"

"Something is happening," Vic said. "The Void. It's here."

"The Void?" Arachne's voice sounded astonished. "The Creator is here in the Above World?"

"Except it's not creating," Vic said. "It's destroying."

Arachne took a few steps, her spider feet silent as she moved across the floor. It was easy to see how she was once a deadly predator.

"And what about you, Pythia? Can you not see why it is here?"

"That's just the thing. It's like my vision is fogged or full of cobwebs. You wouldn't know anything about that, Arachne, would you?" Pythia moved with Arachne so that she stayed in her line of sight. She motioned with her hand and Cal and Vic moved with her, taking slow, careful steps.

Arachne hissed. "If you're asking did I cause it? The answer is no." She moved again and they followed. It was as if she was restless and needed to pace the cavernous room.

"But if you are wondering if I can fix it? Maybe. Only someone very powerful could cloud the vision of the Oracle of Delphi. Powerful and…connected."

"Connected?" Cal asked.

All of Arachne's eyes turned toward him. "You do smell delicious. When I was human, I loved sweet things."

Cal's amber eyes grew wide.

Vic huffed. "He's taken."

Arachne's eyes landed back on Vic. "Who is both powerful and connected to the Oracle?"

Vic shrugged. "Lots of people. Hades, Zeus, my mom."

"Being connected and being friends or an advisor are not what I mean. I am speaking of inextricably linked."

Pythia put her hands on her hips. "You can't possibly mean Apollo."

"But Apollo was taken away by my father and thrown into Tartarus," Vic said. Had Apollo escaped? If so, she had to let her parents know immediately because her mother could be in danger—again. Her heart sank.

"Apollo has not escaped. I tended to him myself."

"What? Wait? Tartarus is here?"

"Spider silk is stronger than any human chains," Pythia explained. But she still didn't fully answer the question.

"Pythia and Apollo are connected because of the Temple of Apollo. But Apollo is a twin," Vic said. She had begun to pace, but caught herself. No sudden movements.

"You can't mean Artemis?" Cal said, surprised. Vic couldn't disagree. Apollo's twin was a waitress at The Rooster. She was eclectic and pleasant and had served them scrambled eggs and coffee on more than one occasion.

"It does not necessarily mean she complied willingly."

It was difficult for Vic to stomach the image of someone as amiable and non-threatening as Artemis to be coerced.

"Okay, so say it was Artemis who cast this spell or whatever you want to call it. Why?"

"Because they don't want the Oracle to see what's coming."

Unlike the ancient gods, Vic rather enjoyed getting to the point. But that's not how the ancient gods and goddesses worked. They spoke in riddles and half-truths. They gave you a crumb trail that you had to follow before you could get to the gingerbread house. Where sometimes you were pushed into an oven by a crazy witch, and other times you were saved by a handsome prince.

"But do you see what's coming?" she asked the giant spider. Pythia had said Arachne had been given gifts. She entrapped the Titans and Apollo, but Vic had a spidey sense that stronger than iron spider silk wasn't the only gift given to Arachne. She touched the bracelet.

Arachne noticed.

"Very good, Princess of Darkness."

"Your silk. Does it have some kind of special powers?"

Pythia moved slowly toward her friend. "Myself and the Fates are not the only ones with the gift of foresight. The gods may curse us, but in the same vein they also often bless us. If one knows what to do with the blessings."

Vic had always found it incredibly difficult to imagine Pythia as the Oracle of Delphi. She knew it had been millennia ago, and it was during Pythia's youth. But it was very hard to imagine the woman she considered so independent and strong, to be subservient and condemned to a life inhaling toxic fumes in order to perform rituals for the gods—and even some mortals. Although she had been revered, she was relegated to a thing—not a person. She was a means to an end—a tool to predict the future. And while she could still be the tool or use divination tools—it was now her choice.

"Have you ever heard of the Divine Web, my child?" Arachne asked.

Vic had to think. Her father had told her lots of stories when she was growing up. Her mother too. But she could not recall any stories about the Divine Web.

"I have," Cal said. He slowly stepped toward Arachne. "My mother—my human mother—used to tell it to me when I was little."

Arachne turned all eight of her eyes back to Cal. "Go on then, Delicious Boy. Tell us the story of the Divine Web."

Chapter Eight

Cal

There was once a young woman named Anna. She lived in a small village not far from the Cradle of Civilization. Her father was a farmer and the one to have raised her, as Anna's mother had died during childbirth. Her father had taught her many things: how to till the soil, grow vegetables from seeds, milk cows, behead and de-pluck chickens, even how to sew and weave! Anna was very much like her mother. She was beautiful and smart. And like her mother, she loved her father very dearly.

Until one day, as her father baled hay, he clutched his chest. One hand at his heart, the other holding his pitchfork, he called out for his daughter who was in the barn feeding the pigs, and not far from the field in which he worked.

Anna sensed the terror in her father's call. She dropped the pail of slop and ran as fast as she could to the field. They had no farmhands, it was always just the two of them. When she arrived, her father had fallen to one knee in the pile of hay. His hand was clutching at his coveralls, and his forehead was beaded with sweat.

She was sixteen now, and recognized that her father was having a heart attack.

He reached for her hand, dropping the pitchfork, and his grasp was clammy, his lips already becoming tinged with blue. There was no way she could run into the square and retrieve the village's only doctor.

So she prayed to the goddess Athena to save her father. She was willing to do anything. Anything at all to save her father.

Athena, who sat atop Mount Olympus, heard the young farm girl's plea. Athena received lots of pleas for aid, but what Anna didn't know is that Athena had already been watching her. She had gotten wind of the girl's talent for weaving. And Athena was the goddess of both war and weaving. She herself wove all of the Spartan's shields out of silver mined by Hephaestus. Her work so detailed and intricate that the shields appeared to be one solid piece.

Athena watched as the girl cried, cradling her father in her lap, and called out to the goddess. She felt kindred to the young girl, so she took pity on her and granted her, her desire. The village doctor happened to be driving past—right on the road to the north of the pasture in which her father had been baling hay. He heard her father's cry and had been worried by the tone. He made his way down to the field and saw Anna cradling her father in her lap. Luckily, the doctor had arrived just in time.

Anna praised Athena, leaving the goddess offerings of grapes, bread, and wine outside the kitchen door that night. Little did she know that her wish would later come with a price. The goddess carefully wove a red thread into her tapestry.

That price would come four years later, after Anna had married and was pregnant with child. Her beloved father was still alive and had helped her husband, the doctor's son, to build them a small cottage on the same land, so that they would always be close by.

As Anna labored, the midwife noticed her heart rate seemed to drop dramatically then rise again. Her father and her husband prayed to the goddess Athena, that she spare their precious daughter/wife and granddaughter/child.

Athena's curiosity was aroused. The farmer she had spared was now calling out to her to save his daughter.

The cost of a life was the life of another. So Athena returned to her tapestry. She took out her magical shears made of gold, and she snipped out the red thread that she had woven in four years prior.

That night, Anna and her child survived. But her father—at least having seen his first grandchild—had a heart attack in his sleep and passed away by morning. The doctor, who had saved her father's life those years earlier, had left only hours before after having checked on Anna and his son after the birth of his first grandchild. Unbeknownst to Anna, her father had gone willingly when Athena showed up at his bed. He had been frightened four years prior because he was his daughter's only family. But when the doctor, who had been taken by Anna's kind, hard-working personality, introduced her to his son, and they had married, the farmer had taken solace in their union. He'd seen the birth of his first grandchild, and this time neither he nor Anna resisted his death.

That is the Divine Web, the interconnectedness of man and god, woven infinitely together and endlessly intertwined.

Cal finished the story with a sad smile. Rachel had so ingrained it in his mind as a child, he could recollect it quite vividly.

"That's a horrible story!" Vic exclaimed. "Anna lost her father anyways!"

"But that's the point, isn't it?" Cal said. "She and her father resisted his death because then Anna would be alone. But then the doctor happened to be nearby and saved her pop's life. He then introduced Anna to his son, and instead of either taking Anna or their baby, Athena instead returned to take Anna's father. And they were both okay with it because now Anna had a family of her own."

Vic huffed. Her black hair fell in tendrils outside of her beanie. "But Athena is a goddess! She could have saved him and not extricated a price. As far as I know, there is no rule book saying that one life must be substituted for another."

"Except if you bargain that life," Pythia said knowingly. "That is another matter altogether."

"Still, Athena could have let the father live—and Anna and the baby—and they could have continued to enjoy their time together!" Vic crossed her arms and scowled. This was precisely what annoyed her about the gods.

"If anyone knows the price for exchanging one life for another, I would think it would be you Little Princess," Arachne said. "Did you or did you not Take mortal souls in exchange for your mother's life?"

"Yeah—but"

"And did you not call upon the ancient magic to save the life of your lover?"

"Well, I wouldn't use the word lover…"

Cal stepped forward and stared at Arachne, realization sending chills throughout his entire body. "You're in charge of the Divine Web."

"Wait. What?" Vic whirled, forgetting to move slowly.

Arachne stomped her spider feet and clicked her pinchers.

"Very good, Tasty Boy."

"When you lost to Athena, they not only turned you into a spider, but put you in charge of the Divine Web. And I bet it's no coincidence that the thread in the story was red. The Thread of Destiny is also red. It's Fate. But I thought the Fates were the weavers of Destiny."

"You are very clever, Son of Sky and Night. The Fates determine the beginning, middle, and end. But I determine the interconnectedness of all beings."

"That's why it's a web. If the doctor hadn't been there to save Anna's father, then he wouldn't have thought to introduce her to his son. If she hadn't met his son, she may never had married as content as she was living with her father. And if she hadn't met the doctor's son, she may not have had a baby and their lives may not have been endangered. Then the father would never had to call upon Athena for help," Cal said.

"Exactly. And Vic Taking human souls and calling upon the magic to save you, has called upon Fate and Destiny many times." *Click-click* went the pinchers. "And now she wears a piece of the web around her wrist. When the time is right I will come to collect."

Vic's face darkened and Cal feared that she'd sprout her wings right then and there would be a giant bat-girl-spider throw down. Which would be awesome. But bad. More bad than awesome.

“And yet you still have not told us why the Void is here and why Pythia’s vision is clouded.”

“Pythia helped you track down Apollo, did she not?” Vic glanced at Pythia. “She knew that aiding you, pitting one god against another, would exact a cost. Even the Oracle knows that.”

Pythia pursed her lips, but nodded confirmation.

“As for the Void…you have asked for the magic’s help many times in the last several months.”

“Not enough times for a giant black hole to follow me home!”

“True. But you saved Persephone as she was on the brink of death. You have saved Cal more than once. That’s at least three lives in which you have spared. But that is not all. Come. I will show you.”

Arachne began to walk away, her eight giant legs making huge strides across the floor. Vic huffed but followed her anyways. Cal jogged to keep up with her and Pythia brought up the rear, her expression sad. Cal couldn’t shake the feeling that Pythia already knew what was coming and not because she could see the future.

The spider led them out of the cavernous room and down a short hallway into another giant room. Vic came to an abrupt stop, almost causing Cal to run into her. The room was full of an enormous, glistening white spider web that took up the entirety of the cavern.

Arachne climbed onto the web, centered herself in its apex and turned to face them. The web was made up of hundreds—thousands—of hexagons

“What do you notice?”

Right away Cal answered. “It’s symmetrical.”

"Yes, all except," Arachne moved across the web. It barely moved beneath her spider feet. "Right here." She pointed with a pladipalp. There was a small hexagon consisting of another hexagon inside itself and another inside of that. On the outer hexagon, one side was larger than the other.

"That hexagon has more strands."

"Indeed," Arachne said, clicking her pinchers in pleasure at his astuteness.

"Okay, so a tiny part of this giant web is slightly asymmetrical. So what?"

Cal understood why he had been brought along on this trip. He knew the story of the Divine Web, his mother knew it too and had told it to him over and over, so that he would be prepared when the time came. "Sacred geometry."

If a spider could smile, he was pretty certain Arachne was now smiling.

"Impressive."

"I hate math," Vic said, clearly irritated by the puzzle Arachne was carefully laying out in front of them.

"Sacred geometry is in everything. Both man-made things and natural things. Buildings, nautilus seashells, even in the centers of sunflowers. It's the mathematical make up of all things. Fractals. Some say it's proof of the Divine."

"That is correct, my tasty morsel."

"The Divine Web," Vic breathed.

"The eastern philosophy calls it yin and yang. The energetic principles of the universe that keep everything in balance. Others have called it the butterfly effect," Pythia moved and carefully touched the web.

"That a butterfly flapping its wings on one side of the world can cause a tsunami on the other side," Cal added, more for Vic's benefit. He wasn't sure if the butterfly effect was covered in Hades' homeschool curriculum.

"The interconnectedness of all things." Arachne turned to Vic. "So you see, it is not solely the gods that exact a price, but the universe itself. The Void has come to collect."

"But then how do I stop it? If I call on more magic, then it will just create a further imbalance."

"That is the question isn't it? Can you outsmart the universe?"

Cal's mind was moving a mile a minute. "The Void can't be destroying everything just because Vic took a few souls and called on the magic to help her. That's not proportional. It isn't balanced."

Arachne clicked her pinchers happily. "Very good."

It was him. The Echidna had said that he never should have been born. That's why Aphrodite had tried to kill him. But Cronus had wanted to keep him alive. Was it for this very reason? To destroy everything? Some of the gods saw his existence as a threat. But others saw his existence as something that could be used for their own agendas. The old rivalries between the Titans and the Olympians had been reignited. But why?

"It's me, isn't it? I'm causing the imbalance in the universe."

Chapter Nine

Daphne

Daphne watched from the safety of her tree as the snow came down in cyclones of white. A warm fire blazed from the stone fireplace

Daphne laid on her back in the middle of the study's floor, staring up at the glass ceiling. She could lay like that for hours. Or she thought it was hours. It was hard to keep track of the time when everyday was more or less the same.

The sky was bright, the clouds full of snow and the white moon cast everything in an effervescent, almost magical glow. If she squinted she could see lightning flashing inside the bellies of the clouds.

Something was changing. She could feel it in the air. In her tree. In her bones. Whatever the tree felt she felt. Over time they had somehow merged into one thing. When Zeus offered to turn her into a tree to escape Apollo, she had been reluctant. That seemed like trading one kind of prison for another. But Zeus had assured her that she would be safe, and he'd also assured her that it wouldn't be forever. Trees lived a long time. But they didn't live forever.

She closed her eyes, allowing the fire light to dance behind her eyelids.

I am Daphne. I love being outdoors and I hate that Apollo has taken this from me. I love to feel the warm summer sun against my cheeks and the cool blades of grass between my toes. The brook runs clear and the droplets linger on my skin before being absorbed. The scent of fresh earth and pine on the wind, with just the hint of a crackling fire. I used to run with my sister Diana. Oh, how we would run for hours and hours. From sun up to sun down.

That's how Apollo found me. Who knows how long he had watched. Days? Weeks? Months? Years?

At first, I'd been fascinated and flattered. Apollo was handsome, with his ringlet of strawberry blonde curls and his dimpled smile. It was as though the sun itself shone through and out his bright blue eyes. It was almost dizzying.

The sun god wanted to pursue me.

But Diana, who was older, was a bit more wary. Something about the way Apollo watched me bothered her. He'd know my every move. My every glance. Nearly my every thought. Diana warned me, said that I should be careful. That I was in over my head. When he kissed me it tasted like liquid sunshine and warmed me from the inside out. It made me drunk for him.

Diana grew even more concerned. She tried to get me to stop my nightly visits with him. Said that he looked at me as if I were something to devour and it scared her. I accused her of being jealous. When I left that night, she cried. It's the last memory I have of her. When she went down to the brook, a water sprite, ever loyal to Apollo, took her life and I found her face down in the crystalline water, her dark brown hair spread around her head like a halo. My stomach sank. If he had been smart, he would not have left the body for me to discover. Perhaps, he had wanted me to know exactly what he was capable of.

I accused Apollo of having killed my sister. He said that it was for me, that she was jealous and trying to come between us, so that she could have him for herself. But I knew Diana, and deep in my heart I knew what Apollo told me was a lie. All that he had ever told me was a lie. I was just another mortal lover to add to his list of conquests.

So I pulled my sister's body out of the brook and laid her lifeless body near her favorite laurel bush. And then I did the only thing I knew how to do—I ran. I ran and I hid. And he always found me. Until, finally, I asked Zeus to help me. And my gods, he did.

Apollo never did find me. The loss of Diana is still like a fresh wound in my heart. If only I had listened to her, we could have lived a normal life together. But instead she is dead and I am a tree.

Daphne woke with a start as the tree rattled from the roots up. It shook the books on their shelves and the paintings on the wall.

Someone passing through the veil between the Above World and the Under World. She scrambled to her feet and hurried down the stairs to the second floor window.

Through the snow she saw two motorcycles with hellhounds astride. The one was the tall thin hound from earlier and the other was a heavier, older man, but still formidable. They wore short sleeved t-shirts and the snow melted on their skin as soon as it touched them.

The tree rattled again as a shiny, old black Cadillac with winged back fenders came through. It hit the ground with a bump. Daphne shivered. Even she knew who that was. And he didn't come to the Above World often. As the two motorcycles and car drove through the field toward the road, the snow melted around them leaving tracks which were quickly covered up once again by the torrent of falling snow. If you hadn't seen it with your own eyes, you would never even have known they were there.

She watched as four red tail lights disappeared on the main road. Outside, the wind howled and the tree shook. But this time it was only from the storm, and not because of someone passing between worlds.

Something was happening. There was a shift happening between the worlds. Not only could she feel it in her bones and see it in her reflection in the mirror, but she could see the shadows behind the snow-filled clouds. She knew that something was coming. Sitting down on her small sofa, Daphne pulled a blanket around her shoulders to watch the chaos unfold.

Chapter Ten

Vic

"That was totally and utterly pointless!" Vic said as they climbed into the truck.

The snow was coming down fast now and she cranked the small truck's heater to max. This time Cal was squeezed in between her and Pythia. He was always on the quiet side, but now he was unnervingly quiet.

Vic, however, was seething.

In the small, circular clearing she threw the truck into reverse and turned around to head back down the mountain. The tall pine trees curved out of the way to let her pass.

"Don't you dare listen to that overgrown arachnid, Callum Bishop. You are not the reason for the Void being here. You are not the reason any more than I am!"

How could Arachne say that this was Cal's fault? So Uranus and Nyx made a lovechild, shouldn't it be *their* fault if the universe was imbalanced? That was like eating a bunch of fast food cheeseburgers then blaming the fast food restaurant when you had a heart attack.

Arachne hadn't even told them how to fix it! She didn't say to put a bow around Cal's neck and offer him up to the Primordial Gods like a sacrificial lamb. She didn't say to throw an olive branch and a dove as peace offerings into the Void.

All she did was start spinning her silk and say that the universe has a way of restoring itself.

At that point, Pythia must have noticed the steam coming out of Vic's ears, and decided to move them along.

Now Vic hurtled the truck down the mountainside as snow came at the windshield, eerie and space-like in the now dark evening.

The trees continued to move—no, they seemed to jump—out of her way as if they could sense her anger and frustration.

"Well, at least we now know what has caused the cobwebs in my vision," Pythia reached over Cal and patted Vic on the knee.

The Oracle's touch sent a jolt of calming energy through her.

"It's hard to believe Artemis would do such a thing."

"The twin relationship can be like no other. Imagine being inextricably linked to someone whether you like it or not. Perhaps, she thought clouding my vision was necessary. Maybe she knew we needed to visit Arachne."

Vic snorted. She found that hard to believe.

She'd gotten barely any help or answers from the spider-woman, let alone any solutions, and she owed the woman one kill a month during the winter months. It was hardly worth the effort to get so little in return.

She rounded a corner heading toward the narrow road that led to the main road. The snow was getting worse and she knew that she needed to slow down. Just before she reached the road, something dark and shadowy flitted in front of the truck. Vic slammed on the brakes, thinking it was an animal, causing the truck to careen wildly over the freshly fallen snow. Cal reached over and jerked the wheel to the left so that they very narrowly avoided hitting a tree.

"Are you okay?" Cal asked at the same time Vic asked, "What the hell was that?"

"What? I didn't see anything."

Vic's heart was pounding in her chest and she slumped back against her seat. She glanced at Pythia, but the Oracle only pursed her lips.

"What did you see?" Cal prompted. He'd leaned back, removing his hand from the steering wheel and instead placing it on Vic's thigh. Her pounding heart began to slow.

"I don't know. A sasquatch?" Vic asked. She loved the lore, myths, and legends of the mortal world because little did they seem to know all of it was actually real. And the ones who did know it was real tended to be met with great skepticism and even ridicule. Humans were curious creatures.

"You think you saw Bigfoot?" Cal responded.

"Yes. No. I don't know. It was a huge, dark shadow. I can't believe you didn't see it. It walked right in front of us!"

Cal bit his lip and sighed. "I suppose now's a good time to tell you that earlier before you came to get me, I swear I saw a skeleton or something in this forest earlier. Not only that, but all the lights went out at school and all the people disappeared."

"What do you mean disappeared?" Vic felt an uneasiness deep in her belly. Something was definitely happening in Olympia.

"As in poof. Gone. It was only a split second. And suddenly everyone was back and the lights were on."

Pythia frowned.

Vic reversed and then put the truck back into drive, so that she was heading back down the snow-covered trail and onto the main road.

The silence stretched out in the truck's little cabin before Cal asked, "What do you think it could mean?"

"I'm not sure. But nothing good, I can tell you that much."

...

Over time, Vic had come to like her life in Olympia. When her father had given her a mission to save Persephone, and sent her to the Above World, she'd been prepared for an adventure. What she hadn't been prepared for was falling in love with the quirky small town, growing soft spots for its residents like Richard and his wife, or her teachers and classmates, or for meeting Cal.

She knew from a young age that her life was different...extraordinary even. And she also knew that she herself was unlike anyone else. She knew that she was a powerful young goddess, but a part of her craved for something normal. Something plain. Regular. Most little girls grew up hoping to be princesses, or fairies, or maybe even knights who could slay dragons. And while she could definitely slay a dragon—an Echidna was basically a dragon anyways just without the wings and fire breathing part—she actually wished that she didn't have to.

So to know that something was seriously amiss in the town of Olympia, created a sadness deep inside Vic. At times, she felt more at home in the fresh mountain air town than she did in the Under World. Not unlike her mother, who usually spent half the year in the Above World—spring and summer—and half the year in the Below World—winter and fall. Persephone was an Above World creature. And while Vic resembled her father in every way imaginable, her tender heart and simple, nature-loving soul were very much from her mother.

Vic dropped Pythia back off at her shop in town and then dropped Cal off at his house on the way back toward the manor. She needed time to think and promised him she'd text him later.

However, when she pulled up to the manor, an old, pristine black Cadillac was in the driveway along with two Harley-Davidson Sportsters. The snow around them was all melted away. The rest of the driveway covered in nearly six inches of snow.

Hades was here.

"He better not have ate all my cookies," Vic grumbled as she parked her truck in the barn-turned-garage and climbed out.

The kitchen door opened itself before she could even rest her fingers on the knob. For the most part, Vic didn't use magic for mundane things. Occasionally, she'd been known to enchant a pen to take notes for her, or to use voice mimicry to call herself off sick at school. But she did not feel the need to use it to open doors, pour herself a glass of water, or any other trivial thing. It seemed a waste of perfectly good magic.

She stepped into the house which was sweltering due to the presence of the three Under Worlders now sitting at her kitchen table. Shutting the door behind her, she removed her beanie and her coat, shaking off the snow. The more time Vic spent in the Above World, the more her physiology adjusted.

"Daughter." Hades stood in greeting. Vic eyed the plate of crumbs that had sat in front of him and raised an eyebrow.

As always her father looked impeccable. Hades had olive toned skin and deep, warm brown eyes that may or may not have the ability to turn red when he was exceptionally angry. Some devil stories have it right. His jet black hair was slicked back like some kind of 1940s Mafia man and he was wearing a three piece suit. Hades always wore a three piece suit—this time it was navy blue with a pale pink button down shirt and mint green pocket square and tie that fit him like a glove—speaking of which, his leather driving gloves were tossed onto the table. Her father always insisted on wearing leather driving gloves whenever driving himself. He had on dark brown wing-tipped shoes. To a mortal, he appeared to be about forty to forty-five years old, but Hades was indeed millennia old.

"Dad," Vic moved to the table and kissed his cheeks as he hugged her warmly. "Brim. Asher." Vic nodded at the hellhounds.

While Asher had been her only childhood friend—there weren't many kids that ran around in the Under World—Brim had been more like her body guard slash nanny. He was a hulk of a man with buzzed blonde hair and a full wild beard. All the hellhounds—yes, there were more, many more, like a hellish Knights of the Round Table—had lots of tattoos across their arms, knuckles, and necks. She'd always thought of the tattoos like body armor. Hellhound chainmail.

Vic released herself from her father's embrace and was relieved to see that there was still a half plate of gingerbread people sitting on the counter.

"Thanks for not eating all the cookies," she said as she helped herself to one. Both she and her father had an insatiable sweet tooth. It was a way to self soothe their intense emotions, particularly the sad or angry ones.

Hades chuckled smoothly. "It wasn't easy to resist Richard's wife's cookies. That woman spoils us."

Vic grabbed two more cookies and brought them to the table. She leaned against the case opening between the kitchen and the living room-turned-bedroom hoping that this wasn't going to be a long visit. Although, that didn't look encouraging.

Hades got straight to the point. "Asher says you nearly killed yourself trying to inspect the Void."

Vic laughed, but it was hollow. "Hardly. It's not like I can actually kill myself. Besides, I had a plan."

Asher let out a snort then tried to cover it up by coughing.

"Victoriana, you know that you should have immediately called me and the Council. That's what we're here for."

"Well, you weren't able to stop it from eating up Aphrodite's ship! How are you going to stop it now that it's here? In Olympia? In…my home?"

Hades bristled at her use of the word home.

"Maybe not. But I'm—the Council—is certainly more qualified than you and a single, quasi-experienced hellhound."

Vic scowled at Asher. She'd known he'd tell her father, but a part of her always hoped that he wouldn't. That his loyalty would lie with her, but it never did. Not then and not now.

"It's still destroying. Why would Chaos use the Void to create the entire universe only to use it later to destroy it? Why now?"

"Why now indeed." Hades began to pace. Another trait that he and his daughter shared.

"Is there anything else I should know?" Hades raised an eyebrow.

Vic shoved another cookie in her mouth, chewed, swallowed and sighed. She went over to her bed and flopped onto her back. This was going to be a long night.

"Pythia took us to see Arachne."

"How is the old arachnid?" Hades narrowed his eyes. He pulled a cigar from his jacket pocket and began to roll it between his fingers.

"Thin. And a mom?" Vic wasn't sure where all the little spiders had come from. Or even what kind of spider would mate with another spider as tall as a house and as wide as a car. "It was a complete waste of time. I'd gone to see Pythia this morning and she said her vision was fogged."

"Fogged?" Hades' eyes narrowed again.

"I don't know. She said something like it being full of cobwebs and before I know it, she's suggesting that we go visit an old friend who might know why. On the way to pick up Cal from school—"

"At least someone still values his education."

Vic sat up, pulling a pillow onto her lap. "I'll have you know that I have a 4.0 grade point average. Some of us are so brilliant, thanks to our father's thorough home schooling education, that going to class is a colossal waste of time. You know like when the entire world is being sucked into a black hole."

"Dramatic," Asher mumbled.

Vic ignored him.

"So on the way to pick up Cal she told me we were going to visit Arachne. I more or less knew the story of the weaver who had challenged Athena. I did not expect a woman who could transfigure into a spider and who looked like a living and breathing ghost."

"Did she have any answers for Pythia?" Hades pulled out a pack of matches and Vic glared at him. He placed the packet on the kitchen table. She got up and pulled a high ball glass from a cabinet, then pulled a mostly full decanter of whiskey from the same cabinet. She poured her father three shots' worth of whiskey and then placed a single ice cube in the glass before placing it on the table in front of him.

Apparently, cookies weren't going to be enough to get her father through this conversation.

"No, she didn't have answers. At least any that I considered helpful. She said the issues with Pythia's vision were most likely a spell or something cast by Artemis. Artemis! Of all people."

"You don't know all the faces of Artemis," Hades replied before taking a sip of the smooth golden liquid.

"Yeah, like the Artemis who used to ride on the back of hellhound bikes," Brim chipped in. Asher had gotten up and grabbed the whiskey along with two more high ball glasses and brought them back to the kitchen table. He was now in the process of pouring a shot's worth for himself and Brim.

Vic raised an eyebrow. It was very difficult for her to imagine the eclectic waitress at The Rooster on the back of a hellhound bike. The Artemis she knew was quiet but friendly, with strawberry blonde hair that was closer to strawberry and less to blonde. She wore polka dot leggings with hand knitted sweaters with unicorns on them and feather earrings and pink cowboy boots. Now, Athena with her corsets and leather skirts seemed a much more likely candidate than Artemis to be a passenger on the back of a hellhound bike.

As if sensing his daughter's thoughts, Hades continued. "You have to remember, we are thousands of years old, Victoriana. The gods have lived many lives, myself included."

As much as she hated to admit it, Vic knew that some of the depictions of her father through history were accurate, even if they were monstrous.

"Artemis was the goddess of the hunt and the goddess of the moon. She could give chase like no other. She moved like an animal herself—wild and free. This Artemis is one who has assimilated to the current way, more content to blend in than to stand out. Sometimes, it gets tiring standing out all the time."

Didn't Vic know that? Not only did she not look like anyone in Olympia with her jet black hair and olive skin, but she was pretty sure none of them had bat wings they could summon at will. It was nice to meet someone like Cal, who didn't treat her like the Princess of Darkness, but just treated her like…Vic.

"Did Arachne say anything else?" Hades prompted.

"She went on about something called the Divine Web. She said the Void was destroying because it had to restore balance to the universe."

Brim downed the contents of his glass. "Didn't one of Aphrodite's crew say that Cal being the son of Uranus and Nyx was causing the imbalance?" The corners of his mouth turned down into a frown. Brim really liked Cal, Vic knew, but his solemn reaction showed her how close the two had truly become in the last couple of months.

"So Cal's causing the imbalance. Easy solution" Asher said.

"Asher." Hades tone was a warning growl.

But it was too late. In one smooth motion Vic had pulled a bronzed-handle knife from beneath her other pillow and had all but flown herself across the room. She now had Asher's hair gripped in her right hand and the serrated blade held at his throat. She was ambidextrous and well-trained with knives, crescent moons, and fighting stars.

"How did you get over here so fast?" he breathed, his Adam's apple bobbing against the blade. A thin trickle of blood came out of his neck.

"You're getting slow in your old age," Vic whispered.

Vic had been training with her new winged appendages. And she'd learned she didn't always need her wings to be visible for them to help her move quickly. She'd simply thought the thought and flew across the short distance. Eagle wings were for longer distances. Little hummingbird wings would do just fine for short ones.

"Take it back," she said.

Hades watched the scene play out with an amused expression. Brim poured himself another shot of whiskey.

Asher's green eyes glared at her and she noticed something new there. Not love or lust. Not pity or sympathy. He'd broken her heart when they were younger, choosing servitude to her father over a relationship with her. She'd even been known to evoke fear in the hellhound, which is what she expected to see now. But what she finally saw was respect looking back at her.

It took a blade to the throat to get the hellhound to respect her. It was almost not worth the effort.

Almost.

"I take it back," he whispered.

Vic pulled back the blade and wiped it clean on her jeans before tossing it back onto the bed.

"You're nuts," Asher said.

Vic shrugged and grabbed another gingerbread cookie person from the plate on the counter. She looked right at Asher as she bit off its head.

"I've been called worse."

Chapter Eleven

Cal

Cal did not disagree with Arachne.

Deep in his bones, he knew that he was causing the imbalance in the universe. But unlike Apollo and Aphrodite, who thought that meant that he needed to die to restore the balance, Cal thought it meant that he was the one who could stop it.

He just didn't know how.

Now, he paced back and forth in his stocking feet across the small attic bedroom. The window was open and snow swirled in, landing on the window sill and his paper-covered desk before melting.

The enchanted velvet blanket hung on one of the bed's posts, looking very much like a normal blackish-blue velveteen baby blanket. Nothing fancy, nothing magical. Maybe a little on the expensive side. But otherwise ordinary.

He paused and brushed a finger across it, letting the silver stars and moons trail across the surface.

His mother—Nyx—had left him no answers. Rachel had known. She'd kept him safe. Told him stories of the gods that would later morph from myth to reality. But his biological mother had left him nothing except this blanket. Maybe she thought if he never knew his true existence, never figured it out, that he would lead a normal life. But then what would have happened as his immortal body outlived the bodies of those he loved? How had Cronus even figured out who he was? How had he found Rachel? His estranged adopted father was smart—but there was no way he was smart enough to outwit the Primordial deities. Had Nyx knew all of this would happen?

He picked up the blanket and it lit up again with the moon and stars design. All the constellations were there. The astrological ones like Taurus the bull and Cancer the crab, Leo the lion. And others like the Big Dipper and the Pleiades—the Seven Sisters. His fingers traced from the Pleiades across Taurus and to the three stars that made up the great huntsman Orion's belt.

Cal paused. If he had once believed the Olympians were nothing but a myth, and that the story of the Divine Web was just that—a story—did that then mean that the stories of the Seven Sisters and even Orion were real too?

As if in response, the constellations seemed to grow brighter. He set the blanket down and went to the window. He opened it further letting the cold almost-winter air swirl into the room. The world outside was bright from the nearly full moon and the now snow-coated landscape. He looked up, locating the North Star, Polaris, which seemed to be brighter than any other star. His eyes travelled south and a bit to the east where they landed on the three stars that made up Orion's belt. He didn't know much about astrology. He did know that the constellation was much more elaborate than the three stars making up the belt, connecting all of the constellation's stars would form a warrior with a shield and a sword.

The only things he could recall of the mythology was that Orion was a marked huntsman and that Zeus had placed him among the stars. Not unlike the Seven Sisters who'd also been placed there by the patriarchal god.

Cal had met Zeus on more than one occasion. The man was formidable. He had longish white hair and a gnarly scar through his eye and cheek. He didn't carry the playfulness of his brother Poseidon or the tactfulness of his brother Hades. The best word to describe Zeus was battle worn.

Snowflakes caressed Cal's cheeks as he leaned out the open window. In the last few months he'd learned there were no coincidences and no mistakes. He had noticed Orion's belt for a reason. The stars above him seemed to wink in confirmation, getting brighter left to right. Too bad he didn't know what it meant or who to go to for more information.

As he shut the window, his calculus book slid off the old wooden desk and hit the floor with a thud. He paused midway to fully closing the window, hoping that the sound hadn't woken his sisters who slept on the second floor below the attic.

He bent to pick the calculus book up and noticed that another book had also slid across the desk. It opened as if by invisible hands and began flipping its pages of its own accord. This wasn't the first time that this had happened, and sometimes he wondered if Nyx lived on the winds and would slip in to help her son find the things he needed to unravel the mystery of who and what he was.

The book was one he hadn't gotten to yet in the researching of his new identity—an old book with a blood red leather cover and the word Olympians stamped in a metallic gold serif font on the cover.

The flipping pages came to a stop about two-thirds through the book. Its pages were worn yellow and even the type was fading. An earthy musk emanated from the pages.

Cal looked closer. The book had stopped on a page with text on the left and an ink illustration on the right. It appeared at one time the illustration had been in color, but that it had faded over time. In it, there was a muscular man wearing a Roman style toga and gladiator sandals that wrapped nearly to his knees. He was holding a sword, but it was pointed down and its tip grazed the ground. The man had his arm wrapped around a beautiful woman. She had pinkish hair, what Cal assumed was once reddish, and wore a short toga as well. There was a quiver of arrows and a bow slung over her shoulders. She had a circlet around her head with a crescent moon in the center of her forehead. The woman was leaning into the man's embrace and laughing, the artist depicting her with a candid expression on her face. It felt more like Cal was looking at a photograph than an illustration. Something caught his eye. He leaned closer, turning the switch on his desk lamp up a notch so that it shone even brighter.

The woman was wearing feather earrings.

There was no doubt in Cal's mind. It was Artemis.

Chapter Twelve

Vic

All of the cookies were gone.

"Are you sure I hadn't told you the story of The Divine Web before?" Hades scratched his chin which was now showing a considerable amount of stubble.

"I'm positive. Arachne and Athena weaving competition, yes. However, a Divine Web rings no bells."

Vic was sprawled across her bed longing to put on her Santa Claus gnome pajamas. Asher was leaning back in his chair so that the front legs were off the kitchen floor and Brim had his head propped up on his left hand, his right hand tracing circles around the rim of the high ball glass.

Even Hades had loosened his tie.

"Everything and everyone is interconnected," he said.

"Yeah, I got that from the story. A butterfly farts in the Philippines and it causes a tsunami in Hawaii which creates a wind stream that causes a tornado in Oklahoma that upends a barn and it falls on the farmer's prize cow. I understand the general gist."

Asher snorted.

"Yes, I suppose that is the general gist. But it isn't just limited to mortals. Mortals have that saying: *Everything happens for a reason*. It's more than that. Not just for a reason but *because* of a reason."

This was probably the most interesting thing Hades had said all night.

"So we have to find out the *because* of the Void. It's not random. And I find it really hard to believe that one person—Cal—is causing it. If everything is interconnected and linked, then Cal is the outcome in a long chain of events and we need to figure out all the links leading up to this. We need to catch the butterfly before it farts," Vic said.

"Exactly—wait what did you say?" Hades whipped his head around to stare at his daughter.

"I said we have to catch the butterfly before it can fart. The butterfly fart is what caused this whole mess, isn't it?"

"Indeed." Hades smile was grim.

"But how do we do that? Gods can't time travel can they? And it's not like we'd go back, even if we could, and stop Nyx and Uranus from getting together in the first place. Because if we did that, then Cal would never have been born." Vic peered around her father to be sure that her earlier antics had subdued Asher from making any snarky comments.

The hellhound caught her glance and held up his tattooed hands in surrender.

"Gods and time travel." Hades was back to scratching his chin. "Asher and Brim tend to the bikes and the carriage. We will return home in the morning. Make space on the upper floors and prepare my room."

Since Vic didn't use the upper floors of the house at all, the furniture up there was all covered with dust cloths. Truth be told, she found it a bit spooky and wouldn't be surprised if giant spiders were residing in any—or all—of the upstairs rooms. She imagined a giant nest resembling the one Arachne had created towering above her from the second floor.

Asher and Brim got to their feet and disappeared out the kitchen door that led to the now-dormant garden and to the giant barn turned garage where Vic kept her truck.

"Black holes affect time," Hades pointed out to his daughter.

"And the Void is a black hole," Vic replied.

Her father rose from his chair and came to sit beside her on the bed. He pushed her wild black hair back from her forehead and peered into her eyes.

"When did you become so grown up?" He held her chin gently and his dark eyes welled with tears, which Vic knew was extremely rare for her father. She knew it wasn't fair when her father had asked her to come to the Above World to Take souls in order to save her mother's life. But she'd also seen it as an opportunity. An opportunity to live differently. Be different.

"It seems like only a day ago that you were climbing the shelves in my study only to jump off the top because you thought you could fly. And now you can fly."

"I wanted to be like you when I was little," Vic shrugged. "You could fly."

He released her chin, but still sat beside her so his shoulder was pressed against hers. "Except you are so much more than I am. I am old, Victoriana. And sometimes I am tired. I feel I always ask too much of you."

"Because you do," Vic said softly.

"And I'm sorry for that. I only ask it because I know you are capable."

Vic felt a warmth spread across her chest. A swelling of pride that she felt in her heart space. Hades knew she didn't want to ever be queen of the Under World. Even though if her parents stepped aside, that's exactly what she would be. But that didn't mean that he didn't find her fully capable of the role.

"You are so much more of a leader than I am. When I was your age I was reckless. Self-centered. Angry. So, so angry. But you, you have skills I so sorely lacked. You are already a great warrior. You have compassion for others, as evidenced by you trying to repent for the souls you had to Take. You're bold and fearless, and willing to go to great lengths to protect those you love. Sometimes I think that you are too kind a soul to rule the Under World." His laugh was mirthless. "And as a father, I want to protect that in you. Protect you from bad things so that you keep that kindness in your heart.

To answer your question, yes. Gods can time travel. The Void is a black hole. I'm sure when you went—without permission from me—to explore it, you felt its pull. It could destroy you in seconds, however, with the proper precautions it could propel you through time."

"But how would I know where to go? Would I go to find Nyx and Uranus? Cronus? Apollo?" Vic's heart had begun to pound in her chest now. Her father was giving her an assignment.

"I think I know when. It's not so far back—at least not to me—but to you it may seem a very far away time."

"Will you be there? Will I see you?"

"You might. But remember the man I am now is not the same as the man I was then. And you may not like the version of me that you see."

Vic licked her lips and nodded. She understood. She knew the myths held elements of truth. And knew her father hadn't always been a good man. She also knew that good men could still make bad decisions and do bad things. It didn't make them bad people. It just took some people millennia to figure out how to be good people.

"How does it work?"

"You will need an object that grounds you to our current time. And an object that allows you to locate the point in time in the past that you want to visit."

"Where will I find an object? How will we decide where and when I need to go?"

Hades fiddled with his tie pin. "I think that you should go to a year before you were born. But not in the Above World. To Mount Olympus. A lot has changed in eighteen years."

He separated the pin from its backing. It was a gold skull and crossbones. He handed the two pieces to Vic. She always felt like her father got a bad rap. He was the Lord of the Under World and that in itself came with a certain amount of notoriety, but she knew it was not easy to manage the souls of people who were liars, cheaters, rapists, and murderers. Certain acts could tarnish a human soul—which she knew firsthand to be an effervescent golden orb of light. But bad things blackened a soul. Sometimes there were other worldly consequences a soul needed to experience in order to try to restore it to its pure state. Other times, a soul was beyond repair—beyond saving—and all they could do was experience the pain they caused others over and over for all of eternity as their penance.

A responsibility like that, Vic knew was not a kind responsibility. She turned the little skull and crossbones over in her fingers. She was thankful for her mother. Persephone provided levity and balance to Hades' dark world. She brought sunlight and flowers, her hyacinth scent trailing throughout the house. Her laugh was like a wind chime singing throughout the castle. Vic had long suspected that her father's assignment from the Titans had caused him a lot of pain. But like Hades with her now, she knew they would not have assigned him as God King of the Under World, if he had not been more than capable.

Vic clutched the pin. "And my future object? So I can return to the present?"

She suspected her bat charm—a birthday gift from her mother—should suffice, but when she fingered it, Hades shook his head.

"It has to be from the present—not even the near past." From his jacket pocket he produced a small black box with a blood red ribbon wrapped around it.

Vic was a pretty simple girl—bat appendages and magical abilities aside—she liked t-shirts, jeans and boots. Sometimes she wore leather bracelets around her wrists, but it was more to help with keeping her wrist stable during knife throwing than anything.

She carefully took the lid off the box. Inside, on a black velvet cushion, was a gunmetal ring with an oblong setting. At first she thought the setting held tiger's eye, but on closer inspection she realized it held a piece of wood. The ring was large enough to fit onto her right index finger. It instantly felt warm against her skin. Clearly, it was magical. The metal seemed to fuse to her skin, but not in a painful or uncomfortable way.

"It's from the tree that protects the veil."

The wood reflected gray, black, amber and gold in its glass-like surface.

"Between the ring and the pin, you should be able to travel to any time between the two points." Vic looked up at the sound of the kitchen door opening. Asher and Brim walked in, their hair and shoulders wet from snow.

Hades patted her knee. "We can discuss this more tomorrow. You should get some sleep."

...

While Cal's domain was air, Vic couldn't very well rule the Under World—that responsibility still, thankfully, rested on her father's shoulders. One of the reasons that Vic wasn't surprised when her father told her that they could use the Void for passage through time, was because not only was she already comfortable passing between worlds—basically dimensions—on her trips between the Above and Below Worlds, but because her affinity was for dreams.

She was an avid Dream Walker. However, it wasn't something she ever did on purpose, so she had little to no control over it. It was often something that triggered by her anxiety and upon waking raised more questions than it answered.

She was having one of those dreams now.

Vic stepped into the room and found her mother staring into a vanity mirror. She was slowly brushing her long corn silk blonde hair. The room was not familiar. Part of the agreement between Demeter—Persephone's mother—and Hades was that the two could stay together if Persephone split her time between the Above and the Below.

A woman walked in and she resembled Persephone in every way just a bit older. This was Demeter. The only other difference was her auburn colored hair, but she had the same cornflower blue eyes as her daughter. As well as the same pointy chin and up-sloped nose.

Demeter appeared to look through Vic, squinting with a frown, before placing a smile on her face and turning to rest her delicate hands on her daughter's shoulders. Their two reflections now visible in the mirror.

Vic turned to see what it was that had irritated Demeter. There was nothing behind her except a portrait on the wall of a young—and certainly dashing—Hades with his red three piece suit and black tie, his slick backed hair slightly longer than he kept it now.

"Ae you sure, my daughter?" Demeter raised an eyebrow. "You do not wish to entertain the advances of Apollo?"

Persephone smiled sweetly and placed down her hair brush. "Apollo is vile, Mother. He persists even when told his advances are unwanted. Look at poor Daphne."

Demeter clicked her tongue. "He is a little on the aggressive side."

"Mother. He is horrid. He tried to make the mortals in Egypt forget about all the other gods—all of us—except for him. He even adopted that ridiculous name. Akhenaten. He is selfish and dangerous."

Persephone rose in a graceful sweeping motion and Vic stifled a gasp.

She was wearing a long white gown with lace shoulder straps. Demeter walked over to a box that rested on a velvet-covered foot stool and pulled out a circlet of white carnations, roses, hyacinth and baby's breath. Long white ribbons cascaded from the circlet.

This was the day that Persephone would wed Hades and forever link the Above World to the Below World. Her parents were together for millennia before they'd decided to conceive Vic.

And here, even on what was supposed to be a special day, a day of joy and celebration, Demeter challenged her daughter's decision. Vic hadn't ever properly met Demeter, but this didn't bode well for her planning on doing so any time soon.

Persephone wrapped her pale fingers around her mother's. Vic had always thought of her mother like early morning on a spring day, or like a gust of fresh air in a room that had long gone dusty and stale.

"It will be okay. Hades is a good man, Mother. I see it in his heart."

Vic knew that, contrary to modern literature, Hades had not tricked Persephone into eating the pomegranates of the Under World, but that she had done so willingly.

Demeter smiled, but Vic noticed that it did not reach her eyes. Was it true that the goddess would have rather seen her daughter with the likes of Apollo than Hades? Vic shuddered at the thought. She definitely agreed with her mother on this one. He was vile and horrid. She couldn't help but wonder if Apollo's attempt on her mother's life a few months ago had persuaded Demeter to change her mind.

Another maiden walked in and for the second time Vic gasped. Luckily, no one seemed to be able to hear her.

The woman was young—younger than Vic knew her to be now—with hair that was more reddish than blonde. Her eyes were green, but what really gave her away was the array of colorful flowers she'd weaved into a sash that was draped over her shoulder and across her chest and abdomen, along with the peacock feathers that dangled from her ears.

"They're ready, Persephone." She handed Vic's mother a white bouquet of perfectly rounded bundles of hydrangea.

"Thank you, Artemis. Such a good friend you are."

Vic had watched her fair share of reality TV since living in the Above World—especially before meeting Cal—and this was the part where the audience would collectively gasp at the revelation.

"I'll just be a moment." With a simple sentence, Persephone dismissed her mother and her best friend from the room.

Outside, Vic could hear a harp and a lute begin to strum an upbeat tune.

Persephone looked into the mirror and motioned. Vic froze.

"I know who you are, Child. You do not think that I would recognize my own daughter if I saw her?"

Vic's heart pounded in her chest.

"I do not see you with my naked eyes, but I see your reflection in this mirror. Don't worry, I don't think Demeter noticed. Your widow's peak and black hair is that of Hades, but your chin and nose resemble my own. You are our daughter. Come to visit me on our wedding day. Come."

Vic shuffled forward. "Not on purpose. I'm dreaming. I think."

"A Dream Walker? Marvelous! What else can you do?" Persephone smiled in the mirror and Vic stepped closer knowing full well that this was her mother—but not. This was her mother before.

"A little magic. But I'm a beast with a knife. Oh, and I have wings like Dad."

Persephone laughed delightedly. "I would not want it any other way." She leaned closer to the mirror, her fingers drawn to the glass.

"You look worried. And your dress—it is not even close to this time. Or this world. Has something happened"?

Vic stopped behind her mother, afraid to get too close, longing to throw her arms around her. The lavender and hyacinth wafted off Persephone and tickled Vic's nose.

"The Void. It's in Olympia. The Above World Olympia. Daddy said I have to travel in time. Back to the year before I was born. The year Nyx and Uranus created something that they shouldn't have and threw the entire universe off balance."

Persephone frowned. "Then what the Oracle said is true. Come closer, *ma fille,* and listen carefully."

Chapter Thirteen

Cal

It was early enough that the sun had yet to rise.

Cal could hear his mother moving about in the kitchen below, the comforting sounds of her sifting out flour and rolling out dough. His mother was an intuitive baker—she didn't even use timers. She simply knew when something was baked to the correct doneness. She wasn't a goddess, but Rachel worked a magic entirely her own.

The Rooster opened at 6 a.m. for students and teachers on their way to school. Cal threw on a pair of jeans and a hooded sweatshirt, grabbed his coat and book bag, shoving the book with Artemis and Orion into the front flap, and jogged down the stairs.

When he reached the kitchen he was breathless in his excitement. He tried to smooth down his dark hair which stuck in various directions.

Rachel smiled. She was covered in flour and a mug of tea sat on the counter, but it had probably long gone cold.

"You're up early."

"I was going to head to The Rooster. Did you want me to make your delivery?"

His mother moved the curtain over the kitchen window. The world was covered in layers of white snow.

After Cronus—Christopher—had left them, his mother had downsized from the large colonial house and into a small house closer to the center of town. And while he could walk to The Rooster, he could not cover the distance to the high school in several feet of snow and on foot. He wouldn't be able to ride his bike, but he did have his driver's license. He just was missing the car part.

"That would be nice. But can you make the other deliveries?"

Cal raised an eyebrow.

"The school district called and classes have been cancelled for the day. A snow day."

That's not something Cal ever experienced when he lived in Southern California. There had been a hurricane day—week—once, but never a snow day. His sisters would be so excited when they woke up.

"You'll have to be very careful. I assume the roads aren't clear enough for the busses to make safe passage. I have The Rooster's order, Miss Martha's tea house, and the market's all ready. You'll have to come back for the others."

Three giant plastic containers with the names of the businesses written on the side with vinyl letters contained countless pale blue boxes with his mother's business logo stamped across the side in white: Sweet Treats by Rachel.

His mother helped him carry the containers to the garage and get them situated in the van. She made him some hot cocoa while he grabbed his coat and scarf. He still took his book bag, hoping he could at least do some reading while he was at The Rooster. When he was ready to leave, his mother handed him a to-go cup of hot chocolate, a list with instructions for each of the vendors, and a kiss on the cheek.

Before he could actually physically leave, Cal shoveled the driveway at least enough for the van to get in and out. Cheeks cold and flushed, he was thankful for the hot chocolate by the time he was pulling out of the driveway.

The sun was beginning to come up now and it made the freshly fallen snow sparkle and glisten. Houses in town were decorated for Christmas. Large inflatable reindeer, snowmen, and Santas filled yards and multicolored lights were strung around the perimeters of rooftops. The town had wrapped red ribbon around the lampposts and decorated them with evergreen sprigs. If felt a little as though he had slipped back in time.

He drove slowly. The side roads were not clear, only the main road and even that seemed to be covered in an icy coating.

He followed his mother's list. First stopping at the market. He pulled up to the back door and called the number his mother had written in her familiar script. Sam, the manager, came out and helped Cal to unload the boxes, complimenting his mother on her incredible baking talent.

"I'll be sold out of all of this by ten o'clock!"

Cal thanked Sam then headed to Miss Martha's. His mother's instructions were to leave the boxes on the back portico of the tea house. Miss Martha didn't like to be disturbed in the morning, so she would bring the boxes in on her own and have her daughter, who helped manage the shop, get them set up and displayed for when the tea house opened.

With that out of the way, Cal headed back to the main road and in the direction of The Rooster. The Rooster was essentially a diner. The sign was—of course—a gigantic rooster wearing a Kiss the Chef apron and holding a frying pan. They only served breakfast and lunch and then were closed the rest of the day. The patrons were often a mix of high-school seniors and senior citizens.

Cal popped the trunk of the van and pulled out the plastic container full of boxes. As he entered the diner, a tiny bell rang above his head. The Rooster had a hostess stand with a chalk sign telling you to seat yourself and a pocket full of plastic menus. A countertop with bar stools ran along the length of the restaurant giving a little peek into the kitchen beyond. The front of the restaurant was full of booths. The signature colors were red, yellow, black, and white.

The smell of bacon and coffee consumed him as soon as the door closed behind him in a gust of cold air. It was less busy than usual, there was a table of three older men, an older couple who looked to be about grandparent age, a table with two teenagers, and another table consisting of a tired-looking young man and woman, two small kids, and a baby in a high chair that was attached to the table's edge. One of the kids was pouring mounds of sugar out of the packets and directly onto the table.

Cal rang the silver bell on the counter top and the cook popped his head around the entrance to the kitchen.

"I have your Sweet Treats order!" Cal called out. His mother's note said the head cook's name was Carl.

"Hey, Elise! Rachel's son's here. Can you grab that and get the display case set up for the day?" Carl called off into some unseen area. He turned back to Cal. "You can just set that on the counter. You staying for a bit?"

"I am," Cal replied.

"Great. That will give Elise a chance to unpack everything. You can seat yourself. Breakfast is on the house. Someone will take your order."

"Thanks!"

That was something Cal had really come to love about living in a small town. In California, he'd felt a little anonymous, but here, people knew who you were. They knew your family. And more importantly, they cared about one another.

Cal grabbed a menu and chose a booth that was in the corner farthest from the door to avoid the cold draft from customers coming and going.

Artemis approached the table. Her hair was pulled up into a frizzy up-do and she had two ball point pens crossed in an X through her hair. She was wearing a baggy emerald green sweater with snowmen printed all over it. The snowmen had on red bow ties and black top hats. Her leggings were sparkly silver and her cowboy boots were bright red. She had double piercings in her ears and wore silver moons in the first set of holes and rainbow feathers in the second set of holes.

It was always hard for Cal to imagine her as the Goddess of the Moon or the Goddess of the Hunt, or anything really except the Goddess of Taking Breakfast Orders.

"Where's your friend? The dark haired girl? It's weird seeing you without her. What's her name? Vic?"

Artemis was the primary server at The Rooster while Elise tended to run the counter. It was a small operation. Usually,

Artemis didn't bother with niceties. She often seemed not completely present, as if she was perpetually daydreaming of better places to be and better things to be doing.

Before he could answer, she continued. "Are you ready to order?"

He was. He ordered a carafe of coffee and a Western style omelet with a side of hash browns and bacon.

"And orange juice," Artemis added. She never wrote down orders. Cal was pretty sure if she did they would just be full of doodles. "You look a little peaky."

Artemis spun on her heel and disappeared into the kitchen to put in his order with Carl.

It really was strange being at The Rooster without Vic. She'd introduced him to the place, having lived in Olympia several months longer than Cal. But it was also strange doing research without her. The only message he had from her was a text sent last night: Surprise visit from Dad. Yay?

Artemis came by and dropped a carafe of coffee off along with a white mug. He poured himself a cup and watched her walk away. It was hard to picture the Artemis he knew as the same woman from mythology. The Artemis of mythology was a strong huntress. She ran with wolves and stags and used a magical horn to initiate her full moon hunts. Cal was once again reminded of how people seemed to have multiple personas.

There was Hades the doting father. Then there was Hades as Lord of the Under World. Vic as his girlfriend and Vic as Princess of Darkness. Arachne as a weaver and Arachne as a giant arachnid. His mother as, well, his mother and a champion baker and his mother as a protector and keeper of a very special secret—him. The more he learned, the more he was beginning to see how people were not ever just one thing. Not only in their daily lives, but throughout their lives.

Once Artemis had brought his food, which was only a few minutes after bringing the coffee, he thanked her and pulled out his book, knowing that she wouldn't be back unless he flagged her attention.

He sent Vic a text to let her know he was at The Rooster in case she wanted to join him, then opened the book.

Artemis, the huntress, and Orion, the hunter, were inevitable as lovers. They were equally matched in skill, Orion having been taught as a toddler to use a bow and arrow. Orion was a demi-god, the son of the god Poseidon (studying the illustration, Cal could see the resemblance) *and a mortal woman, the daughter of King Minos. It was love at first sight when the Moon Goddess and the hunter met.*

During an archery competition on Crete, Artemis was enamored with the demi-god's talent. His talent was so unparalleled to any other archer in history. So beloved was Orion to Artemis, that even her mother, Leto, granted them her blessing. They would lose themselves on hunting trips and their shared skill resulted in a passionate love affair.

Much to the dismay of Artemis' twin brother, Apollo.

(Cal shuddered. Dun-dun-dun.)

Apollo was jealous of his sister showing love for another man. So he came up with a simple solution. He would have Artemis kill her lover. While out on the shores of Crete, he noticed Orion swimming in the sea. Knowing Artemis couldn't refuse a challenge, he told her there was no possible way she could hit that thing in the water that was far off there in the distance. Accepting the challenge, Artemis sent an arrow all the way to, and right through the object. Unknowingly and unwittingly killing her lover. When his body washed up onto the shore she asked for Zeus' help in placing him among the stars, to immortalize him as well as to antagonize Apollo with his constant presence as punishment for his treachery. It is said that Artemis never took up another lover, broken hearted as she was to have unsuspectingly betrayed her one true love. This is why we see Orion in his hunter glory in the night sky.

Now Cal was thoroughly depressed. He pushed some hash browns around on his plate. Artemis seemed like a pretty nice lady and if this story was true, she definitely had a sucky go of it. He couldn't even fathom if someone had tried to get him to kill Vic. Actually, he could fathom because that's exactly what Cronus and Apollo had more or less tried to get him to do.

The bell sounded above the door to the diner and Cal felt his heart beat just a little bit faster at the rush of warm, not cool air, as Vic walked in bundled up in her parka and a knit beanie with a pom-pom. Except she wasn't alone, her father and two hellhounds trailed behind.

The diner fell silent for a moment as the group entered, but then resumed their breakfasts as if it wasn't unusual to see an Italian-looking Mob boss and two tatted up guys walk into a diner at 7 a.m.

Vic spotted Cal and slid into the booth beside him, pulling off her beanie. Hades and Brim crowded onto the bench on the opposite side of the table. Asher noticed a wooden chair pushed up against the wall and grabbed it, flipping it backwards before sitting down at the end of the table.

Hades smiled. "Good morning, Callum. It's been so long since I've been in a place like this!" Vic's father looked around as if he'd just entered a magical kingdom. Never mind that he resided in what most would consider an *actual* magical kingdom.

Artemis spotted her new customers and Cal closed the book as she approached.

"Well, look what the cat dragged in," her lips curved in a polite smile.

"Now, now, Artemis, you know that I certainly wasn't brought here by a cat."

"How's Persephone doing?" Cal watched Artemis closely. Her green eyes seemed sincere as she spoke.

"She's doing well now, thank you."

"That's good to hear. Vic, hello. I'll grab another carafe of coffee and four more mugs." Artemis disappeared behind the counter and returned with two more carafes of coffee and several mugs. She took the other orders—enough to feed a small army, apparently hellhounds ate as much as a pack of wolves—and then headed back to the kitchen.

Vic poured herself a cup of coffee and dumped five spoonfuls of sugar into the cup. Cal noticed as she did that she was wearing a new ring on her index finger. It was gunmetal with a stone that resembled a sliver of wood.

Cal quickly gathered from the pleasantries circulating the table that something had gone down between Vic and her father—which he'd probably find out more about later—and that Brim and Asher were basically just along for the ride.

Hades sipped at his coffee, a concoction similar to Vic's laden with sugar. "So Cal, how goes the quest for new information about your identity?"

Cal rested his elbow on the book. "Slow. Just, you know, the whole never should have been born thing throwing off the delicate balance of the universe bit is a conundrum."

"Indeed. If it were only as simple that."

Carl prepared food quickly and Artemis reappeared with a large tray full of plates. As she distributed them around the table, Cal heard the bell above the door ring once more. He looked up, but no one else seemed to notice or care as preoccupied with their food as they were.

What he saw made him freeze. It was just like being back at the high school when everyone disappeared around him. Except no one disappeared now, it was just that all sound seemed to drop away around him. An impossibly tall black shade stood in the doorway to the diner. Its eyes burned bright red, hot as coals in its face, and it seemed to look directly at him. There was a loud snap and the sounds around him flooded back in and the shade was gone.

Chapter Fourteen

Vic

It was definitely weird seeing Artemis after seeing the younger, more goddess-like version in her dream.

When Cal had texted her that he was grabbing breakfast at The Rooster and that he wanted to share something with her, she knew it would be impossible to shake her father. After all, he was going to see her off when she entered the Void. But to both her surprise and her chagrin, her father was all for a family breakfast at the classic small town diner.

Now Vic sipped her sugar-laden coffee and watched Artemis over Brim's shoulders. The resemblance was there, but the Artemis in her dream had obviously been her mother's best friend. It was millennia ago, of course, but what had changed? What had reduced their friendship to nothing but niceties?

Cal leaned into her ear. "You're staring."

Vic pulled her gaze so that it was focused on him instead. "You said there was something you wanted to talk about?"

She'd noticed his elbow resting on top of a red book. He'd clearly been reading about something before Vic had shown up with her hellion family. Figuring he was at The Rooster, she assumed it also had to do with Artemis. All this time, they'd been so focused on Apollo and had paid his twin sister little attention.

Cal paled a little at her question and gave a near imperceptible shake of his head. This was something he wanted to discuss with only her, but what he didn't know is they didn't have much time left before she'd have to go, and she wasn't sure how long she'd actually be gone.

Her father had told her that time travel was dangerous under normal circumstances, and doubly dangerous if more than one person went. They could get separated into different places or different times. Even more difficult to make sure they both landed in the correct time and place back in the present. It would be best if she travelled alone. And even that held its dangers. If she lost her present time object, she could become trapped, or worse, the Void would notice her as an anomaly in the past and absorb her into the timeline—essentially erasing her from existence. And yet, her father still thought it was their best, and potentially only option, to stop the Void's destruction.

Hades was talking about how much he enjoyed snow—the Harvest Festival incident aside when the sky had rained a pomegranate-colored snow—and Asher was going on about how delicious the maple peppered bacon was.

Vic was already feeling unmoored from her present time. She'd heard the bell above the door ring and she'd seen the shade step in, its eyes glowing red hot. If what Cal had said was true about the skeleton he saw and the lights and people disappearing at school, then it wasn't just Olympia that was in jeopardy. She wondered if her father had noticed—the shade was a creature of his domain after all—but Hades just seemed to carry on. There was no way for Vic to tell if her father had seen it. And if he hadn't seen it that was even possibly more disturbing than if he had.

Each time Artemis came to the table to take away dishes or replenish the carafes of coffee, Vic tried to match her with the open-hearted young woman she'd seen in her dream. The lines around her eyes and the furrow of her brow. The slight softening of her body, not the muscular huntress she'd been when Persephone and Hades had wed. Her bow toting muscles obvious in the shape of her arms and shoulders. The sparkle in her sea green eyes. All gone in this present day Artemis. Something had happened that had fundamentally changed her. What was it?

Vic was anxious about traveling in time. She was a firm believer that certain things probably shouldn't be messed with: black magic, exes, the multiverse, and the delicate threads of time.

She poked nervously at her eggs.

"Well, I think that we should be going," Hades stood and threw a crisp pile of money onto the table that was much more than needed to cover the cost of their breakfast.

"Are you coming?" Vic asked Cal, but he shook his head and tapped his book.

"I have some reading I'd still like to get done and I promised my mom that I'd pick up the rest of her deliveries and drop them off."

As her father and the hellhounds walked away she leaned over and gently kissed his cheek. "I'll see you later then?"

Cal nodded. "Tell your dad thanks for breakfast."

Vic scooted out of the booth and followed her father out the diner door. She felt weird not telling Cal what was going on, but she also didn't want him to unnecessarily worry. Besides, Hades said that if all went according to plan, then Cal shouldn't even notice that she was ever gone. What could be days or weeks of time for her, would be only seconds or minutes for him. Not all that different from how Below World and Above World time functioned in relation to each other. She tried to tell herself it wasn't that different than the two dimensions, but she knew traveling a thread of time was much more nuanced than passing between her two homes.

When she stepped outside the sun was shining brightly, masking everything in blinding white. She got into the passenger seat of her father's car.

He was waiting patiently, his black leather driving gloves already on, along with a pair of aviator sunglasses.

They followed Brim and Asher along the road heading toward the location of the Void. It was hard to believe it had only been a couple of days since she had convinced Asher to go with her. She could have asked Cal, but he was still trying to figure stuff out. Figure himself out. Asher had been available to help, but he also provided brute strength. Where Cal was logic and sense, Asher was impulse and adventure. Sometimes you needed the one and sometimes you needed the other.

Vic toyed with the idea of telling her father about her dream. He could also Dream Walk, but for some reason the way Persephone had responded to actually seeing her, that was new and different. It somehow felt sacred. Instead, she settled for staring out the window at the snowy landscape.

One thing about Hades was that he did not insist on small talk. He knew it was important for people to be alone with their thoughts; therefore, he'd mastered the art of companionable silence.

Asher and Brim turned their bikes off the main road. The snow melted around their tires as they moved, creating pools of green and brown. The forest was full of dirt bike and ATV trails. Hades drove along the edge of the forest, the snow parting as he passed through it and closing up the path behind them.

Over the tree line Vic could see the Void hovering in the sky like a giant black moon.

The Cadillac met up with the Sportsters and came to a stop.

"Are you ready?"

Vic shook her head. "No."

"It will be fine. Just remember what we discussed. You have the pin?"

Vic unzipped her jacket and flashed the skull and crossbones pin that was fastened to the collar of her hoodie.

"You don't need to worry about running into yourself, since the time is before. Which also means that your mother and I also won't recognize you."

Vic nearly snorted. Fat chance. Persephone had recognized her right away in the dream. And she wasn't born for several hundred years after Hades and Persephone had wed.

"It may feel uncomfortable at first. But once you land, the feeling should dissipate fairly quickly. Look for familiar landmarks. It's hard to say exactly where you'll land, but look for structures or people you know. Don't forget that they won't recognize you," Hades repeated.

They'd talked out the details at length, at least as much as they could. She was counting on no one recognizing her. It would allow her to move about the other time freely, searching for the answer as to why the universe was out of balance. And hoping that it wasn't because of Cal.

"Alright. Let's go," Hades kissed the top of her head and got out of the car heading toward the tree line. He looked out of place in the middle of the forest wearing his black three piece suit. She hoped that she looked less conspicuous where she was about to end up.

She got out of the car and marched across the snow coming up beside her father.

"Everything will be fine," he said.

She wondered if he was trying to convince her or convince himself.

Chapter Fifteen

Daphne

Zeus had promised it wouldn't hurt.

He was right. When she'd gone to Zeus seeking his protection from Apollo, she'd been scared. What if he wouldn't listen to her? Or worse, what if he did listen, but wouldn't help her?

Luckily, her fears had been unfounded.

She'd received an audience with Zeus and Hera. They'd listened to her carefully, in the temple on the mount. Her gifts of fruit and wine laid at their feet.

After Daphne had shared her story of Apollo's plot to kill her sister and his relentless pursuit of her affection, Hera's brow had furrowed. The goddess queen was beautiful with rich brown hair the color of chocolate and eyes like sapphires.

"Husband, this cannot continue. It's like dealing with a petulant child."

"Indeed. What is it that you ask of us, Daphne?" Zeus leaned forward. He had pale blue eyes with a jagged pink scar down his cheek. Daphne wondered how the god had gotten such a fierce wound and tried her best not to stare.

"I would like to be under your protection. Far away from Apollo and safe from his interference in my life."

"And what are you willing to give up for us to make that so, Child?" Hera asked.

As long as her loved ones were safe from Apollo that was all that truly mattered.

"Everything," Daphne replied simply.

Hera had smiled then and Zeus had nodded. A servant stepped toward her and handed her a giant brown teardrop-shaped seed.

"Hermes will take you to a location and once there you will plant this seed in the earth. You will water it with honey wine and it will provide you the protection you seek," Zeus explained.

Daphne rubbed the seed between her thumb and index finger.

"Will it hurt?"

"Not at all," Zeus had smiled.

...

Hermes had flown her to a giant field surrounded by forest. There he'd waited as she knelt in the earth and dug with her bare fingers a hole deep enough for the seed to be placed. She put the freshly turned earth back over the seed and patted it carefully. Hermes handed her a small decanter of honey wine and she poured it over the planted seed so that its golden liquid completely saturated the earth.

She'd barely returned the glass decanter to his outstretched fingers when it began to happen.

The seed began to sprout little green shoots. They quickly sprang up out of the earth and reached out like vines, grabbing her by the ankle. The vines continued to wind up one ankle and then another. As they spread around her body, the seconds old growth began to brown and harden. She was rooting to the earth. She'd wanted to scream, but the vines had filled her mouth.

They wrapped around her entire body, hardening into tree bark as the spell rooted her to the earth. Her legs and torso stretched and she shot into the sky leaving Hermes as a small speck on the ground below. Her arms lengthened like branches and her hair twisted into leafy foliage. As the tree continued to grow and blossom, she felt herself—her human self—getting smaller. Mortals referred to this self as the soul. Her soul fell into the hollowed out trunk of the tree, landing roughly on the wooden floor.

Inside the tree's trunk was anything she could possibly need. Books, furniture, even a tea kettle. Daphne pushed herself to her feet and looked out the window. She could still see Hermes below in his winged sandals, holding the empty glass decanter. Later, Hermes would visit her once a year and deliver her whatever she needed. Food, her blank journaling books, new blankets to replace the threadbare ones.

She looked around at her new surroundings. She would be safe here. More importantly, so would her family. And Apollo would never be able to find her.

...

Daphne watched with curiosity when the God of the Under World stepped up to her trunk. She knew that not only had Zeus protected her, but he'd used her to protect the veil between the worlds.

He felt around her trunk and walked among her roots which where gnarled and protruded from the earth. By now, she'd been here a long time and seen Hades come and go many times. But this visit was different. Clearly, he was looking for something.

She watched with curiosity as he bent down and picked up a piece of her bark that had curled up and fluttered to the ground. He placed it in his pocket, then pressed his hand flush against the tree trunk. She felt the warmth of the Under World radiate from him and it gave her tree a little jolt of extra life. Her time as a tree was coming to an end and the Lord of the Under World seemed to know it too.

As he got into his car and drove off to the road, she wondered what he planned to do with that little piece of her bark.

An Interlude of Sorts

Artemis & Orion

"Who is *that*?" Artemis leaned forward, a strand of strawberry blonde hair falling over her shoulder.

Persephone looked over her best friend's shoulder and squinted at the row of competitors below.

"The handsome one." Artemis pointed to a man with longish brown hair. He looked young and even as he engaged in warm up stretches, his muscles looked like rippled cords. His piercing sea blue eyes were unmistakable.

"I do believe, dear friend, that is one of Poseidon's demigod children." The man bent over in a forward bend, his toga leaving little to the imagination. "I use the term children loosely," Persephone amended.

Artemis cackled in delight.

The God Games were by far Artemis' favorite celebration. Although it was unfortunate, that she wasn't allowed to participate since she was a pure bred and could have an unfair advantage over the mortal and demi-god participants. Her skill with a dagger, bow, and arrow was second to none and she tended to love showing off her skill.

"Enjoying the view?"

Persephone whirled around and Artemis noticed the imperceptible scowl before it disappeared from her face. "Apollo," she responded in greeting.

Artemis' twin brother could try the patience of nearly anyone, even her calm and mild-mannered best friend. Something about him—okay, lots of things about him—tended to rub people the wrong way. He was conceited, manipulative, and obsessive, contrary to his halo of strawberry blonde curls, big blue eyes, and dimpled smile. He looked like a cherub, but was more a devil than even Hades. She liked to think of herself as the good twin and Apollo as the evil one.

"Orion is a handsome one. All the good looks of Poseidon and the royal stature of his mother, the daughter of King Minos. I hear he's quite the shot. Some say even better than you," Apollo lowered his voice conspiratorially to his sister.

Artemis snorted. "Unlikely. Besides, he's not really your type, is he?"

"Everyone is my type," Apollo grinned but it had malice. He grabbed a goblet of wine from the tray of a passing servant and disappeared from the viewing box.

"Your brother makes my skin crawl," Persephone shuddered.

"That's typical for most insects," Artemis glowered.

A horn sounded the warning that the competition would be starting soon. At least now she knew the man's name, Orion. The God Games were a set of skill and athletic competitions designed for mortals and demi gods to win the favor of various gods and goddesses.

There was a rustle behind them. “Good day, Ladies.”

Artemis turned and was met with a man that was slightly taller than her and olive toned in skin. He had wild black hair and dark brown eyes that were almost black as well. He had a bushy black beard and where the other gods wore togas of white, he wore a toga of black.

“Oh, hello, Hades. It’s nice to see you here in the light of the Above World,” Artemis said in greeting. Some of the gods seemed afraid of Hades, but Artemis always found him pleasant. Especially since he seemed interested in her best friend.

“Hades. How delightful,” Persephone grinned shyly.

“Not as delightful as seeing you on this fine day,” he smiled. Artemis noticed it was genuine too—not all teeth like her brother’s smiles at Persephone—but this one crinkled the corners of Hades’ eyes.

“For you.” he handed her a deep burgundy-colored rose with the thorns already carefully removed. “Enjoy the games.”

“Oh. It’s lovely! Thank you, Hades.”

He tipped an invisible hat to her and then meandered away to visit with Ares and Athena. Persephone stuck her nose into the bloom.

“That man really has the hots for you, Seph.”

“You think so?”

Her giggle was drowned out by the sound of Hermes’ bugle signaling the start of the games. The first competition also happened to be Artemis’ favorite: archery. The competitors lined up across from a row of archery targets. The first round was always a traditional scoring competition. Each competitor received ten arrows. Each ring of the target held a numeric point value and the top five scorers, or half of the competitors, would move on to the second round. That's when things usually got really interesting.

The competitors were made up of all types of people: men, women, young, and old. There were no requirements for the initial entry. At Hermes' command, each competitor let sail their first arrow. Artemis noticed Orion's ease with the bow. The way he pulled it back and released it looked as natural as breathing. Persephone handed her a pair of binoculars and Artemis looked to see that Orion's first arrow hit the center of the target. Bullseye.

Artemis cheered.

The second arrows were released and again, Orion hit the center target. This continued with nine of his ten arrows hitting the center target, the tenth being borderline between the bullseye and the next ring out. Hermes announced the five competitors moving to the next round: Orion, an older man named David, a young woman, a boy, and an older woman named Katarina.

"Well done!" Artemis and Persephone cheered and clapped.

The competitors were granted a quick reprieve before the next competition. This part would require the contestants to engage in different challenges while on horseback. Two competitors would be eliminated after this round, leaving the final three.

A servant walked by offering grapes and ambrosia. Artemis took a golden goblet and a handful of grapes. She'd kicked off her sandals, and had her legs folded up beneath her.

Hermes' bugle sounded and the horses were brought forth by a stable boy. Orion was assigned a white horse with gray spots. It happened to be one of Artemis' favorites for her hunting parties. Calleigh was a fierce spirit and Artemis felt a kinship with her, able to communicate with the animal simply by using her mind. And she was fast. A thrill of delight went through Artemis when Orion gracefully mounted her horse.

The competition had five rounds, each increasing in difficulty. The first round was to simply shoot an apple off a standing target's head while on horseback. Artemis could practically do that in her sleep. After several eyes had been lost, they'd changed the competition to a wooden post with an apple on top, as opposed to a stable hand.

David was up first—he was a peasant shepherd—and he hit the target easily while astride a satin black mare. The young woman who Artemis didn't recognize, narrowly missed the target. This did not immediately eliminate her, as each of the five rounds were worth a certain amount of points determining on where the competitor ranked. The boy and Katarina both hit the target.

Calleigh with Orion on her back stomped in a circle. The riders rode bare back and Calleigh's formidable spirit was showing. "Be still," Artemis silently urged. The horse gave a petulant stomp, but settled nonetheless.

Sensing that his horse had settled, Orion started her into a gallop and when he reached the wooden marker he let his arrow fly and hit the apple cleanly.

Artemis clapped and cheered. As if sensing her master, Calleigh whirled so that Orion was facing her as he waved to the cheering crowd. His blue eyes caught Artemis in the viewing box and she felt her cheeks grow hot as his gaze fell on her. He smiled. And then Calleigh whirled around, ready for the next competition.

This time the competitors had to hit a moving target on a platform while they were still on horseback. The contraption had been created by Hephaestus and was mechanized so that it could move the apple around a large ring.

Again, David went first. He got his horse into a gallop and cleanly hit the moving target. The woman missed again, and Artemis figured she wouldn't fare well in the remaining three competitions either. Her skill was textbook and less real world applicable. The boy also missed the target, but Katarina hit it easily after righting her horse who had tried to run off course. Astride Calleigh, Orion galloped into the ring, his bow at the ready. The mechanized device moved erratically around the ring, but Calleigh was used to real hunts and she intuitively knew where to place Orion so that he could easily strike the target.

Artemis and Persephone cheered.

"He really is quite good," Persephone noted. "That's your horse isn't it? That he's riding?"

Artemis nodded. "Calleigh has a warrior spirit."

"Ah, a kindred spirit then."

The next competition was a surprise target. Each competitor would bring their horse to a gallop and a bullseye would be dropped from a tree by a stable hand hidden in the brush and holding a string that acted as a trigger. The danger here was a matter of timing. On occasion a competitor had gotten knocked clear off his horse.

Again, David started. He brought the black mare into a gallop and at the third tree a bullseye dropped. He pulled from his quiver and let his arrow soar, but it narrowly missed, sailing to the right of the target. The young woman also missed the target when it dropped, her arrow going high and to the left and disappearing in the brush. The boy also missed, his arrow landing short of the target. Katarina galloped into the tree line and when the bullseye was dropped, she hit the target on one of the outer rings.

Artemis watched as Orion patted Calleigh's neck and whispered something in her ear. Her ear twitched at his breath and Artemis wondered if Calleigh was listening as she listened to her. Orion pranced the horse in a circle before squeezing his heels into her side and she shot off like from a cannon, galloping along the tree line. At the fifth tree, Artemis noticed Orion pull back his arrow seconds before the bullseye dropped—as if he could sense it, hear the rustle of the leaves—and let it launch, hitting the target dead in the center before the board even was fully released.

The crowd went wild.

"This Orion seems to have nearly as much talent as you, my dear friend," Persephone noted.

"It wasn't necessarily kind for him to be assigned Calleigh. The fact that he can convince her to follow his desires and not her own, is a feat in itself."

Artemis clapped harder, impressed with the demigod's skill.

He played up the crowd waving and smiling broadly, not in an off-putting way, but in a way that made him seem warm and friendly. Artemis' heart beat just a little bit quicker in her chest.

The fourth round was similar to the third, except that it included two targets being dropped at random. Sometimes the stable hands dropped them seconds apart, sometimes in quick succession, other times one could drop to your left and another to your right. It was all about reload speed as well as accuracy.

David circled the black mare and began to gallop down the tree line. His targets came in quick succession giving him only seconds to reload his bow. He hit the first target, but was wide on the second. The young woman's targets came down in quick succession as well, she was prepared, and hit them both, although neither was a bullseye. The boy missed both of his targets, which came down in opposite cardinal directions. The crowd gave him a hearty applause nonetheless.

Katarina's targets also came down in opposite directions. She missed the first, the arrow soaring clear above the target, but hit the second one which had swung down to her right.

Orion trotted Calleigh around. He began to gallop down the tree line. Just as two boards began to drop, Orion pulled not one but two arrows from his quiver, loaded his bow and released. One arrow sailed left and hit the target in a near bullseye. While at the same time, the second arrow sailed to the right and hit the target dead center. Again, the crowd went wild. They cheered and yelled and stomped their feet. The viewing box shook.

"Did you see that?" Artemis leaned forward excitedly. "He shot two arrows at the same time. And hit both the targets."

Persephone smiled. "Indeed. It does seem as though it is a match made in heaven."

The fifth round of this competition involved hitting skeets released in the air. The stable hands would release five discs into the air simultaneously and the competitor had to hit them all before they struck the earth.

Again, David went first leading the mare into the ring. Once he had her going at a trot, the stable hands released the discs high into the air. David rapidly loaded his bow and hit all five discs. The crowd cheered. The young woman went next and Artemis already had rather low expectations for her. She hit three of the five skeets, missing one wide and the other hit the ground before her arrow found it. The boy gave it his best shot, hitting two of the skeets. Artemis had to give him credit. For a child, he was indeed skilled and it showed great courage to go up in competition against those much older. Katarina went next and she hit four of the targets, losing the fifth to the ground.

Orion rode Calleigh into the ring and brought her to a gallop. The stable hands released the discs high into the air and Artemis held her breath. Orion's hands were lightning quick, he shot off three arrows in quick succession before the targets had even started their descent back to earth. His hands nothing but a blur. He hit the fourth target as it just hit its apex and began its descent. Then he dug his heels into Calleigh and she shot forward, he loaded his fifth arrow, and directed Calleigh in the opposite direction away from the fifth target. What was he doing?

Then, with a jovial wink to the crowd, he turned so he was astride Calleigh with her head to his back and her posterior to his front, and let the fifth and final arrow sail. It hit the target several feet from the ground.

The crowd went berserk.

Including Artemis, who had jumped to her feet and was waving her arms, whistling, and stomping along with the common people. "Did you see that, Seph? Did you see that?" She howled.

"I can hardly imagine what he'll do for the final round with talent like that," Persephone replied.

The five competitors lined up on horseback. The young woman and the boy were dismissed, leaving David, Katarina, and Orion as the final three contestants.

The final round of the competition was about both skill and inventiveness. It was more about showmanship than the other competitions.

“Let’s get a better view, Seph!” Artemis urged her friend.

“You go, Artemis. I will keep Persephone company in your absence,” said a smooth voice. Hades had appeared at her friend’s side. The two were opposite in so many ways. Where Hades was dark, Persephone emitted light. And yet her friend’s eyes seemed to brighten whenever the Lord of the Under World came around.

“Oh, alright. You two better behave yourselves!” Artemis wagged a finger at the two of them, and then headed down the wooden stairs of the structure. She grabbed another goblet of ambrosia wine when a servant passed her on the stairwell.

She wasn’t going to miss this final round. She needed a front row seat. The ground level was crowded, but Artemis, like all the gods, commanded a certain amount of presence. People made space for her as she sidled up to the makeshift ribbon fence.

Her dress was long and she’d left her sandals at the viewing box. The grass was warm between her toes and the sun made her hair glisten like copper coils. Her golden circlet with its crescent moon pressed into her third eye.

She noticed Orion glance in her direction and something seemed to melt in his gaze before he looked back to Hermes who was giving the competitors their instructions.

Artemis sipped her wine as the competitors drew straws to determine the order of the performance. Katarina pulled the longest straw, so she would go first, and Orion the shortest, so he would go last. Katarina mounted her steed. Stable hands pulled one of the archery targets to the ring.

Hermes sounded his bugle. The crowd hushed. Katarina trotted her horse along the perimeter, gaining speed. She pulled an arrow and loaded it, then carefully adjusted her body weight so that she was riding her mount from the side, her head parallel to the ground. She let her arrow sail and it hit the bullseye.

Cheers erupted around Artemis, jostling her as people spilled their wine and grapes and olives and they were smashed beneath the crowd's feet.

Artemis applauded. Katarina was a good shot and that was definitely a trick worthy of a medal. Katarina slowed the horse and righted herself on her mount. She took a congratulatory lap around the ring, waving to the crowd.

Now, it was David's turn. Artemis wasn't sure how he was going to top that. From his expression, he wasn't sure how he was going to top that either.

David rubbed at his beard. He leaned toward one of the stable hands and whispered directions, before climbing atop his horse.

The stable hand mounted a chestnut colored horse and slung a sack over his shoulder. Artemis knew that the sack contained apples. It was a classic trick, a bit more exciting than skeet shooting. More room for error since the apples weren't aerodynamic like the disks. However, an additional layer of challenge with the apples being tossed while also in motion and not being launched into the air from a standstill.

The two men took up on separate sides of the ring. At Hermes' bugle they brought their horses to a gallop. The stable hand pulled out an apple and tossed it into the air, David pulled an arrow from his quiver, loaded his bow and hit the apple clean through. The stable hand had another in the air already, the velocity of the horses playing further tricks with the apples—eliminating the clean ascent, apex, and descent of shooting skeets. David hit the second apple. The stable hand pulled a third apple and tossed it over his shoulder, David hit that as well, snicking the apple neatly in half as it fell.

The crowd cheered once more. David did a lap around the ring waving to the crowd. Artemis applauded approvingly. She could appreciate the simplicity of a clean trick.

Now, it was Orion's turn. Artemis wasn't sure how he planned to one up himself this round. He'd already shot facing the back of his horse and shot two arrows at the same time. Short of knitting a scarf while shooting, she wasn't sure what other trickery he could bring to the table.

That was until the stable hand approached her.

"Artemis, the competitor Orion has asked for your sash." The boy fidgeted nervously from foot to foot.

"He did, did he?" She raised an eyebrow and looked over the boy's shoulder. Orion had a guilty grin on his face that made him look all the more endearing. He held up both hands in surrender.

Artemis set her goblet down and untied the mint green silk belt from around her waist. She presented it to the stable hand with a curtsy.

The crowd hooted and hollered. And Artemis felt a blush rise up her neck and to her cheeks.

Orion had mounted Calleigh and the stable hand handed him the green sash. Orion leaned over and whispered more instructions to the stable hand who nodded then ran off.

What did he have up his sleeve?

The stable hand reappeared by the ground target that Katarina had used. He raised his hand to the crowd. In between his thumb and index finger he held a single green olive. He stepped off to the side. Hermes sounded his horn. Orion then proceeded to tie Artemis' sash around his eyes. Hermes held up four fingers. "How many?" he called.

"No less than none but no more than ten," Orion responded and the crowd laughed.

He spun Calleigh around so that she danced in a circle, once, twice, thrice before he brought her to a standstill. The crowd grew quiet. *Was he mad?* Artemis wondered. *Surely, he was.*

Orion dug his heels into Calleigh's sides and she took off like a shot. As he neared the target, the stable hand tossed the single olive into the air. The breath seemed to be sucked from the crowd as they watched in amazement. Orion pulled an arrow from his quiver and loaded it by feel alone, he then waited a beat as the olive hit its apex, and then he released the arrow. There was a collective inhale of breath and then the arrow pierced the olive and pinned it to the bullseye of the ground target. The crowd went insane.

People were cheering and screaming.

Someone took up chanting his name: Orion. Orion. Orion.

The ground shook as people stamped their feet.

His smile was easy, knowing from the crowd's reaction that he'd made his mark. He slid the blindfold down and brought Calleigh to a slow trot around the ring. When he reached where Artemis was standing, he handed her back the sash with a flourish.

"My lady. Thank you for your assistance," he smiled as she took it from him.

She almost didn't know what to say but before he rode off to the winner's circle, she replied. "Not bad. For a demi god."

...

After that first meeting it was a whirlwind romance. There were double dates with Hades and Persephone on the banks of the Mediterranean. Wine and fruit, laughter and good company.

And the hunts! The best part were the hunts. Artemis had always championed herself a solo huntress, but with Orion it was as though they were two moving parts of the same whole. They moved in perfect synchronicity.

Artemis preferred to lead a hunt on the full moon. She and Orion would ride through the forest with a sea of animals among them—Artemis didn't hunt flesh and blood animals, she hunted the shadows. The shades of animals that once were alive. She took their essence and filled the horn she wore around her neck. Foxes, deer, coyotes and bears ran alongside Calleigh and Orion's steed, Hennessey.

The lovers would be gone for days, hunting shades and howling at the moon. At night they would make a bonfire and fall asleep curled in one another's arms. Artemis had never felt that she'd truly had an equal. The other gods, they thought because she was Apollo's twin, that they were equal in every way, but it simply wasn't true. She hunted the darkness. Her brother was the darkness.

Orion had explained to Artemis that the first person to put a bow into his hand was his father, Poseidon. He had a natural talent at the young age of three and found that he had much enjoyment in it. He was also an excellent swordsman, and he and Artemis would duel at length trying to disarm the other. Because his father was Poseidon, naturally, Orion was also an excellent swimmer. Artemis would lay in a wooden canoe, reading a book and sipping a glass of wine as Orion swam laps around her, his body rippling in the water below.

"My friend," Persephone said one evening as they sat in her room. "I've never seen you so happy."

Artemis laughed and squeezed a pillow to her chest. "I've never felt this alive in all the hundreds of years that I have lived. To be in love is like magic for the soul."

Persephone smiled. "Indeed. It is magic for the soul and harmony for the heart."

What they didn't notice was the small fairy that had fluttered into the room through the open window and that now rested on the window sill. She was made entirely of golden light and was about the size of an acorn. She listened to the two women as they discussed their love lives, then once she felt she had enough information, she flew directly to the Temple of Apollo.

There the little fairy told Apollo everything that she had overheard and he rewarded her with two gold coins. Fairies were fickle creatures and the fairy felt no remorse for spying on the sun god's twin sister.

Apollo paced the temple seething. He may have to relinquish Persephone to that insufferable Hades, but Artemis was his. They were two split from one. He would not share her with another. So he formed a plan that would make his sister realize that she was his one and only true destiny.

...

"Come on, Art. Just one afternoon. I'm sure your strapping lover can survive one little afternoon without you." Apollo frowned at his sister.

"Don't be so jealous, little brother," Artemis laughed, but there was no real amusement in it.

"I even brought your favorite wine from the Champagne region. Do you know how difficult that is?"

“For a god? It shouldn’t be very. Fine. If I spend some time with you, will you leave me alone?”

“I promise,” Apollo smiled, but the smile didn’t reach his eyes.

Artemis followed her brother to the shores of the Mediterranean. The day was sunny and the ocean was a crystalline blue. Apollo laid out a blanket near a rocky alcove. He poured his dear sister a glass of her favorite wine—harvested from grapes that peaked in the winter time. They drank and talked—of the Oracle, and of Apollo’s attempts to convince the Egyptians’ to worship him as their one true god. Artemis tried to listen, but being with her brother bordered on torture. He really only cared to discuss his favorite topic. Himself.

“Oh, look!” Apollo jumped up and ran over to the rocky alcove. Half-hidden in some brush were a bow and arrows. “How’d that get there?”

Artemis sipped her wine and glanced wearily at the bow and arrow. They weren’t hers. Hers were gilded in gold.

“Let’s see who can shoot the farthest!” Apollo teased.

“Brother, surely you know that you cannot win such a competition. Why would you even entertain the idea?”

But Apollo knew that his sister was hard pressed to refuse a challenge. Especially when it came from him.

Apollo loaded an arrow into the bow. “Give me a target. Any target.”

Artemis sighed, looking around. “How about that olive tree over there?” She pointed down the shoreline to a cliff overhang with a single olive tree hanging on for dear life.

“Easy,” Apollo grinned. He took aim and let the arrow soar. It came up about two feet short.

“You’re a terrible shot, brother.” Artemis laughed.

"Oh, like you can do better! These arrows are only made of wood and flint. They can only travel so far."

"Do not blame the tools for a lack of skill."

"Fine. You shoot. How about, that, out there?" Apollo scanned the Mediterranean and pointed to what looked like a dead log floating in the sea.

Artemis sighed. He would not leave her alone until she obliged. It was one of the more infuriating qualities of Apollo, although, truthfully, all of his qualities were infuriating.

He handed her the bow and an arrow. She loaded and took aim. The log seemed to buoy with the sea's currents, but she knew she could hit it easily. She pulled back her arm and released the arrow. It whistled as it cut through the air and stopped as it came into contact with the deadened log.

"See?" Artemis handed the bow back to her brother.

"Indeed, I do. You are second to none, my sister goddess."

Artemis stared off at the horizon, as Apollo poured more wine. She noticed that when she hit the target, it had begun to sink. She found it odd that a hollowed out old log would sink from a simple arrow hit.

...

"But I have not heard from him all day, Persephone! Something is wrong. I know it."

"Maybe he simply lost track of time?" Persephone asked.

"No. Orion would not break a date with me. He would send a messenger." Artemis was distraught. The sun was beginning to set and she had not heard from her lover all day long. Her heart pounded in her chest and her palms felt clammy. Something was wrong. She just knew it.

"Let us go look then."

Artemis grabbed her best friend's hand gratefully and held it to her chest. "I'm frightened."

"I'm sure all is well. Let us go search for the elusive Orion."

The two women searched the grounds. They checked the stables, but both Calleigh and Hennessey were in their stalls. Artemis patted Orion's horse nervously. The gnawing feeling in her gut growing worse.

They checked the vineyards and the temples, but still did not find him. The lights in his small stone hut were all extinguished and the chickens hadn't been fed.

Artemis bit her lip as they made their way down the path that led from Orion's home to the shores of the Mediterranean.

As they came over the dunes, that's when Artemis saw it. A large form curled up on itself near the shoreline. Was it a whale?

She began to run and Persephone was quick on her heels. As she grew closer, Artemis realized the lumpy object took on a human shape. Bile rose in her throat. She ran harder.

"Orion!" she screamed. But he did not stir.

She reached the body, his legs draped in seaweed, his hair matted with salt and water. In the moonlight she could see that his lips were tinged with blue.

"What happened?" Persephone panted coming up to her friend. "Is he…?"

"I don't know, I don't know." Artemis leaned her ear down to her lover's mouth and felt no breath. She moved to his bare chest and did not feel the familiar rise and fall.

Persephone knelt beside the lifeless body, searching. "What's this?" she asked, plucking something from Orion's side. It was a wooden arrow with a flint tip. The tip was covered in Orion's blood.

Artemis backpedaled from the body and vomited.

"Art?" Persephone whispered.

"It was me. Oh my gods, Persephone, I killed him!"

Artemis began to sob uncontrollably, her shoulders heaving.

"Surely, it was an accident!" Persephone exclaimed. She knew her friend. She harmed no one.

"It doesn't matter. Accident or not, he's gone!" Artemis cried. Then a horrible realization dawned on her. "Apollo," she sneered.

Artemis scrabbled across the sand, grabbed the arrow and snapped it into two. She scrambled to her feet and threw it as hard as she could into the sea.

She hiccupped and wiped the back of her hand across her nose.

"Shall we return him to the sea?" Persephone whispered. She gently moved the matted brown hair back from Orion's forehead.

"It doesn't feel right," Artemis replied softly, staring off at the horizon where the fathomless sea met the dark sky. "He is my equal. His heart is mine, and mine is his. Although this was by my hand, dear friend, it was murder. Treachery. A soldier's death is at sea. Orion is not a soldier."

"No, he is not. He is beautiful, wild, and free," Persephone agreed.

Artemis came and knelt beside her. "He is too big for the ocean. He is made for the sky."

She looked at Persephone and knew her friend understood. Zeus was not the one to help them. She took her best friend's hand and together they whispered. "Goddess of the night, we ask you to take this man's soul and scatter his remains across the sky so that he may be forever free. May his light serve as a reminder of the treachery that befell him and may he always be a beacon to help lost souls find their way. We ask you, Goddess Nyx, to give this hero a burial in the sky."

They repeated it two more times. Then they waited. The bright moon shone down on Orion's lifeless body, casting him in an eerie blue glow.

The shadow of a woman appeared down the shoreline, floating as if she was one of Hades' shades. Artemis stood.

The woman nodded at the young goddess, and knelt beside the dead man's body. She removed her cloak from her shoulders and motioned to Artemis. Together, they draped the cloak over Orion's body. As they did he seemed to disappear. Artemis gasped, but Nyx encouraged her to keep going. They covered his entire body with her cloak. Nyx held both Artemis' hands and moved them over Orion's body. She chanted inaudibly in an ancient tongue much older than even the beginning of time.

As they chanted, tears ran down Artemis' cheeks and her chin, dripping onto the invisible body. After a few minutes, the cloak seemed to rest flat against the sand, the body underneath gone. Artemis began to cry harder, but Nyx took her chin, and turned it toward the night sky.

There shining brightly above her were a new spattering of stars that appeared in the shape of a man holding a sword and a shield. A hunter. A hero. A protector.

"Thank you," Artemis whispered. Nyx nodded. She picked up her cloak and draped it back over her shoulders. She too knew what it was like to feel great loss and to feel the sting of betrayal from a loved one.

Artemis closed her eyes and the moon above dimmed its luminescence, so that the new constellation Orion stood out brightly against the dark sky. *May the stars serve as a reminder to your betrayal. May they serve as a beacon for true love's compass. May they watch over you and protect you during times of darkness.*

Nyx heard Artemis' silent prayer and took her hand. That night, the Olympian goddess of the moon and the Primordial goddess of the night, stood as equals.

Chapter Sixteen

Cal

Cal's coffee was cold. He was still sitting at The Rooster. He'd have to get going soon and finish his mother's deliveries.

Artemis appeared from the kitchen, dropped a tray of food off to a table of senior citizens, then stopped at his table. She put the empty tray on the counter and scooted into the booth where Hades had sat only ten minutes ago.

"What's on your mind, kid?"

"You're Artemis."

She looked at him as if he'd gone dumb. "Yeesss. And you're Callum Bishop."

"I mean your Apollo's twin sister."

Her face clouded. She knew what had happened to Persephone and she knew that her brother had a role in both nearly killing her once friend and trying to return the Titans to power.

"In DNA only."

"Were you the one who clouded Pythia's vision?"

She shrugged. "Not exactly. Some things need to be figured out on your own. She may have denounced the House of Snakes, but she is still Apollo's Oracle."

"Did you know my mother?"

At this point, he was starting to feel like he had nothing to lose. Artemis didn't strike him as a very forthcoming person, in fact, she seemed pretty closed off every time he'd seen her. But when Hades had came in, he'd noticed something shift in her demeanor. There was an old familiarity and a sort of softness.

Artemis looked sad. "A long time ago, I met your mother. She helped me…bury a friend."

Cal considered this. Was the story in the book wrong? Was it Nyx, not Zeus, who had cast Orion into the stars?

"Is that why you always seem so sad? Because of your friend?" Cal felt silly now, with the book resting beneath his elbow. He'd been wrong to come here and try to open old wounds.

"Some losses. They stay with you."

Cal's mouth went dry and he nodded.

"I know the Void is here. We can feel it. We are connected to it. I can feel it pulsing here." She pointed to her pulse point in her right wrist. "I can't give you the answers—that's not how a hero's quest works." Her lips quirked into a smile.

Cal gulped. "A hero's quest?"

"That's what you're on, isn't it? You're looking for the truth. You're afraid that you're the imbalance in the universe, causing the Void to destroy. But I'll let you in on a secret that the imbalance started long before you were even a star in your mother's eye. I am a Titan and an Olympian. Just as Cronus and Aphrodite, and Apollo. The Titans may be in Tartarus, but as you have noticed, we are all not one or the other. The problem is that some of us have not learned to co-exist. We take and we take, and that eventually creates an imbalance where the universe has nothing left to give. My mother does not deserve the same fate as my brother." She paused and looked down at her hands, which were knotted on the table. Her sparkly apricot nail polish was chipped. "Who we love should never serve as a punishment."

The bell above the diner door rang as a couple came in, shaking snow off their shoulders.

"I should go. You should too." She pointed to the book. "That's one of my favorite illustrations. Although, I do think the artist took away some of my athleticism and replaced it with some voluptuousness, but it's a good painting of us."

Cal's mouth fell open as Artemis walked away. She'd known he had the book the entire time. He scooted across the bench and slipped his coat back on. He grabbed the plastic transport container from the counter and headed into the parking lot.

He tossed the container into the van and climbed into the driver's seat.

Artemis had been forever changed since her brother tricked her into murdering Orion. Even for a goddess, there was no way to bring back a lost loved one. The Titans and Olympians were deeply entwined, and now Cal was a Primordial entwined with an Olympian. Maybe that was the problem. All these thousands of years of illicit love affairs, betrayals, and feuds were causing the imbalance.

Maybe he and Vic were just the tipping point.

Chapter Seventeen

Vic

The howl was deafening.

They'd gone over the plan one more time. Hades embraced her and whispered into her hair. "You can do this, Princess."

She nodded. Hades suspected that the Void had been trying to restore balance for much longer than anyone had realized. Aphrodite had just tried to harness its power. If Vic could find out when the Void had started destroying, then maybe she could also figure out why.

Her father kissed her forehead and released her.

She double-checked the skull and crossbones at her collar and rubbed her thumb over the surface of the ring on her index finger.

"Tell *Maman* I love her," she whispered, even though she knew Persephone already knew.

Hades nodded once and Vic summoned her wings with a single command: *Fly.*

They unfurled from her back and lifted her off the ground. Above the cloud line, the Void pulled her like a siren's song. It howled louder as she let its suction pull her in. Once she was even with the black hole she lowered her wings, not wanting the strong winds to tear the fragile skin. The air scooped her up and brought her closer.

The blackness before her was absolute and dense. Not even a speck of light inside the Void. The black hole was nearly ten feet in circumference. She stuck out her fingertips and they disappeared, swallowed up by the dark. It reminded her a bit of the passage into Arachne's cave. That made her feel a bit better. Her father had assured her that she should end up on the timeline with all her fingers and toes intact.

Trusting her father, she pushed her hand all the way through, then let her wings fold in as the darkness of the Void fully enveloped her. But even her father couldn't prepare her for the odd sensation that followed.

Her body felt as if it was being pulled in multiple directions. She felt larger than life as if she would spill out of time, but then also felt so small it was as if she was nothing more than a speck on the timeline of the entire universe.

There was no noise, only pitch black. No up or down, left right, forward or backward. And yet there was still the sensation of movement.

After a while—or what Vic assumed was a while—she heard the whispers of voices and a bright light broke through the darkness. She shielded her eyes. Things seemed to move faster and the small dot of light grew bigger as Vic seemed to approach and the voices grew louder.

The Void unceremoniously dropped her out, as if she were laundry falling down a chute. She shot her wings out like a parachute and it helped to slow her fall. She was getting better at this.

Landing on the ground, she curled her wings back in and checked that she still had both her father's pin and the ring that would ground her to the present time—her present time.

The outside light was startling after being in the darkness for what had seemed so long. She stood and looked behind her. The Void was still there just as her father had said it would be. She glanced around her. She was in a forest. She took a few steps and noticed the giant gnarled tree that acted as the gateway between the Above World and the Below World. She was in Olympia.

It wasn't snowing and instead the air was warm. Spring maybe. She was glad she'd left her parka behind. The trees were covered in new green buds and the world smelled of fresh soil. She could see the main road from where she stood.

There was a rumble beneath her feet and Vic crouched behind some low shrubs. A black Harley-Davidson Iron 883 Sportster roared through the tree. If she'd ended up in the right timeline, she was not born yet for a couple of years. That meant Asher was just a toddler. The man on the bike had red hair and even nearly two decades earlier, Vic could still recognize him as Brim.

He was a thick build and had less white in his beard. He roared off toward the road and Vic wondered where the hellhounds went before she was regularly transported back and forth between the worlds.

Vic noticed more movement and stayed crouched low. The movement was coming from the tree. The old tree seemed to be reverberating after Brim's passage. As the tree vibrated Vic thought her eyes were playing tricks on her. It was as though she could see inside the tree. And inside was what appeared to be a wood nymph—a petite woman with greenish blonde hair. The nymph's eyes were large and she peered out as if realizing that someone was watching her too.

The tree held a woman? But how did she get there? And more importantly, who was she?

Chapter Eighteen

Cal

Was Artemis right? Was Cal on a hero's quest?

Did heroes deliver baked goods to their mom's clients using her minivan? Not in the books he read. But Artemis was right. He was searching for the truth. Yet for everything that he'd learned, he felt less and less close to figuring out just what that was.

As he drove back to the house, he tried to list in his mind the things that he knew. He knew that his parents were Primordial deities. He knew that his mother had left him with his human mother to keep him safe. It was obvious the Titans and Olympians pretty much hated one another. But not all of them felt this way. Although, pretty much all of them agreed that they hated Apollo. Pythia had made a prophecy some months ago that the Sword and Air would rise as one. Clearly, that was Vic and Cal. They already had cheated death on more than one occasion. But Cal couldn't help but think they'd been kept alive on those close calls for a reason—there was something else the two of them were meant to do.

But what were they meant to do? Artemis had seemed so tired. She's been alive for thousands of years, and while some could live thousands of years and never fall in love, Artemis had to live thousands of years having lost the love of her life. Maybe it was just time for a change. But what change, and how could he and Vic help to make that change?

A sole tree in the middle of a snowy field caught his eye. It was the tree that acted as passage from the Above World to the Below World. His van wouldn't drive through the snow—it didn't have the heat of the Under World that caused the snow to melt around the tires. So, instead he pulled off the side of the road and put on his hazards. The roads were pretty empty because of the previous evening's storm.

He looked at the tree, standing by itself. To a passersby it looked like a tree that had been struck by lightning one too many times. But Cal knew that looks could be deceiving. He didn't know much about the tree though. How did it get there? Did it always grant passage between the two worlds? The forest line was so close, yet the tree stood alone and apart. Looking at it against the freshly fallen snow, it looked ancient and scarred. Tired.

Zipping up his parka to his chin, he got out of the car and began the trek from the road and across the field toward the tree. As he walked he noticed the mushy tracks indicating that Hades and the hellhounds had been here probably after breakfast. The cold was biting and the wind whipped, promising more snow to come.

Crossing the field, the wind was relentless, and bit at his nose, cheeks, and chin. He held up his hand to protect his face and as he did so, the wind seemed to go around him as if his hand motion had thrown up a shield against it. He was the Air after all. He'd redirected it without even meaning to do it. As he approached the tree he couldn't shake the sensation that he was being watched. He looked along the tree line, but through the bare trees, he didn't see anyone in the forest.

He reached the giant tree. It was really old. He'd even used the tree to cross into the Below World before. Passage was only granted with a hellhound so that people weren't just randomly falling into the Below World.

The snow around the roots of the tree was all melted. The age of the tree had caused its bark to take on a gray cast. In fact, he wasn't even sure that he noticed it in bloom this fall. It just always seemed perpetually bare.

He pulled off his glove and pressed his hand to the ridges of the trunk. The tree seemed to shudder in response. Was this how the creatures had gotten into the Above World? But how had they passed through without a hellhound?

The hair on the back of his neck stood up, and again he couldn't shake the feeling that he was being watched by someone or something. There was a rustle from the forest behind him and he turned slowly. But there was still nothing there. Not even a bird or a rabbit. Something howled in the distance.

He put his bare hand back against the tree and he heard a giggle this time along with the shudder.

Something was definitely going on.

He heard a distinct voice in his head say: *Try knocking.*

Figuring he'd experienced stranger on more than one occasion, especially since meeting Vic, he did just that. He tapped his knuckles against the tree trunk. At the base of the trunk a small arched doorway materialized. It was much too small for him to fit through, but he decided to crouch down and stick his head inside. As he did so, his body seemed to shrink until he was just the right size for the doorway. Magic.

When he crossed the threshold the door swung shut behind him, trapping him inside the trunk of the tree.

He noticed he was standing in a small foyer on top of what appeared to be a hand-woven rug. The house smelled like tea and scones and books. It was a small house, he could see it in its entirety from the entryway, and everything inside seemed to be made of basic materials like wood, metal, and fabric.

"I told you knocking would work," came the same voice that had told him to try knocking.

A small woman with large brown eyes and greenish blonde hair appeared at the top of a stairway that ran along the outer edge of the tree trunk and to a floor above him.

"Who are you?" he asked. Then realizing his manners. "Hello, I'm sorry for barging into your home."

"I'm Daphne. Or at least I was. I'm actually not sure who I am anymore. It's been a very long time since I needed a name."

"Are you the guardian of the portal between worlds?"

Daphne descended the stairs and entered into the small kitchen where she immediately began preparing a pot of tea.

"Have a seat, God of Air."

"You know who I am?"

"I knew you would be coming for quite some time. I guess you could say I've been expecting you."

She pulled two small teacups from a cabinet.

The house was extremely modest and didn't seem to have many furnishings. The woman was dressed in a simple canvas jumper and was barefoot.

"Were you put here by Hades?"

"Hades? Heavens, no. Zeus gave me this home so that I would be protected. The exchange was then that I would watch over the beings who travel in and out of the Under World. A small price to pay to be rid of that nasty Apollo."

"Apollo?" Cal stepped farther into the house. How was it that one god could cause so many problems?

"Indeed. He killed my sister because he thought that she was coming between us."

"I have heard that he's the jealous type."

"More like the insane murderer type. So, I beseeched Zeus and Hera for protection. So that Apollo would not find me and so that the rest of my family would be safe." Daphne's eyes turned sad. "They're probably long dead by now."

She poured two cups of tea and brought them into the small sitting area that had two wooden rocking chairs and a little table. She sat in one of the chairs, her feet barely touching the ground, and Cal sat in the opposite chair.

"Are you here to give me news?" Daphne asked.

Cal sipped the hot tea, hoping to take the chill off. It tasted like grass.

"I'm not sure. I know something strange is happening. I've seen creatures in the Above World that shouldn't be there."

"Yes, the veil is growing thinner. I've noticed that as well."

"Thinner? Does that mean it can grow so thin that it disappears entirely?"

Daphne sipped her tea. "In theory. Which is good for me because then it means my time as guardian is over."

"What about for everyone else?"

"Well, it would mean that all the demons and shades from the Under World could walk around the Above World. Or that any regular human could just slip into the Below World."

That would be a total and complete nightmare.

"Can we stop it?"

Daphne tapped her chin thoughtfully. Her mannerisms made her seem really young, but from her appearance Cal could tell that she was easily hundreds of years old.

"I don't think so. You see, the portal was never really meant to exist. The mortal and immortal worlds used to be comingled. But that was at a time when the mortals worshipped the immortals as their deities. Now…well, now they sing in bands with mortals, and work in restaurants with them. The two worlds have become so blended, but it wasn't ever meant to be this way." She paused and sniffed. "You smell like snickerdoodles."

"So I've been told," Cal replied.

"The more time the immortals spend among the mortals, the more diluted the immortal magic becomes. That includes this tree and this portal."

"Are you saying the immortals are becoming mortal?"

"That's one way of thinking of it, but not quite. They still seem like highly magical beings by comparison. But compared to the old days when gods were worshipped and given offerings and had temples constructed in their honor, they have become weak."

Cal put down his tea. "There's an imbalance in the universe. Is that the cause of the imbalance?"

"The earth is tired. Gaia was not made to support multiple dimensions for millennia. So there is a tear between worlds. And not only the Above World and Below World. The immortal and mortal worlds as well."

"So then, we close the portal. The immortals stay in their dimension and the mortals stay in ours."

"Ah, but you are an immortal too. Do you think such a choice would be so easy?"

Cal had already forgotten. And no, he didn't think a choice would be all that easy. But then he thought of Artemis and how tired and heartbroken she seemed. Or how all the minds of the townspeople had to be altered after the Harvest Festival. The people wouldn't even have been in danger if there was no connection between the worlds. Let alone would they have needed their minds altered. It seemed the Void was just trying to do what should probably have been done a long time ago. How many human wars had been caused either by the gods or in their names over the millennia?

"I think saving humanity would be the easy choice."

"At your own expense? What if you chose the immortal world? You would never see your human family ever again. Your mother. Or your sisters. But if you choose the mortal world, you will never be able to see Vic again. Or ever have the possibility of meeting your immortal parents."

"I see your point."

"I've had a long time to think about this, Callum Bishop. I always knew this day would come. The decision has to be made by two together. Two opposites. One of heaven and one of hell. One light and one dark. One from Above and one from Below."

So that was the rest of Pythia's vision. He and Vic would have to make a decision about the two worlds together. He wasn't sure he could convince Vic to leave her mother and father forever. He didn't even consider it fair to really ask her.

And he knew she would never ask him to leave his mother or sisters either.

"Some decisions are worth the difficult conversations. Perhaps it's time that the mortal world experienced some peace and did not have the gods meddling in their affairs. Maybe a human girl would be better without someone like Apollo pursuing her relentlessly. Maybe Rachel would have been better off if Cronus had never crossed her path, or Nyx before him. Maybe sometimes the gods simply ask for too much."

The way Daphne talked it seemed like she'd been waiting a lifetime to be able to say these things. And Cal was right. He knew his mother would never not want to have raised him. But her life could have been a lot simpler if Nyx hadn't left her with a baby all those years ago.

"Would you like some more tea? I'm afraid my days here are limited and I'm trying to enjoy all the creature comforts of home while I still have them." She picked up the pot and poured him another cup before he could respond to her question. "Your friend and I had a very similar conversation."

"My friend? You mean Vic?"

"She was just here. Well, maybe it wasn't just here. It could have been twenty minutes ago or twenty years ago. When you live in a tree it's difficult to keep track of time." Daphne shrugged. "But I think you'll find if you talk to her, that she may have already made up her mind."

Cal didn't doubt that. He just wondered in which direction she'd made it up. Would she choose to stay with him or would she choose to be with her family?

Chapter Nineteen

Nyx & Uranus

The night and the sky were intimate lovers. But it wasn't always this way.

Uranus and Gaia birthed the Titans. The Titans then birthed the Olympians. And eventually the two groups waged war on one another, nearly ravaging the earth in the process. The Titanmacy lasted one hundred years. The blood of her children seeping into the earth caused much pain for Gaia. So much pain that the waters dried up, plants wilted, and animals died. Her heart so broken that she could not provide the nourishment the land needed, thus creating the Desert of Lemnos in northern Greece. A desert world in an otherwise lush landscape.

Gaia withdrew and after trying for hundreds of years to coax her back out, Uranus grew wary. The sky and the earth were opposites. And although opposites attract, it's not always a sustainable attraction.

Uranus turned to his beloved friend, the Night. She was always there—cloaking the earth and hiding the pain every evening. The Night is a loyal companion to the Sky.

When Nyx became pregnant with child she told Uranus. A child of Night and Sky would be born of the Air. This child was special. He was not a Titan nor an Olympian. He was not a child of Gaia. He was a child of Heaven—of Light and of Darkness.

Nyx knew that this child would be much needed when the timing was right. One time, she sat with the goddess of the moon and placed her lover in the stars to provide a guide in the darkness. This child would also be a light in the darkness. Literally, his mother the darkness and his father the light of the heavens. He would represent the duality of the worlds. All the pieces would fall into place when he realized his true identity and only then could the earth begin to heal herself.

Knowing this child would change everything, Nyx made the difficult decision to hide her child in the folds of time, knowing that the universe would call to him when the time was exactly right. She tore a piece of her cloak—the night sky—and wrapped him inside it. She watched and waited for a young woman to take care of her child. So she could remain close enough to observe, but far enough removed that her son would have a good life.

The woman she decided upon to raise her child was a tailor's apprentice. She lived a simple life and worked very hard, more importantly she was always kind to all of her customers, even the disagreeable ones. Nyx decided to leave her baby with this woman for safekeeping, but she also left him a clue. In his blanket she animated the constellations, making the constellation of Orion particularly bright. The moon goddess would know when change is needed. She would recognize the hero in Nyx's own son because she had so passionately loved a hero herself. Callum's mother just hoped that when the time came, he would know enough to make the right decision.

Chapter Twenty

Vic

There was definitely someone looking at her.

And through a tree no less. Trees were supposed to be solid, opaque things. The wood nymph blinked at her again.

"Well don't just stand there," she finally said. Her voice was as clear as if she were standing right beside Vic.

"Um, hello?"

The nymph rolled her eyes and pointed toward the roots of the tree. Vic squatted down and peered at the trunk, noticing a knot in the bark that oddly resembled a keyhole. She placed her fingers against it and a small door materialized in the side of the tree.

She pushed and it swung open.

Knowing full well how these things tended to work, Vic placed an arm and shoulder through the small doorway and then her head before dragging the other half of her body all the way through. Each body part magically shrinking to the size needed to accommodate her inside the wood nymph's house.

"There. Now isn't that loads better?" the nymph asked.

Vic nodded. She was sitting on her butt in front of the now closed door, which had swung shut behind her once she was inside.

"You live here? In this tree?"

"I do. Funny you never noticed in your comings and goings. Funnier that you happened to notice right now."

Vic looked down at her ring with the amber colored petrified wood. It was from this tree. She had thought the ring was the present day object. But maybe she had it wrong and the Void put her exactly where she needed to be.

"It's a lovely ring. I remember the day your father found that curved little piece of bark."

Vic looked up at the wood nymph. She didn't look like a typical wood nymph. Her skin was human-like and not wood-like. She had what appeared to have once been blonde hair, but it was tinged with green. There were circles under her eyes and the nymph seemed tired. She wore a simple canvas jumper.

"Are you a wood nymph? Because you don't look much like a wood nymph to me."

"I am not of the tree. I simply live in the tree."

"Are you human?"

"I suppose that's what you could call me. I'm not sure what I am anymore."

"Are you trapped here?" Vic stood up. The trunk had a staircase that ran along the outside wall leading up to other floors. There was a little table with two rocking chairs, and windows looking out, which Vic realized is how she saw the woman in the first place. Some creatures could only be seen when they wanted to be seen.

"I am protected here. I was put here at my request. They wanted a guardian between the worlds and I wanted protection. It was mutually beneficial."

"Aren't you lonely?" Vic asked. "I don't imagine you get many visitors."

"No, not particularly. Hermes will visit on occasion. And I can see you, your father, and the hellhounds."

"What's your name? You have a name, don't you?" Vic sat in one of the rocking chairs. She was obviously here for a reason, so she figured she may as well make herself comfortable.

"My name is Daphne."

"It's nice to meet you, Daphne. I'm Vic." She flipped through her mental rolodex of Greek mythology. The name Daphne was familiar.

"Would you like some tea?"

Vic didn't really, but she didn't want to turn down someone's hospitality. "Sure."

Daphne busied herself in the kitchen. Vic looked around. There weren't any photos or anything on the walls of the little house. The furniture was sparse and worn. There was a threadbare, knitted blanket draped over a small linen couch. The windows somewhat made up for the quaint furnishings, letting in lots of sunlight and casting the entire room in a cozy, golden glow.

"Have you lived here a long time?" Vic asked.

Daphne picked up a tea pot and poured into two small cups.

"Hundreds of years? A thousand? I think I've lost count. I have journals where I've kept track. More to help me remember who I am, than anything of particular interest."

Daphne brought over a small tray with the teapot, pink sugar, unicorn milk, and two cups.

"Will you be leaving here soon?" Vic asked picking up a cup and placing a heaping spoonful of sugar into the amber colored liquid.

Daphne nodded solemnly. "I do think it will be soon. But what is soon over the span of hundreds of years? Hours feel like minutes and days feel like hours. Or is it the reverse?"

For a moment, there was nothing but the clink of spoons against tea cups. Vic felt bad for Daphne. She may have asked to be protected, but this seemed more like a punishment than a protection. When Vic was younger and had misbehaved, she'd be sent to her room where she couldn't be with the family or Asher. This seemed like that.

"Do you know why you're here?" Daphne asked Vic after taking a sip from her cup.

"I'm not sure," Vic replied honestly. "I'm not from this time, I don't think. The Void has begun destroying in my time. I don't hear its howl, so I must be in a different time. I was hoping to find out why the Void is trying to destroy everything and if there was anything that I could do to stop it."

"Would you like to hear a story?" Daphne had gotten a dreamy look on her face and Vic wasn't sure she had even heard what Vic had just explained to her. She sniffed her tea cup, but it just smelled like earth with a hint of nutmeg and sugar. She couldn't imagine that Daphne would poison herself. Maybe all the time living alone made her a little erratic. It was probably strange entertaining a guest when one never had guests, or even much human interaction for that matter.

"Sure. I'd love to hear a story," Vic said and smiled hoping that it reached her eyes and looked encouraging.

"There was once a beautiful princess."

Uh-oh. Vic hoped this wasn't some delusional story Daphne had entertained herself with the last eight-hundred years.

"But she was unlike any princess before her. She was beautiful, but she was also tough. Her knife and sword skills were second to none. Her father taught her to be both tough and smart. He filled her head with books and knowledge. Enlightenment. Light. He taught her to be a fierce fighter, but to also use her mind. People were amazed at how this princess was made. She was made of light and dark, but her home was in the darkness. The people called her the Princess of Darkness. The princess would grow up and expose the lies and betrayals of her people. More importantly, she would question everything. She would slay monsters—terrible monsters—in her quest for the truth. Despite her hardened exterior, the princess had a heart of gold. Her father had taught her to love openly and freely. And that even though love was a risk, it was always a risk worth taking. As the princess grew older, she began to realize she had been raised for a responsibility much, much bigger than just helping her father rule his kingdom. She'd been raised to make a very difficult decision. The princess would live in another realm, and in that realm she would meet a handsome man—not a prince—unlike any man she had ever met. And together, they would need to make a difficult decision that would affect both of their lives forever."

Vic's brow furrowed. It was pretty clear she was the princess in the story. Her father had certainly done all of those things. But what was the decision?

Daphne noticed her confusion, and continued. "The earth had grown tired. Blood had been shed over the millennia. Wars had been fought in the names of the people of the princess's world. And when the earth grew tired, it also grew weak. The two kingdoms started slipping together, but that was a bad thing. The princess' kingdom was a dark and scary place. She knew the people in the world that shared the other kingdom were not prepared for that type of darkness. Perhaps it was time for the kingdoms to rejoin and remain in their own world, and leave the earth to recover in peace."

How did Daphne know that the demons and shades had begun to appear in the mortal world? Had it been happening for much longer than even Vic realized?

"On the Winter Solstice, the princess will have to make a decision."

"Wait. What did you say?" This wasn't the first time Vic had heard these words.

Daphne repeated it and Vic's skin erupted in goose bumps. Those were the words her mother had whispered to her. The solstice was only a few days away. In the dream, her mother had told her that she will have to make a big decision on the solstice. She told her she knew that no matter what, she would make the right decision, and to not be afraid. Her last words to her before Vic woke up were: *The dark and the light will rise as one. One from below and one from above. They will determine our fate. And we must accept whichever destiny they choose for us.*

"Do you know my mother?" Vic asked Daphne.

She shook her head. "I'm afraid not."

"Will the decision—whatever it is—will making it stop the Void from destroying? Will it save Olympia?"

Daphne nodded. "It should." She reached out a hand. Her hands were very tiny and delicate looking compared to Vic's calloused ones. "But, Princess, you know what the decision is that needs to be made."

Vic bit her lip. She did know, she just didn't want to be the one to have to think about it. She was the first pure Olympian born in thousands of years. Was it a coincidence that two Olympians and two Primordial deities gave birth to children within the same two decades? Had Hades and Persephone and Nyx and Uranus known that this time would come and that their children would be the one to end it? How was that even possible?

As if reading her mind, Daphne repeated what she said earlier: "Minutes seem like hours and hours like days. When you live for thousands of years, you grow weary. You become tired, and sometimes careless. The two worlds were never meant to be entwined this long. Perhaps, the only way to see that it needs to end, is with fresh eyes. What fresher eyes than the eyes of youth?"

"And if we don't end it?"

Daphne frowned. "I think you know what the result will be. You've already seen it. The veil between grows thinner, Princess. Soon it will not be at all."

Chapter Twenty-One

The Council —19 Years Ago

The steel hexagon doors slid open.

Hades looked up. He had been studying a map of the Above World. The map was covered in red Xs. These were the areas where the veil between the mortal world and immortal world were thinning. Over the millennia, the Olympians had assimilated somewhat with human beings. It wasn't on purpose necessarily. It was more out of necessity.

When human beings stopped worshipping them as gods who could provide things for them: protection, rain, crops, wealth, even love—they'd grown restless. The gods were meant to be needed. They were no doubt an egotistical bunch, but if the humans didn't need their help anymore, then what choice did they have, but to live among them and perhaps provide help when they could.

The man who had entered the room was formidable. He was taller than Hades and even taller than Zeus, but he carried the air of the God of Gods. He had a full white beard and piercing blue eyes. His skin was very pale, but he was of an athletic build. He dressed in the old ways, complete with a white toga and a laurel wreath around his head.

There was a hiss as the doors opened again. Persephone entered looking her usual ethereal self: pale skin, straw colored blonde hair, and a long lavender sundress. She always looked and smelled like a dose of spring time. She was accompanied by a woman with jet black hair and pale skin. Her eyes were striking green and she wore a midnight, velvet cloak. She was also much taller than an Olympian, nearly as tall as the man who had entered just before.

"The others should be here any moment," Persephone said. She pressed a button on the wall and the hexagon-shaped table moved and shifted on an unseen mechanism to form into an octagon to accommodate the two extra guests.

It was always weird for Hades to see Persephone in the War Room. She was the antithesis of anything hard, cruel, or calloused. This room was sterile. It was designed for tactical planning and difficult decisions.

"It's good to see you, Uranus." Hades said extending his hand. The older god took it.

"You remember Nyx?" Uranus replied releasing Hades hand.

Hades nodded. "Thank you both for coming."

Nyx nodded as she took a seat at the table. The doors slid open a final time and in walked Zeus, Poseidon, Ares, and Athena.

Zeus always had a stoic air about him. He'd obtained a nasty scar in a battle with the Titans, which ran down the side of his face that no amount of magical ointments or elixirs seemed to heal or fade. His hair was nearly to his shoulders and white like Uranus. Hades wondered if that's what the burden of their immortality had done to them.

Poseidon was less serious than either of his brothers. He always had some degree of an impish smile on his lips. His eyes were the color of the ocean and his hair was sun-bleached and curled at the ends from the salt of the sea.

Ares, on the other hand typically went through various *phases*, as Persephone liked to call them. His current phase was a bit of moody grunge rock. His dark hair was long and wild instead of its usual Mohawk. He wore a ripped black t-shirt that showed off his numerous tattoos, along with a flannel shirt tied around his waist and black combat style boots. Ares was the God of War, but as less mortals called upon him to win their battles, he'd turned his aggression toward various music careers.

Athena rounded out the Council Members. Zeus was the General, Hades dealt with the darker side of things and its repercussions, Ares was the strategist, Poseidon provided a perspective that was lighter and less intense than the others, and he could also manipulate the weather that Zeus could not. And Athena brought wisdom. She was younger than the rest of the council and often restless. She was also a wordsmith which was key for treaties and doctrine. She'd even written numerous novels under various pseudonyms over the millennia.

Each Council Member took a seat at the table, except for Hades who remained standing. The River Styx ran underground and slightly above them, providing the faint rushing sound of water.

"Let us begin," Zeus said with a nod.

"Well, I think you all know the reason that we are here." Hades pressed a button in the surface of the table and a holographic version of the map he'd been studying projected into the middle of the table so that it could easily be seen by each attendee.

"The Xs mark where the veil is beginning to thin."

Athena squinted. "So many?"

"Indeed. The hellhounds are rounding up shades and demons at least once a week. Here," Hades pointed to an X near a mountain range. "A mortal slipped through and ended up on Mount Orthrys. Luckily, thanks to some quick thinking from Pythia, a simple potion seemed to be enough to convince the mortal that he'd been hit by a falling rock while on his hike."

"It's been too long," Ares said simply.

"What choice did we have though? We exist on the needs of the mortals. If they have no need for us…" Athena's voice trailed off and her gray eyes clouded.

"Then do we even exist at all?" Persephone asked softly.

"If Apollo hadn't introduced monotheism in Egypt in the first place, would we even be in this mess?" Ares asked.

Hades didn't disagree. Considering Zeus was the father of Apollo, he just said, "He definitely has not matured at the same rate as the rest of us."

"He is selfish," Zeus said simply. "And his careless and reckless behavior has put many in danger over the millennia. Not excluding his own twin sister."

"Artemis," Nyx said softly. "Hopefully, she takes some solace knowing that Orion's soul is safe in the sky each night."

"Thank you for that," Zeus turned to Nyx. "I thought Artemis was destined for fratricide that day. I think your kindness saved her."

Nyx smiled and shrugged. "Orion protects her from further betrayal. He is her light in the darkness. I do think she longs to be with him though."

Hades reached over and squeezed Persephone's hand. He could not imagine having her taken from him too soon. Apollo deserved a fate in the domains of the Under World, but that fate was reserved for the souls of mortals.

Uranus was studying the map which was rotating slowly.

"What do you suggest we do, Hades?"

Hades sighed. "I think that it is time."

Poseidon's eyes grew wide. "Surely, Brother, you cannot mean…"

Hades nodded. He put his hands in his suit pants' pockets and began to walk around the table.

"I do mean that. I think that it's time the gods stayed in their own kingdoms, and let the mortals live a life without us. They have science and philosophy and little need for Titans and Olympians anymore. We have not held up our own end of the bargain, many of us meddling in their lives even without their bequest. We have caused wars out of our own boredom, changed history with our need to be worshipped, and allowed our blood to poison Gaia."

Athena picked at a string on her sweater. "I can't argue with any of those things. The gods were meant to help accelerate humanity. And now we have accelerated them past the need of even their creators."

"But what if they do need us?" Ares challenged. "What if something happens?"

"Like what? Look at the Greek and Roman empires. Both have fallen. Countless other cultures that worshipped gods have all fallen. If we cannot save them, then what is the point of us?" Persephone asked.

Zeus turned to Uranus and Nyx. "You are older deities. What do you think?"

Nyx sighed. Her cloak moved like water over her body, revealing shining stars and moons. "I do fear that we are obsolete. There was a time when the humans relied on us for something as simple as the rising and setting of the sun. Now, their science has proved the rotation of the earth and explained their seasons. Their science, religion, and philosophy has made us practically obsolete."

Uranus nodded solemnly. "I must agree that I fear at this time we have the potential to do more harm than good. Perhaps it is best if our kingdoms were permanently sealed off from the mortal world."

"What about demi-gods? Like my Orion?" Poseidon asked. "They can function in either world."

"But even Orion felt more at home in the mortal world, Poseidon. He loved to hunt and chase, and practice his weaponry. In the mortal world, those like Orion are considered heroes. Perhaps, they could help to continue to move human kind along in our stead." Persephone was keen to remember that not only had her best friend lost a lover and kindred soul that day, but that Poseidon had also lost one of his sons.

"So we are all in agreement then, that the worlds remain separate and that the passage between mortal and immortal must come to an end. The Under Kingdom and the Kingdom of Mount Orthrys should remain together. How then do we go about doing this?"

"It is something that no Olympian, a Titan, or a Primordial can do on their own. We need it to be closed by an heir of their own accord, for non-selfish and pure reasons. It is the way the Void originally intended it," Uranus explained.

"If no one can do it on their own, then how is it supposed to be done?" Ares asked.

"The Oracle said that there would be a child of the heavens and a child of the darkness. One light and one dark. These two will cross paths and between the two of them, they will close the dimensions," Hades explained.

"Assuming that they can agree," Poseidon said. "It seems there are a lot of variables."

"The Oracle is never wrong," Athena pointed out.

"And, as you can see, Persephone is already with child," Hades gestured to his wife.

"And so am I," said Nyx glancing at Uranus. "I'm due in two more months."

"A child of the heavens and a child of the darkness," Zeus mused. "So that settles it then? You must not interfere in the upbringing of the children. You must not tell them or influence them in any way."

Nyx nodded. "We plan to leave our son with a mortal woman. It is safer for him that way. To think of a Primordial born after all this time…" She let her voice trail off. It pained her to give up her son, but she knew it would provide him with all the opportunities that he would need. And if she was lucky, some day he would return to her.

"And we will take the binding vow," Hades said to Zeus. "Persephone and I both."

"Very well," Zeus said. He stood and Hades snapped his finger. A red demon servant holding a tray materialized beside him. On the tray was a coil of rope and three goblets of a blood red pomegranate wine.

Zeus picked up the rope and gestured for Hades and Persephone to come closer. He took the rope and wrapped it around their left wrists, then wrapped it around his own left wrist until all three of them were bound to one another. He summoned some bright blue electricity from his fingertips and touched the loose end of the rope. A blue aurora formed around their entwined wrists.

"Hades and Persephone, with this binding vow, you both swear to not influence your—" He looked at Persephone.

"Daughter," she answered.

"Your daughter's decision regarding the closing of the dimensions. She must come to her own conclusions, purely and of her own accord. Shall this binding vow be broken, you will both meet a sudden and abrupt death upon the transgression. Do you so swear to uphold this vow?"

"We do," said Hades and Persephone at the same time.

The blue electricity snaked up their arms and to their hearts where it encircled their hearts in its brilliant aura. If they broke the vow, this would be their sudden death. With their free hands they each took a goblet from the tray.

"To death and life, to truth and lies." They said in unison. Then all three of the gods took a drink.

As they drank the blue light broke free from Zeus' fingertips. It glowed white hot for an instant than faded.

Zeus put down his goblet.

"It is done."

Chapter Twenty-Two

Cal

Cal now had a new understanding of Cronus' ambitions. He hadn't just wanted an alliance. He'd been biding his time because he'd realized what was at stake. That if Cal aligned with Cronus and Apollo, then perhaps he would not close the veil between realms. Unfortunately for Cronus, he'd vastly underestimated Rachel's influence on her adoptive son, as well as the significance of Vic. There was much to be said for relationships established on a foundation of mutual trust. Something Cronus didn't understand.

He now stood outside of the tree, restored to his normal full-human size. His mom's van was still on the side of the road with the hazards flashing. It felt like he'd been inside the tree for hours, but based on the position of the sun, it appeared it had only been minutes.

The tea had warmed him up and he didn't feel the cold now as he made his way back toward the road. He knew he had to find Vic and share with her what he'd just learned, but something told him that it wasn't yet time. Maybe she had some self-discovery she had to do on her own too.

Even though he now had a greater understanding of his role in everything, he still had some questions.

He got into the driver's seat of the van. The car was still warm from his arrival. He turned off the hazards and pulled back onto the deserted road.

Artemis' mother was Leto and Leto was a Titan. Which meant that both Artemis and Apollo were both part Titan. So it made sense then that if Cronus hoped to see the Titans back in power and worshipped by mortals again, that he would choose someone as egotistical as Apollo—willing to betray his own family without even thinking twice—but who was also a Titan.

As he drove along with his mind wandering, he lost his full attention on the road. He saw a flash in front of him and was startled, jerking the wheel of the van to avoid hitting what he assumed was a deer. The jerk of the wheel was enough sudden movement to catch a patch of ice on the road and send the van spinning into a snow-covered ditch.

He swore and pressed the gas, but the van just spun its wheels. Frustrated at his carelessness, he climbed out of the van. There was no way he would be able to dig out the van. He'd need a tow truck.

He peered in the direction he had just came and there was no sign of a deer or other animal anywhere in sight.

What was it then that he had seen? He stepped into the road. It was lightly covered with loose snow. He walked a ways, following his tire marks. He knelt down. There was no hoof prints or any prints of any kind.

He stood up and looked into the woods. There was a flash of something dark. Was it a shade that had gotten through the weakening veil? There were no oncoming cars, so he trotted across the lanes and into the edge of the forest.

"Hello?" he called out, unsure if that was a smart or a stupid thing to do.

Nothing answered him. But he distinctly heard the crunching of snow. As if someone was walking. Snow fell off a tree branch, making a soft whooshing sound as it fell to the ground below.

He followed the sound—which sounded very much like footsteps, but which left no prints in the snow. It seemed to leap from tree to tree, encouraging him to go deeper into the forest. Cal was fairly certain there were numerous fairy tales and horror movies that began this very way.

As he followed the sound, he got farther and farther from the road. Deeper into the forest the sound seemed to get closer. He stopped when he reached a pile of stones that seemed to mark some kind of entrance to a tunnel. The stones were carefully arranged and lightly dusted with fresh snow. There were some pine tree branches around the entrance.

Cal had kind of had his fill of visiting caverns after the visit to Arachne. Caves where gods were concerned often meant monsters. Caves where gods were not concerned meant things like Bigfoot. Either way, Cal's knowledge of caves was pretty simple: caves equals bad things.

Disappointed, he stood up to head back toward the minivan. He'd call a tow truck on his way and if he was lucky it would be there shortly after he got back.

There was a long, low howl from the entrance to the cave followed by a whimper.

Cal hesitated.

If there was an animal in distress he couldn't just leave it. Maybe he actually *had* nearly hit something out on the road.

With a deep sigh, he ducked under the entrance to the cave, nestled inside the hillside. He pulled out his phone and shook it to turn on the flashlight function. He had not brought along his flashlight for his mother's deliveries and breakfast with the Hadens.

The cave sloped downward and the floor and sides were packed dirt. It appeared that someone had intentionally made this entrance. He knew the cave systems were vast in Olympia, both in the mountains and underground. His geography teacher had spoken of them several times and was both an avid hiker and spelunker. That fact gave him slight reassurance that the cave entrance could have been intentional. Maybe it was part of some spelunking park system or something.

He paused and listened. He could hear breathing echo through the tunnel. He continued on, the outside light growing dimmer and dimmer the deeper he made his way. He looked at his phone screen. No service. Of course not. Definitely a horror movie. Maybe he heard the howl of the mythical dire wolf and was about to stumble into its lair. If he'd simply been paying attention while he was driving, he wouldn't even be in this situation right now. *Just make sure it's not hurt,* he told himself. *Then you can get back to the forest and call for a tow truck.*

The tunnel veered to the left and then sloped downward. It smelled old and musty—and inhabited. There was something dark smeared across the dirt floor. It could have been the blood of the animal he'd hit...or the blood of a kill made for dinner. He couldn't tell if it was fresh or not. There was no tinge of metallic in the air, so he convinced himself it was old. He gulped.

He really was ill-prepared. He had no weapons. A phone and the ability to create some...wind drafts?

As he neared another corner he heard the distinct sound of breathing.

No, not breathing.

Panting.

He paused, fearful to round the corner.

Deer didn't pant. They also weren't carnivores. Which left very limited remaining options. A puma or some other kind of wild cat, a wolf or maybe a bear, or if he was really lucky, just a regular dog that happened to be lost.

He could just turn back. That's what normal, sane people did. They turn around and go in the opposite direction of danger as opposed to toward it.

But something had caused him to nearly crash in the road. He was sure of it. And he was nearly certain he'd saw the same creature in the woods. What if it was wounded and needed his help?

He sighed. Long gone were the days that the only things filling his mind were school, surfing, and girls.

Pressing his back against the cool dirt packed wall, he counted to three then slowly peered around the edge of the wall, using the phone's flashlight to cast an indirect beam of light in the direction of the panting.

There was a bed of pine needles, twigs and clumps of fur. There was a small pile of what he hoped were animal bones. On top of the bed was a very large white wolf. Its ears were perked up even though its eyes were closed. Even if it didn't see him, it clearly could smell him with his fresh-baked scent that Arachne was so keen to point out, and it could definitely hear him.

Cal liked animals. When he was really young, they'd had a golden retriever up until the first time that they moved. Once they began moving more often for Cronus' work—or so-called work—they'd given her to a family friend with a farm. Now, Cal knew that had been the right thing to do. It wasn't fair for a dog to live in such an unpredictable environment, but at the time, he'd been heartbroken and cried for weeks.

The wolf lifted its head and peered in Cal's direction. There was no use in hiding, so he crept slowly around the corner. He crouched down. He didn't exactly want to look like prey, but he also didn't want to appear too threatening to cause the wolf to act defensively.

She looked at him, her eyes pale blue and her expression mild. She raised her snout and sniffed at the air.

"Did you bring me here?" he asked her.

She tilted her head. He knew it was probably a bad idea, but he stuck his hand out in a fist. Dogs could nip your fingers, but this way she could still smell him.

The wolf sniffed and then licked the back of his hand.

"You did bring me here, didn't you?" He looked her over without moving closer. She didn't appear hurt and there was no metallic tang in the air indicating fresh blood. So why had she brought him here?

That's when he noticed that the wolf was wearing a collar. So she was...someone's pet?

She nudged at his hand with her nose, and he extended his fingers. She sniffed his palm. He wasn't afraid, although if he was in his right mind he maybe should have been. This wolf was not a domesticated dog. She smelled like the forest—

the bite of snow mixed with pine needles—and was bigger than any wolf he'd ever seen. Not that he'd ever seen any not in a movie or at the zoo. But she appeared at least twice as big as any dog that he knew. Her paws looked as big as his hands with his fingers outstretched.

Her nose was cold and she nudged his open palm. He tentatively turned his hand over and very slowly patted her head. She put her ears back and closed her eyes. She didn't seem like much of a threat. Still, he was leery with any animal. Because animals were still wild creatures.

He slowly moved his hand to her collar. Her collar was a deep navy blue canvas material and the charm hanging from it was a silver crescent moon. Four letters were engraved on it: Luna. So he was right, she was a female wolf.

"Luna? That's your name?" She nuzzled his hand. "Were you told to find me? Why?"

He half-expected her to talk, he'd seen weirder things in the last few months. But she didn't. And yet, he was sure he'd seen her on the road and that she had led him here.

The moon charm seemed to be a dead giveaway for Artemis. Did this wolf belong to Artemis?

"Do you belong to Artemis?" he asked Luna. She licked his hand. He took that to mean yes. So then what did Artemis and Luna want him to find?

He looked around the small cave. There didn't appear to be anything else besides the bed and the bones. He moved his flashlight over the walls. There was no writing or drawings of any kind.

Still kneeling he petted Luna's head again. She looked well fed. He rubbed her ears and her neck which is when he noticed the charm on the wolf's collar giving off a peculiar white glow. He touched it and realized that it wasn't just a moon charm, but a moon locket.

It felt cool in his hand and the glow seemed to slip through the cracks of the locket. He ran his thumbnail along the seam of the front and back piece until he came to a little closure.

"Do you mind if I open this, Luna?" he asked the wolf. There was a gray spot of fur on her chest also in the shape of a crescent moon. He wondered if this wolf was millennia old like her owner. She licked his cheek, so he took that as a yes.

He pulled open the front and back of the locket and the cave was filled with a brilliant white light. The light was clearly coming from the locket, but he couldn't tell what object was creating it, unless it was simply the locket itself.

He tilted the open locket and something small and warm dropped into his palm. It was the object emitting the light. He'd never seen anything so brilliant. Except. This was Artemis we were talking about. And the object did glow as bright as any star. But how was that even possible? And why would Artemis have a star?

He thought back to the story of Artemis and Orion and how Orion had been turned into a constellation. Was this star actually part of that constellation? Was it like some sort of keepsake for Artemis?

Luna nudged his hand and shifted her body weight. When she did, a small green vial with a cork stopper rolled out from underneath her. She'd been laying on top of the other object.

"What have you been keeping, huh, girl?" he asked her.

He picked up the vial as Luna readjusted her weight and curled her tail back up and over her hind legs. Carefully, he dropped the star back into the moon charm and snapped it shut. After he did so, Luna laid her head back down and over her front paws so she was nearly laying in a ball.

The vial wasn't very large. About the size of a double shot glass. The cork needed a little working to twist out of the vial. Inside the vial was a small rolled up piece of paper. As he unfurled the paper, at first it appeared blank. He was sure that couldn't be right. He held his phone flashlight over it, but there was nothing there. Luna moved her head and light from the charm shone onto the paper, revealing an unfamiliar, looping handwriting.

Dear Son,

If you find this letter then you know you are near to making the biggest decision of your life. In fact, of all of our lives. But I have no fear that you will make the right decision. By now you hopefully understand why I made the choices that I did. If you should have any doubt whatsoever, I gave this star from the constellation of Orion to Artemis. I helped her to put her lover into the sky to serve as both a protector from danger and a compass if one should lose their way. The stars always shine no matter how deep the darkness.

Love, Your Mother

The note was not addressed to him, and yet, clearly it was for him. He knew that it was for him and that his mother, Nyx, had written it who knows how long ago. Sometime before she had left him with his human mother.

He read the note a second time then carefully rolled it back up and placed it in the vial. He replaced the stopper.

"Do you mind if I take this Luna?" The wolf didn't acknowledge him, her duty having been served. He wished he could take the star with him as well, but he felt weird taking the collar or the charm from the wolf.

He patted the wolf one final time on the head, then turned to head back up the tunnel. As usual with these things, walking back was much quicker than the walk down. He emerged at the cave's entrance and looked around. Cal couldn't see the road from here. He'd followed the sound of footsteps earlier, and now he realized he had no idea how to get back to the road or to his mom's minivan.

There was a jangle behind him and Luna was standing beside him. He took a step forward and she moved so that she was standing in front of him blocking his way into the forest. He went left and she went to her right. He went to his right and she went to her left.

He knelt down in front of her. "Am I supposed to take the star to help me find my way?" She stood and stared at him with her piercing blue eyes.

Cal removed the charm from Luna's collar. "I'll give this back to Artemis when I'm done with it, okay?"

She nudged the back of his knee with her muzzle then turned and walked into the forest disappearing between the trees.

By now the sun had set and it was dark save for the reflection of the moonlight on the snow. In the forest, the snow was beautiful. It glittered and sparkled. The air was cold and crisp with a hint of pine and earth. Silence surrounded him. And it felt very much as if he was in the time before time. Before there were gods and people and machines and all of the other things that made modern life modern.

He flipped open the locket like it was a compass and stepped to the left. The star seemed to stutter and then dim, so he tried stepping to the right and the star grew brighter. So as long as the star stayed bright then he assumed that meant he was headed in the right direction.

Letting the star of Orion guide him, Cal made his way back to the road without incident. His phone still had a little bit of battery, so he dialed a tow truck and got into the van to wait. He flipped the moon locket closed and ran his thumb over the engraved name. He was fairly certain the note from his mother and the guiding star had more to their purpose. He just didn't yet know what that was.

Chapter Twenty-Three

Asher

Hellhounds were created from the River Styx. The river could take the form of a woman and the hellhounds were essentially her children.

Asher knew he was a child of the Under World, and that unlike Vic, he could maybe pass for human at a glance, but if someone really looked they would notice things. The way he could turn locks without touching them. The fact that he always smelled like home—leather and incense. Or the fact that when snow fell onto his bare skin, it melted instantly. Asher was the type of guy that people would cross the street to avoid, and it wasn't just because of the full sleeve tattoos.

Sometimes he felt that their fear was warranted. Most of the time it wasn't. He had no ill intent toward humans, except for the souls he saw that were black. You could see it when you looked into their eyes. Hellhounds were the ones that retrieved those souls upon their death and brought them to the Under World for Hades to place in one of the three domains. They pulled the souls out by simply reaching into the chest cavity and then using a bone knife to disconnect them from the human vessel. A healthy soul was gold and almost effervescent. It was a live thing. But a soul that committed acts against humanity: stealing, raping, murdering…those souls became tarnished. You could think of it as dead bits. The more bad things a person did—truly evil things—the more it deadened their soul. These souls did not feel light; they felt heavy, laden with their transgressions. Hellhounds reaped the souls and transported them to the Under World in a small crucible.

Asher had wanted to serve Hades his entire life. He could have chosen to be assigned to Vic—he didn't have to choose until he was sixteen. But his loyalty lay with the God of the Under World. He hadn't realized how attached Vic had become to him. They were best friends since Vic could walk and talk. But hellhounds were not made to be friends with people, except other hellhounds. Sure they liked to be with their pack, but even Asher liked to be a lone wolf most of the time. There were things he saw and had to do, that he just couldn't confide in someone like Vic. The way she looked at the world—with so much light and hope in her eyes—pained Asher every time he looked at her. He loved her in his own way and still did. It just wasn't the way in which she needed. She needed something soft to temper her hard edges, but Asher acted more like a flint to her steel, often evoking her temper and violent rages that seemed typical of creatures born in the darkness. He always knew her outrages were not personal, even when the things she said and did stung. Being a hellhound didn't mean that he didn't have feelings. It was just that his duty always took precedence over such things.

Now, after the breakfast with Vic and Cal, where clearly they had all noticed the shade that had entered the diner, Hades had sent him to collect as many Under World creatures that had leaked into the Above World as he could.

These creatures didn't operate on the mass chaos level, they found someone who was open to latch onto and then influenced their soul. Some things were meant to stay below ground.

The cold Above World air felt good against his skin. Hellhounds had heightened senses not unlike their canine counterparts. He could smell the sulfur stink of an Under World creature from at least a mile away.

He rode his Sportster down the main road toward the high school. The sulfur smell became more prominent as he drew near. It was hard to believe that for several months Vic attended classes here like a normal, human girl did. Asher couldn't imagine such a mundane existence for himself, but it seemed to soothe something in Vic. Maybe growing up surrounded by such darkness—no matter how hard Hades and Persephone had tried to shelter her from it—had caused her to crave a certain amount of levity in her life.

Asher pulled up to the parking lot on the west side of the school. It was empty—Vic had mentioned something about final exams and a winter break. There were a couple of security lights that lit up the school exits and parts of the parking lot. He parked his bike near the curb to the sidewalk and got off.

He opened his saddle bag and pulled out a length of enchanted chains, made from Hephaestus' own hands. Then he pulled out a short sword also made by Hephaestus. The fires to Hephaestus' forges were fueled by souls in the Under World.

Throwing back his head, he took a big inhale from deep within his stomach. The smell seemed to be coming from the football field. He lowered his head and stuck to the building's shadows. He wasn't worried about his bike—a hellhound's bike was magically linked to the hellhound; it wouldn't operate for anyone else. Not even another hellhound.

His feet were silent as he walked across the shoddily shoveled sidewalk. Hellhounds moved soundlessly. Even their motorcycles could be rendered silent. There was an equipment shed near the stadium, and he suspected the smell was coming from there. And because of its strength he surmised that it was also from more than one Under World creature. He found this odd since Under World creatures tended to lean more toward the solitary.

There was no way he could catch all of the creatures that had slipped into the Above World, but Hades had insisted that he catch as many as he could and return them. Sometimes people summoned these creatures which had always baffled Asher. People thought they could make a deal with Hades, but Hades didn't make deals. He doled out punishments in proportion to the transgression. He'd always been fair. When people thought they were selling their soul to the devil, they were actually just bargaining with demons who preferred darker dealings.

He made his way to the equipment shed. There was a single, two-light parking lot lamp post near the door. The stench was overwhelming. He cracked his knuckles. Catching a demon or a shade was much more complicated than retrieving a dead person's soul. Although demons and shades weren't incredibly intelligent, they could still think. And run away. Or fight back.

Thus, the short sword and the chains.

There was a window in the side of the equipment shed. Luckily, hellhounds didn't cast shadows. He stood on top of an overturned wooden crate that sat along the edge of the structure. He peered into the window. It was dark inside, but he could make out various pieces of sports equipment and boxes. A large tractor to cut the fields, as well as several moving shadows. Maybe three. Maybe four.

He hopped down from the crate and moved toward the equipment shed door which faced the stadium.

There was a pad lock through the shed's latch. That was the thing about shades and demons. They didn't need much space to slip into the Above World. The thinnest tear in the veil could let them in. Shades could slip under the crack in the door, but demons could simply appear, disappear, and reappear in whatever realm they were in—just not in between the worlds. They needed an opening in the veil—whether via invitation or not.

Lucky for Asher, locks didn't stop him either. He simply moved his fingers over the pad lock and the mechanism inside tumbled, releasing the steel bar that was placed in the small rectangular base. He moved the lock, and opened the door's latch, then placed the opened lock on the hook attached to the door frame. There wasn't really much to the lock, really anyone could get into the shed easily enough if they really wanted to. But he knew from his few months moving around Olympia, that Olympia was a town full of people who were good and kind. They looked out for one another and helped one another. Sometimes he thought it was very unfortunate for them that the gods had decided to take up residence in Olympia because all of their troubles stemmed directly from the presence of the gods. He dropped the chains near the door. They were just an extra precaution. Hopefully, he wouldn't need them because transporting creatures back to Under World tended to be nasty business.

He slid open the door without a sound.

His eyes adjusted almost immediately to the near pitch blackness of the shed. There was shuffling and scuffling inside. He saw two horns hidden behind a crate full of footballs. He was pretty certain it wasn't a Viking helmet.

Asher pulled the door closed behind him.

He reached into his pocket and pulled out a Twix bar and a pack of Sour Patch Kids. All creatures from the Under World, god or otherwise, had a severe sweet tooth. It was almost like the sugary sweetness counterbalanced the dark energy that seemed to hum in their blood.

His exponential hearing picked up the sound of sniffing. Carefully, he placed one of the Twix bars on the top of a box to his left and then slipped behind it. Demons and shades tended to be simple creatures.

There was more shuffling and he heard something skitter across the floor, most likely a tail belonging to a demon. Then there was the scratch of claws reaching for the Twix on top of the box. Demons were not tall, they were usually between two and three feet in height. He heard the crinkle of the wrapper letting him know that the Twix was being taken.

He had two options, kill the demons or bring them back to the Under World to face the wrath of Hades. Death was often the kinder of the two options.

Asher sprung up swinging the short sword. He made contact with the fleshy side of the demon. It was a red-skinned demon with horns and fangs. Its skin was covered in scales. Demons had blood but didn't bleed, as he pushed the blade into the side of the beast it simply registered surprise and then there was a puff of brimstone and a flash of light as the demon instantly turned to charcoal-colored dust around the blade.

He picked up the Twix bar and pocketed it with the rest of the candy. He was nearly certain there was more than one Under World Creature in the shed. Narrowing his eyes, he scanned the room looking for any shadows in the darkness. There it was. Moving along the wall, tall and thin with spindly arms and legs. A shade.

Shades were even dimmer than demons—no pun intended. Asher popped open the box of Sour Patch Kids and sprinkled some across a stack of boxes along the wall leaving a trail to where he knelt down behind the tractor. The only thing about shades is that he had to focus because if you blinked you could completely miss one in the dark.

The spindly black shadow peeled from the wall and made its way toward the Sour Patch Kids trail. Asher popped one in his mouth and wiped the blade of his sword across his pants. Demons turned to dust upon killing, but they did have life blood. It was black as pitch and thick like maple syrup.

He peered between the boxes and saw the movement of the shade along the candy trail, a single Sour Patch Kid disappearing each time. Sulfur stung his nostrils as it approached. He never understood that. What good was it to be a shadow if people could smell you coming from a mile away?

As the little orange candy kid in front of him was picked up, he launched his attack. He pulled out a white powder created by River and threw it into the air blowing it in the direction of the shade. It clung to the shadow revealing its three-dimensional form. He lifted his short sword and severed the shade right in half at the waist. It curled in on itself and dissolved into nothing. The only indication that it was ever there was the white powder on the floor.

He stood up and looked around, then closed his eyes and listened. He didn't see or hear the presence of any other Under World creatures.

Satisfied, he moved toward the door. As he pushed it open, an unsettling feeling washed over him. His instincts told him he wasn't alone. He sniffed the air, but there was only the faint smell of brimstone. In the distance he could hear the howl of the Void. He had a feeling that whatever it would take to stop it from destroying, would have a steep price for Vic to pay.

When he finally crossed the threshold, his eyes immediately noticed that the chains he'd left outside the door were missing. The second thing he noticed was the white skeletal figure holding them.

So there *had* been a third creature. He reached into his pocket for the remaining Twix bar. The creature lunged and Asher was caught with surprise. Under World creatures didn't often go on the offensive. The Twix bar went flying, its golden wrapper landing in the snow.

This creature was also fast; it encircled Asher's wrist in a length of chain. Hellhounds were the fastest creatures in the Under World, so he had a bad feeling that this creature wasn't from the Under World even though it looked the part. It was also missing the telltale sulfur scent. He lifted up the short sword and swung at the creature, aiming for the side below the ribcage.

The creature hissed and dodged the blow. It pulled on the chains, throwing Asher off balance. But Asher was smart and well-seasoned in fighting. He threw his weight into his fall and in the process pulled the creature down with him. The creature let out a hiss of surprise as it fell. Asher untangled his wrist from the chains and quickly encircled the creature's bone-like legs. It flailed out with its arms but Asher was faster and he swung the short sword down on its neck. The head rolled off and red blood shot out of the open wound.

Red blood? Asher sniffed the back of his hand which was now spattered with it. Metallic. Was this creature a *human*?

He noticed a garbage bin nearby. He tossed the lid onto the ground and then emptied the small amount of garbage from the bag and into the unlined bin. He brought the bag over to the creature and first put its head inside. The eyes were large and black and hollow looking. Then he folded the body up as if he were folding a sweater and put it in the bag. As an extra precaution, he wrapped the bag in chains then hefted it up and carried it the short distance back to his motorcycle.

There he unbuckled one of the saddle bags and shoved and grunted until he placed the bag inside. A faucet was on the side of the building and he turned it and rinsed his hands and face off, removing the blood of the creature.

The unsettling feeling had not subsided.

He flicked the start button and the Sportster roared to life. He had to take this body to Hades as soon as possible. Something was very wrong.

Chapter Twenty-Four

Vic

The Void howled at Vic. Again.

If it was at all possible, it somehow seemed angrier than it had before. She stood on the forest floor below looking up. She'd left Daphne's feeling even more puzzled. The Winter Solstice was only a few days away. She had to close the portal between the two worlds, but what then? Would Cal go with her? Or would he want to stay in the mortal world, having lived nearly all of his life in it already? He would never leave Rachel or his sisters.

But the alternative was Vic leaving behind her parents. And Asher. And Brim. And River. Could she really and truly bear to never, never-ever, see her family again? As much as she'd lamented about wanting to be normal the last year she'd spent in the Above World, she wasn't sure if being normal was worth never being able to see or be with her family.

The entire thing was frustrating. She was still a kid for crying out loud! You couldn't let kids make these kinds of decisions! Close the portal and stay in the mortal world and never see your family again. Or close the portal and stay in the immortal world and never see Cal again. Or leave the portal open and let chaos reign on all the worlds. At this point, it was tempting. Just to spite the gods for putting her in this predicament in the first place.

She rubbed the surface of the ring that contained the wood of the old tree. Daphne had looked so tired. Vic had wondered what would happen to Daphne if she chose not to close the portal. Would she get fully absorbed into the tree at some point? Was that even fair when she was simply seeking protection from Apollo—one of the gods.

The conversation had given her a monster headache and now she had to hope that when she entered the Void for a second time that it would spit her back out at exactly the right point and place in time. She moved her hand to her collar, her fingers searching for the skull and crossbones pin. It was still there. This was her ticket home.

She expanded her wings and flew upward above the forest tree line. It was now evening in this time, the sky turning into a watercolor sunset of peaches, pinks, and lavenders. Olympia was beautiful. At home in the Under World, the sky was a menacing red and it rained fire and smelled of brimstone. The River Styx was black and the tree trunks of her mother's pomegranate trees were also black and the fruits a bruised purple-red. It was beautiful in its own way, but much of the time for Vic, it felt claustrophobic in the Under World. With sunsets like this, the Above World often felt like the magic one.

As she drew nearer, the Void began to tug on her weight, shifting her gravity. The pull felt even stronger than it had when she first had passed through. In the back of her mind she couldn't fight the niggling feeling of something being off, but she continued her ascent anyways until her wings beat erratically like sails in the wind. At that point, fearing injury, she folded her wings against her sides and allowed the Void to relentlessly pull her. She extended a hand and it disappeared into the blackness.

She had two objects. One for the present and one for where in time she had wanted to go. In her mind, she'd viewed it as a round trip situation. But the Void had other ideas.

...

Vic landed with a thud.

This time the Void had unceremoniously spit her out. Not having time to gain any sort of purchase, she'd landed roughly on the ground, but not before crashing through the canopy of tree branches.

The wind had been knocked out of her and the scratches across her arms and neck burned. But those would heal in a few moments, a benefit of immortality.

Had she landed somewhere in the forest surrounding Daphne's tree? Back in her own time?

She pushed herself up slowly and looked around. This forest seemed...unfamiliar. When she was Taking souls six months ago, she'd learned the forest of Olympia. She had to keep to the shadows. Live in the shadows. She'd come to know the hidden paths, nooks, and crannies of Olympia as well as she knew the back of her own hand.

The first thing that she noticed was that there was no snow. It was nearly the Winter Solstice in Olympia. Around her, the air was humid and held a thickness to it. Even the ground beneath her was warm. She felt her hair frizzing immediately into a halo around her head. Annoyed, she quickly braided it with deft fingers. Beads of sweat were already forming around her hairline.

The second thing she noticed was that the forest around her contained a mix of deciduous and tropical trees. There were palm trees with their odd curves and leafy green fronds with bright foliage. Definitely not Olympia.

Lastly, the calls of birds were of a more exotic nature, their caws a trilling singsong that echoed throughout the woods. Birds in Olympia had flown south for the winter, or were common birds with common songs: Cardinals, Jays, Orioles, Wrens. Not birds that cawed. More birds of the chirping variety.

Vic got to her feet and brushed the soil from the seat of her pants. The ground had been warm, but it had also been damp. She was in a jungle. Or a rain forest. She closed her eyes and listened. The tang of salt burned her nostrils followed by the faint crashing of waves against rocks. There was a sea not far away.

She wasn't a hellhound, but that didn't mean she didn't have some super powers of her own. She ran her fingers over the bat charm at her neck. It glowed white and warm against the notch of her collarbone. *Lead me to the sea.* As soon as the thought came, it was as though someone had hooked a fishing line into her solar plexus, and was tugging her gently through the forest.

Vic's power was a mix of skill, dumb luck, enchanted items, and a subtle magic that coursed through her veins. Her magic wasn't of the showy variety. It was like a quiet hum that lived in the background.

Her boots gained purchase on the path—it looked like she was maybe on an animal trail. Maybe a path the animals took into and out of the forest searching for water and food. As she blindly followed her feet, she tilted her head upward, except all she could see was a thick green canopy that nearly blocked out the sun and sky.

The sound of the sea grew louder and she noticed the forest—jungle—becoming thinner as she neared its edge. Through the tree trunks she could see a sandy beach—except the sand was black not white like she had seen in so many pictures. It's not like she'd taken family vacations as a kid. She hadn't even reached the Above World until she was seventeen. But she felt her encyclopedic knowledge would serve her in lieu of actual firsthand experience.

When she burst out of the jungle, the warmth evaporated from her bat charm and she instinctively took a big gulp of sea air. It was refreshing and crisp despite the humidity. It felt...untainted.

She took a tentative step forward toward the sea. It was a cerulean blue and crystal clear. A surprised sigh escaped her lips when she noticed where the sky met the sea at its horizon. The sky was a cotton candy pink, tinged with lime green near the horizon. Hovering not far above the horizon was a tangerine colored sun. It glowed brilliantly and warmly. If the Above World was beautiful in its color compared to the Under World, then this world was full-blown Technicolor. It was Dorothy when she left Kansas and landed in Oz.

It took her breath away. And she stumbled forward, suddenly exhausted, toward the water. She knew she couldn't drink it, but she wanted to feel its coolness against her skin.

When she reached the shoreline, she dropped to her knees. Her sweater was torn from her fall through the canopy, so she slipped it over her head since she had on a camisole underneath. She shoved the sweater into her bag and slipped her hands into the cool water. It was silky against her skin.

She splashed water against her face and neck, then sat back on her heels facing toward the jungle. She gasped. Over the jungle towered a range of jagged, lavender-colored mountains. Not like anything she had ever seen before. Not in Olympia, nor in the Under World, or even Mount Othrys.

So the Void had given her a layover.

Except she had no idea where in the worlds she was.

Chapter Twenty-Five

Cal

If you had asked Cal a year ago about gods and goddesses, or people being placed into the sky as a constellation, he would have told you it was a bunch of hooey.

Legends. Myths. Definitely not reality.

Now he stared at the glowing star sitting on his desk. Just lying there among his textbooks and papers. A glass of water from the previous night was still set there and the star's halo of light reflected off the water.

How was a star supposed to help him?

He flipped onto his back and sighed. Running through the week's most recent events. He couldn't shake the feeling that he was missing something. And something very important.

It was late. The rest of the house was sound asleep. Rachel often retired early in the evenings since she woke so early to bake. Everything was quiet. The moon was full and the world was bright as it reflected off the snow. He glanced at his phone, but its screen was dark. He hadn't heard from Vic since he'd seen her that morning. Usually, they talked regularly, but he had a feeling she had her own stuff to sort out.

Artemis. Orion. Compasses. Apollo. Betrayals. The Void. Close the portal. The thoughts ran through his head on an endless loop. His eyes slid closed.

But then popped open again at the familiar rumble he heard approaching.

He pushed himself out of bed and squinted out the window. A hunched figure on a motorcycle was heading down his street and toward the small house. When they'd first moved to Olympia they'd lived in a large colonial house in a neighborhood, but since the incident with his disowned father, they had downsized into a smaller house closer to town.

The window was cracked open and the familiar sent of incense whooshed in. He'd expected the figure to be Brim. He kind of considered Brim his hellhound and Asher as Vic's. Like bodyguards. Or something. But the figure was more angular with a jaunt to his defiant shoulders.

He watched as the motorcycle approached the driveway, the sound gone. Hellhound trickery. Asher parked parallel to the end of the driveway. The roads had been cleared, but Cal knew that the Harley Davidson Sportster Iron 883 was as hot as the Under World, melting any snow in its wake.

His phone began to flash and vibrate from his bed. Cal lunged for it and hit the answer icon. The number had read 666. Funny.

"Asher?" he asked at the same time that Asher said, "Dude."

"Is Vic okay?" Cal asked immediately, suddenly concerned that Asher's presence without Vic meant that she was in trouble.

"Actually, no idea. And hello to you too."

Asher had no idea how Vic was? He had assumed Hades, and as a result Asher, knew everything about Vic's well-being. The fact that they didn't made the hair on the back of his neck prickle. What was she doing? And why hadn't Asher been sent with her?

"Sorry. Hello."

"We're past pleasantries, now. I need your help, stat. Get your primordial butt down here." The call ended and Cal scowled at the black screen. But he knew better. If Asher was asking him for help that meant something bad had happened. Or crazy. Or crazy and bad. Crazy bad.

He shoved his phone into his pants' pocket then carefully picked up the small star. It was warm in his fingers as he carefully placed it back into its locket. He then took the locket and hooked it to his keychain ring for safekeeping.

Fumbling down the stairs, he shoved his arms into his coat. He all but burst out the door, suddenly shot with a rush of adrenaline.

The winter air was crisp against his flushed cheeks.

Asher was intimidating. Cal didn't like to make assumptions, but if he'd seen Asher at school, he probably would have given him a wide birth. His piercing green eyes clearly sent the message: DANGER! DO NOT COME NEAR! Not to mention his colorfully tattooed knuckles, hands, arms and neck. His hair was shaved on the sides and longer on top, and black was his uniform. If they didn't have Vic in common, they'd be as opposite as…well, as day and night.

Cal came to a stop at the end of the driveway.

"What's wrong?"

"Hop on," Asher commanded. He was also a man of few words. Cal figured most hellhounds were. They seemed more like physical beings. They didn't need words if they had fists.

Cal hesitated.

Asher noticed.

"Listen. I have no idea what crazy ass mission Hades sent Vic on. But she's smart. And she's tough. All I know is Hades gave me an assignment and it did not turn out as expected. We need to get to the Under World and ASAP."

Cal appreciated Asher's honesty. But he didn't understand what Asher's problems had to do with him. Besides, he had his own problems to figure out.

Asher must have noticed the uncertainty in Cal's eyes.

"It's worse than we thought, Dude. The worlds are seeping together and let's just say that the Above World is not prepared for the shit show that's about to happen right in front of their eyes. *The Walking Dead* is child's play compared to what's about to happen."

Cal's brain flashed to shadows and skeletal figures he'd seen at The Rooster and in the forest. He thought of his little sisters. And without further hesitation, he hopped onto the back of Asher's Sportster and they raced down the street toward the Under World.

Chapter Twenty-Six

Vic

She didn't know why, but Vic had felt inexplicably drawn toward those mountains. She didn't know where she was—in time or in worlds—but it felt deep in her bones like she was meant to be here. Wherever here was.

Her boots felt heavy on her feet, but she figured it was probably best to keep them on in case there were crabs, snakes, or scorpions hidden in the sands of the beach.

The water she'd splashed onto her face, neck, and arms had already evaporated from her skin. The humidity pressed on her from all sides. She definitely had not been dressed for a trip to the tropics.

She continued down the shoreline toward the mountains. There was a stone wall that jutted out, maybe a pier of some kind, which meant that if there was a manmade structure then other people had to be around. Or had to have been around at some point in time.

As she walked, she peered at the sun with its strange orangeness. It was unlike anything she had ever seen. For all of the Under World's darkness, this place was like its polar opposite in brightness. The pink sky reflected in the cerulean sea and up close, it mixed into a lavender color, jarring against the black sandy shoreline.

What *was* this place?

In the distance she could hear what sounded like thousands of wind chimes coalescing with the caws of the jungle birds.

Her lips were already cracking with thirst. Hadn't it been only a short while ago—minutes?—that she had been drinking tea with Daphne?

She ignored her incessant thirst and let the sounds of the chimes guide her closer to what she hoped was not only other humans, but answers. The entire time she walked, the sun did not move in the sky. The water lapped pleasantly at the shoreline. It was as if there was no passage of time whatsoever.

Vic tried to wrack her brain for any stories or lessons her father may have given her about places where time stood still, but she was coming up empty. She already knew of several places that defied her physics lessons, but that's because physics only applied to the 3D plane of existence. There was much, much more to the world than that of course.

A gong slowly mixed in with the chimes, its deep tenor sending a vibration through the earth and up through the soles of her boots and then her feet. Nearing the stone wall, she noticed to the right there was a break in the forest line. The trees were sparser and there was a large, white boulder, nearly half her height and double her width that seemed to mark a path leading into and out of the forest.

When she reached the boulder she noticed that it had an engraving on it. An elaborate calligraphy letter L in between a symbol that clearly represented the sun and another that was a waning crescent moon. They were primitive markings, but also worn with time and sea salt air.

Her mind immediately went to the symbols of Apollo and Artemis. L. Did this place—this island or world—belong to the Titan Leto, mother of Apollo and Artemis?

Even more curious than before, she headed down the path and into the forest leading gently into the mountains. As she did, the chimes grew louder and the gong sounded with the beat of her footsteps as if it was drawing her to where they originated.

As she slightly rose in altitude, the humidity from the beach began to dissipate and it no longer felt as though she were breathing through a thick curtain of fabric. The sweat along her brow began to evaporate. Now she was thankful for her boots as they guided her up the rocky, tree root-laden path.

Finally, she knew she was about to discover the source of the sound when the path seemed to grow wider and the trees seemed to bow over it, forming a sort of trellis along the path. Slices of bronze sunlight cut through the dirt path as she made her way.

Her heart trilled with excitement and she placed a hand against her chest to steady its rhythm. Only then noticing the gossamer bracelet that clung to her wrist. The bracelet that Arachne had given her. Had she landed here because of the bracelet? Was she about to discover another string in this so-called Divine Web that they all had unwittingly become part of?

Vic looked back up and was struck still. Before her as if it had just grown out of the forest floor, stood a massive stone temple. It had four massive lavender colored columns and Vic realized immediately that it was actually carved into the mountainside. Steps led into a cavernous area and above the columns was a façade of carvings: suns, roosters, moons, and wolves. It was an odd array of items, but they were carved deliberately and in a repeating pattern. The symbology was not lost on Vic. These were symbols of Apollo, Artemis, and Leto. The symbols of a family. Or maybe of what remained of one.

Palm trees formed a walkway with numerous flowery bushes lined behind them. A peacock walked by, startling Vic so that she stumbled backward on the path. It eyed her suspiciously and then, deciding she was uninteresting, continued its saunter across her path. This place was unlike anything Vic had ever seen in her entire life.

She threw back her head to take in the entirety of the temple structure.

The gong sounded from inside, reverberating off the interior's stone walls.

Tentatively, Vic pushed out of the jungle line and out into the open. She tugged at the spider silk bracelet. If she wasn't meant to be here, surely she wouldn't have landed here.

The steps of the temple were solid beneath her feet. She thought of photos she'd seen of the crumbled temple ruins in places like Athens and Rome. This was clearly well-maintained. Pots of colorful tropical flowers flanked the entrance to the temple. Tall, feathery grasses and ivy-like greenery spilled out. Incense wafted through the air.

This place felt familiar. Like home. And this inner knowing released any doubt that this temple belonged to the Titan goddess Leto. The mother of Apollo and Artemis, who was also one of Zeus's consorts.

The Universe didn't cause coincidences. It was much too smart for that.

Vic let the pull of the gong guide her across the threshold of the temple.

Inside, shelves carved into the walls held hundreds of misshapen candles, all lit. Above her was a massive wind chime chandelier. From the flat, opalescent pieces they appeared to be shells. The chandelier was strung not from its center as typical, but at several points so that it went around and then tapered down from a giant, open skylight. The orange sun shone in at such a slant that it illuminated something gold near the back of the temple.

Normally, Vic would expect this to be a statue of the god or goddess who represented the temple. Something for the people to worship and to whom they could bring offerings: coffee, tea, shells, flowers, handmade statues, berries, or tobacco. But she had seen no people as of yet on the island.

Instead, the shiny gold object that was illuminated was a giant golden gong hanging from a wooden A-frame. Next to it rested a large wooden stick, leaning against the wall, with one cloth wrapped end. A breeze shuffled the chimes and they sang softly in the dimness of the temple.

Between the scent of the incense, the soft candlelight, and the sound of the chimes, Vic suddenly felt very sleepy. For a split second, her training kicked in and she feared she was being set up—lulled into an enchanted sleep. Her limbs felt loose and relaxed.

"I assure you, it's not a trap," said a voice from the shadows.

Vic had grown very still, now her hand went instinctively to the knife at her waist. But her knife wasn't there. She had stopped carrying it after the Takings. She'd taken up another blade, and still used it from time to time, but it wasn't the same. And she hadn't thought she'd need it on this journey.

A cloaked figure stepped out of the shadows and into the ray of sunlight. Except it wasn't a cloak so much as a sort of open-weave shawl that the woman wore. She was tall and statuesque—like the old gods. Like the Titans. Her feet were bare and her gauzy dress was the same cerulean color as the sea just outside.

The woman pushed back the hood of the shawl and revealed strawberry blonde hair. Just like that of her twin children. Leto's hair was twisted in an elaborate braided chignon revealing long shell earrings. One a sun and one a moon. Twins that were a duality of opposites. One yin and one yang. One light and one dark...not unlike Cal and herself. Cal was of the air and Vic was of the underground. Except for the whole family-twin dynamic, instead of the boyfriend-girlfriend dynamic. Although, Vic speculated, if you asked Apollo he'd probably disagree. His love for his twin sister was akin to that of a jealous lover. Vic shuddered at the thought.

Leto's eyes were the same lavender as the mountains, giving her a breath-taking ethereal appearance. Despite living on an island, her skin was fair and creamy. Vic could see why Zeus had been drawn to her beauty.

Now the goddess's eyes appraised Vic in return.

"Are you the one who brought me here?" Vic finally asked. Her voice came out a rasp. She'd forgotten her thirst.

Leto laughed and the sound mimicked that of the chimes that tinkled softly in the breeze.

"You know better than that. Destiny brought you here." She brushed past Vic, heading into an alcove off to the side that led deeper into the temple.

"You're Leto," Vic said trailing behind the goddess at what she considered was both a safe and respectable distance. The gods could be volatile, not unlike herself.

"I am" Her bare feet slapped against the stone floor as she walked. They continued in silence until an arched opening appeared. It had no door and tangerine-colored light beckoned from within.

Vic followed Leto through the doorway and out into the most beautiful garden Vic had ever seen. There was a large, clear pond filled with colorful koi fish. A waterfall tumbled down one side of the temple, recirculating the water in the pond. Hundreds of tropical plants were in bloom and two more peacocks meandered along the cobblestone walkways that appeared to wind through the garden.

Vic spotted both a lemon tree and an orange tree, and a floral scent that reminded Vic of a combination of coconut, watermelon, and vanilla lightly scented the air.

There was an elaborately carved stone bench beside the waterfall. It was a bit taller and wider than a standard-sized bench, and Vic realized as Leto sat upon it, that it was to accommodate her statuesque size.

"What is this place?" Vic asked.

"Home," Leto replied, gesturing for Vic to sit down. "Some call it Aegina. Some Atlantis. Others Delphi. But it's really none of those things and all of those things. It's an island near Greece, but it would appear on no map. Mortal, mythological, or otherwise."

Vic sat down on the opposite side of the bench. In the light, she realized Leto herself looked as though she were carved from the same smooth marble as the very bench on which they sat.

"I suppose you would call it a dimensional island. There, but not really there. Everywhere and nowhere."

A large white bird with an enormous curved beak appeared beside Leto. In its beak was a basket containing two tea cups and a teapot, which Leto carefully plucked out and placed on the long bench between her and Vic. *Was that bird wearing a bowtie? Was he a servant?*

"Thank you, Spies," Leto said, clearly dismissing the bird who teetered off on spindly legs. "Tea?"

"Please," Vic responded automatically. Although, she'd actually prefer a tall glass of ice cold water.

Leto carefully poured tea into the cups. It was a brilliant pink with a slight floral scent with a hint of citrus. Hibiscus tea.

"Are there no other people here?" Vic asked taking a polite sip of tea. It was cold, not hot as she'd first assumed. The scent was soothing and the taste crisp and refreshing, quenching her thirst.

"I'm afraid I am the only one. Sometimes the Universe drops in a visitor."

Vic frowned. "That must be lonely."

"Time has no meaning to someone who lives forever. Long or short, tall or wide. It passes one way or the other."

Vic tried to recall from her lessons why it was that Leto lived on an island by herself, but she kept coming up empty. Although knowing Apollo, Vic supposed anyone who gave birth to someone as horrible as him, should potentially be exiled. Then again, one couldn't necessarily control one's offspring nevertheless their actions.

As if sensing Vic had questions, but was too good mannered to ask, Leto supplied an answer anyway. "When I got pregnant with Zeus' children, Hera was furious. She bid it that I not give birth on any land, mortal or myth. I fled to the sea—my favorite place—fell to my knees at the shore and cried. The salt of my tears mixed with the salt of the sea, and before I knew what was happening an island—this island—rose up in front of me. I tentatively stepped onto the new land, and like a ship, the island floated off into the sea until Mount Olympus was nothing but a spec in the distance. So you see. An island that is everywhere and nowhere, neither here nor there."

So Destiny had led her to the goddess Leto, mother of twins Apollo and Artemis. Both Olympians were also part Titan. The Olympians had a long and contemptuous history with the Titans. Vic was several generations removed and she knew that many of the Titans had been banished to Tartarus. Although some, like Cronus, had escaped, while others like Aphrodite, Artemis, and Apollo had proclaimed themselves as Olympians. Leto herself, of course, remained a Titan. Why would the Universe send her here instead of back home?

Vic didn't even need to ask to find out. Clearly, Leto had both been expecting her and had a story to share.

"When the twins were in my womb, I now knew which was the one whose little fists and feet had bruised my abdomen. If Apollo had had his way, he would have fought his way out much sooner. He was the bigger of the two upon birth, but Artemis' docile nature had allowed her to slip out of the birth canal easily. She entered the world peacefully with an easy smile upon her face. While she was swaddled, her brother struggled. For someone who had wanted out so badly, he now seemed to refuse. It was long and painful and many hours before Apollo entered the world. And when he did, he did so with a high shrill and a red face. His tiny fists waving in the air angrily."

She took a slow sip of tea before continuing.

"When my children were young, an untrained eye could not tell them apart. The only way was to watch them and observe their behavior. While, Artemis was gentle and smiled freely. Her brother was often silent. He did not cry, but he also did not smile. When it was time to nurse, he would push his sister away, trying to claim both of my breasts. Eventually, I had to nurse them separately. I was weary. They were but children. Children do as they do."

"But as they aged, this behavior did not change. Apollo was the harsher, bolder of the twins. Artemis was soft and gentle. She'd wander the island, tending to the birds that roamed here and the fish that swam here. She would have been content to stay. Her twin was restless. Once he'd mastered swimming, calisthenics, and preening, he grew bored. While it broke my heart to send them to their father, I knew that they would never learn or grow if I allowed them to stay. But I also worried that Apollo's increasingly possessive behavior of Artemis—and of me—would eventually lead to her demise. I could protect myself. Titans are infinitely more powerful than the Olympians, despite what mythology may tell you."

Leto's gaze was unfocused and very far away. Vic imagined that she was reliving the moments of her children's youth. The tea cup now loosely held in her hands.

"Before I sent them away, as their mother, I had to bestow or acknowledge their affinities. Artemis, with her quiet wisdom and steady hand, would come to represent the full moon hunt. Apollo, with his flamboyant and aggressive personality, would come to represent the sun. His deceptive personality would later lure unsuspecting souls like the gentle song of a harp. Legends would say the twins drove silver and gold chariots to initiate the rising and setting of the sun."

A small smile appeared at the corners of Leto's mouth and Vic realized that it pained her to speak of her children. She was proud of them—or at least proud of what they had been capable of becoming. But even Vic knew that once you sent children out on their own, who they became was of their own volition. Their own choices. A parent could do their best, but someone's destiny ultimately lay within their own autonomy.

"What no one realized is that the sun is life, but it is also death. It can dry up entire seas, create arid desserts, ruin entire harvests, and destroy civilizations. Over the eons, he has caused much damage and much carnage. It is time for him to be stopped."

Leto's lavender eyes focused on Vic and a cool chill ran down her spine.

"The Destroyer must be destroyed. It is the only way."

Vic watched as Leto lifted a necklace over her head. Instead of a pendant, it contained a vial. She held it out to Vic, who accepted it tentatively. Somehow she already instinctively knew what the vial contained.

"This is my son's umbilical cord blood. The life blood of an immortal spilled on the Winter Solstice by the hand of both worlds, shall destroy the one who destroys."

Vic placed the necklace over her own head, her mind flashing to a dream in which her mother was preparing to wed her father and she had leaned over and whispered in Vic's ear. The part of which Leto was unaware, was that destroying Apollo, would also destroy the veil between worlds. Cal was not the imbalance in the Universe.

Apollo was.

Chapter Twenty-Seven

Cal

It was different this time, driving through the portal to the Under World.

The air shimmered and felt thicker, Asher had to gun the engine to push them through. The tree, which Cal now knew housed a young nymph named Daphne, shook angrily and he imagined her books and china rattling and crashing to the floor.

Heat rushed at Cal and he immediately regretted putting on his winter coat and hat. The Under World was a ripe ninety-eight degrees Fahrenheit. It rained flakes of ash that mixed with your sweat and coated your skin.

They raced passed the three domains of the Under World and to the bone bridge guarded by River. Usually, River wore a large smile—she was the Keeper of the River Styx and granted passage into the inner sanctum, where the Hadens resided—but today her face was grim. Her eyes were focused over Cal's shoulder in the direction from which they had just come.

He took the chance and glanced over his shoulder.

There was a large opalescent doorway-shaped hole shimmering in the air behind them. You could see the snow covered field through it, but only if you squinted. Was this how and where the shades and skeletons were escaping? Cal knew it couldn't be that simple. If it were, the portal would be heavily guarded on both sides.

They rattled over the bridge and up the long drive to the vast rotunda.

Cal's breath was always taken away by the majestic castle where Vic had grown up. In a way it suited her, but at the same time, seemed so different from how he knew her. She was complex, what immortal wasn't? But she was also simple. She loved sweets, her pajamas, and binge watching bad TV.

However, he knew that her upbringing had been anything but simple.

Asher parked his motorcycle in what Cal knew usually was a long line of Sportsters, but today there was only a handful. Were all the hellhounds out hunting shades?

Cal hopped off but before he could head for the entrance to find Hades, Asher grabbed his arm.

"Not so fast. I need your help."

He unlatched the buckle on his saddle bag, rummaged around a bit, and then gestured to its contents. Cal stepped forward and peered into the container. Inside was what looked like a living skeleton. It wasn't just bones, but it had a thin, translucent coating of skin over its body. It was wrapped in chains and bent at an odd angle. There was red smears on its skin.

"Is that blood?" he asked, turning toward Asher.

"Yes."

"It's human?"

Asher shrugged. "Demons have black blood. They don't bleed though. Too viscous. Immortals bleed a shimmery ruby color. Mortals bleed red. They're the only ones who have blood that oxygenates."

Cal repeated himself. "So, it's human?"

"Have you ever seen a human that looked like this?"

Asher dug around some more then lifted the garbage bag that surrounded the body up and out of his saddle bag. He re-cinched it shut and slung it over his shoulder like Santa carrying a toy sack. A very tattooed, very dark, and unamused Santa. He jutted his chin toward the double doors of the castle and Cal rushed to open them.

The crystal skull knockers were cold under his hand. A rush of cool air greeted him and the scent of hyacinth—Persephone's scent—wafted out of the entry way, at odds with the red sky, black clouds, and sulfuric smell that permeated the outside environment.

Asher wedged past Cal and snapped his fingers with a free hand.

Immediately, a short red-skinned demon appeared. This wasn't Cal's first trip to the Under World, but it still fascinated and scared him in equal measure.

The demon was about hip height with black horns and fangs that hung out snaggle-toothed. His eyes were heavily lidded. He wore a black bow tie that marked him as a servant of the House of Hades. He bowed slightly to Asher.

If this was medieval times and Hades was the king, then the hellhounds were essentially the Knights of the Roundtable.

"Fetch Hades."

The servant snapped out of visibility, off to retrieve Hades and bring him to the entry way. Cal hoped that he hurried because he didn't think Persephone would much appreciate it if Asher's sack began to drip blood on her shiny, black marble floors.

The castle was vast. With an array of turrets, bedrooms, chambers, and underground bunker-like rooms. The River Styx even ran beneath the castle, flowing freely through a subterranean passageway. There were artifact rooms and a war room, where the Council—including Hades, Zeus, Athena, Poseidon, and Ares would meet. The gods had adapted with the mortal world around them.

Even though he'd been here before, Cal was always amazed. He knew that the majority of the castle was glass, crystal, metal, and slightly sterile, but that there was a special wing that transitioned into stone architecture and that was a part of the castle that was created for Persephone. She was the goddess of the seasons and she needed warmth and natural beauty.

"Asher, is that you?" A voice akin to wind chimes drifted down from the top of the staircase that encased the foyer.

Persephone's lithe form appeared and she all but floated down the stairs.

Her straw-colored hair fell to her shoulders in waves and she wore a long plum-colored dress with a cream-colored shawl draped over her shoulders.

"And you brought Callum. How lovely."

Cal knew that Persephone looked—and even sounded—delicate, but she had cheated death and her calm disguised an underlying wisdom. She was thoughtful and rational, which was a direct foil to her husband's passion and impulsiveness.

Before Cal could manage a greeting, Asher heaved the body bag from his shoulder and placed it on the shiny, immaculate floor.

"I think we have a problem. I found this in the Above World."

There was the click of heels on tile and a deep voice responded. "Did someone say problem?"

Hades joined them in the foyer. As always, he was dressed impeccably. Cal had never seen him in anything other than a three piece suit. Today, the suit was a crisp navy, with a starched white shirt beneath, slightly open at his neck. Hades' jet black hair was slicked back and his dark eyes were discerning. Neither Persephone nor Hades ever seemed to change or age and Cal realized he and Vic would both experience that same sort of timelessness.

Asher nudged open the bag with his knife.

"There were shades, but then there was also this," Asher said.

Cal hadn't fully seen the body and he recoiled now. Persephone let out a gasp of surprise. The figure was bent over and skeletal. It didn't necessarily look human, but it also didn't necessarily not look human. It had no visible musculature, if the saying "skin and bones" was applicable, then this was the occasion. The head had no hair or any discernible features, just large, round, vacant eyes that now stared at nothing. It was exactly like the creature he had seen—for what, seconds?—in the forest only a short time ago. In the diner, no one else had seemed to even notice it was there. But why could the immortals see it?

"Is that blood?" Persephone asked softly. She had been bent over at the waist and now stood up, pulling her shawl tighter around her shoulders as if she'd just felt a chill.

"Yes. And not shade or demon blood," Hades said. He snapped his fingers and another servant appeared. This one dark green with a single horn in the middle of his forehead, and tiny wings on his back which Cal suspected could never actually lift the portly fellow, short as he was.

"Your Highness," acknowledged the servant.

Hades gestured toward the body bag. "Take this to River. I suspect she will know what to do with it."

The servant nodded and grasped the bag. Cal wondered how the demon would move such a large bag; it was nearly three times his size. But he simply disappeared out of thin air with the bag in tow, as if it weighed nothing at all.

"What is it? If it's not a demon or a shade," Cal asked. He didn't really want to know the answer to that question, but felt he should ask anyways. "Was it human?"

Hades scratched at his chin. "Yes and no."

Asher sheathed his knife and ran a hand through his tawny hair. "It was human and alive once."

"But then that means it escaped from one of the domains. The damned souls have no means of escaping," Persephone protested.

Hades turned to Persephone. "Except the veil is growing thinner."

That's what Daphne had told Cal. That the veil was growing thinner and that it would eventually need to be closed. He would have to choose which side to stay on. The side with his mother and his sisters, or the side with Vic and her family.

"We'll need to station hellhounds around the portal. They'll have to guard it. Hades, damned souls cannot be slipping back into the world of the living," Persephone's cornflower eyes clouded over with worry.

Hades slipped an arm around his wife's shoulders. "I know, my love. Asher, see to the security of the portal. Once you feel it's secure and that no shades or damned souls can slip through, I want you to return to the Above World and follow the trail of any that may still remain on the other side of the portal. And bring them to me. But bring them to me alive."

Asher nodded and disappeared back out the front door.

Why had he brought Cal here? What was it that Cal could even do? He alone didn't have the power to close the portal, and he had no idea where Vic was or when she would be back.

"Persephone, call together the Council. And bring the Primordials. This is much worse than we feared." Hades instructed and Persephone nodded, already heading off down one of the many castle corridors. "Cal, you can come with me. It's about time that you meet your biological parents."

Chapter Twenty- Eight

Vic

Vic landed on the ground with a hard thud that knocked the wind out of her. This time she knew she was in the right place. Well, she was in the right place and was pretty sure she was in the right time.

The snow felt refreshing against her bare skin, but only for a minute, and the sky above her was dark and ominous with clouds that threatened Olympia with yet more snow. Her hand clutched the vial of umbilical cord blood that was around her neck.

Sure, she could have tried to use her wings to soften her fall, but this time the Void had all but spit her out like it had a bad taste in its mouth. It had been too quick and she couldn't get purchase before she was crashing through the treetops, and she did not want to tear the delicate skin of her newly formed wings.

Her immortality was already at work—like a magic elixir—fixing up any bruised areas or potentially cracked ribs from her fall.

The snow crunched beneath Vic as she made it to her feet. She glanced at the ring that graced her index finger. The one that had part of Daphne's tree embedded in its setting. A gift from her father. Her skin around the edges of the ring had turned black, which logic told Vic was impossible.

She looked around the forest, trying to get her bearings. The pines were so thick where the Void had unceremoniously tossed her out that it was hard to see and make sense of where exactly she was. The ring throbbed against her finger.

There was no visible sun, so Vic couldn't even tell exactly what time of day it was. She still had enough light to see. It wasn't yet evening which meant it was at least before five o'clock.

Well, she certainly couldn't stand here all day. She had a mission now. A mission, but no plan. She figured the plan would fall into place once she started moving.

She took a tentative step forward and a searing pain shot up her arm from her finger to her elbow.

Vic hissed and took a step back.

The pain immediately went away.

Curious, she took a step forward and again experienced a shooting pain up her arm. This time without the element of surprise, it took some of the edge off. It was almost like when you hit your funny bone, which everyone knows is not the least bit funny.

She took another step forward and this time the pain intensified, shooting all the way up to her shoulder.

Sighing, she took two steps back.

The pain stopped.

Carefully, she took a step to the left. Pain shot up her forearm. She took a hasty step back to the right and the pain stopped.

Her index finger was turning pink. She glared at the ring.

Then she tried to pull it off, but it appeared stuck as if it was melded to her skin. She gave it another yank, but it didn't even budge from its comfortable spot above her knuckle.

Vic sighed. There was only one direction left to try, besides down and up. If this didn't work then she was at a total loss.

She took a deep breath and gently stepped to her right.

Nothing. No pain.

She turned facing her right and took a step forward.

Still nothing.

Was the ring some kind of tracking device? And if so where was it planning on leading her?

Well, she had no choice. It would be dark soon and she'd be stuck in the woods alone with not even a knife to protect her, so it was the way of the ring or freeze her butt off until morning and hope for the best.

She began trudging in the direction the ring had approved.

After about ten minutes, she began to feel a throbbing in her wrist and as she continued, it eventually permeated to her forearm. Vic stopped.

This again.

Losing patience and deciding the pain was temporary, she tried each of the other two directions, besides forward and backward. When she turned to her left, she experienced no pain, so began making her way in that direction

The forest was quiet. No birds, no crunching of snow beneath an animals' hooves. Just utter stillness.

She walked in this direction for a good twenty minutes before the trees began to break up and she could see a clearing in the distance. A clearing that she hoped, was the familiar clearing of home—of Olympia and Daphne's tree to the Under World.

Evening was setting in, painting everything in a wash of gray-white.

Finally, she saw the charred tree that always looked dead—as if struck by lightning—to any mortal passerby, but which Vic now knew housed Daphne. Housed? Imprisoned? Vic figured it was a fine line based on Daphne's story. Had Zeus protected her or tricked her? Or both? Did it matter?

Vic emerged from the forest line feeling victorious that she'd successfully returned home. Until her eyes fell onto the familiar tree.

Energy shimmered around it, swirling and swaying its bare branches, which reached toward the sky like old, gnarled fingers.

The energy reminded Vic of looking at a black asphalt road or a roof on a hot summer day, the way the heat shimmered above it, almost like a mirage.

Vic squinted, trying to see if the door she'd used earlier or a window with Daphne looking out would appear, but the tree simply remained as it was.

She took a step toward the manor, in the direction of town, but pain shot up her arm stopping her.

Damn ring.

Sighing for the umpteenth time, she walked across the clearing and toward the tree. The shimmering energy thrummed the ground beneath her feet.

Whose energy was this? It wasn't her father's. Her father's magic—his essence—left a sweet scent lingering in the air.

Like air spun sugar. Her mother's left a sort of flowery, herbal smell behind. Vic stuck out her tongue. The energy was crisp and warm. Like snowflakes melting on your tongue before drinking hot chocolate and eating snickerdoodles.

But that couldn't be right. She'd been continuing to walk as she sniffed the air, not paying attention, she was now in the vortex of the wind that whipped around the tree, tossing loose pieces of bark to the ground and swirling the light snowflakes that had just begun to fall.

She stuck out her tongue, opening her mouth wide to the sky as if she could suck the world into her own lungs. Like the Void. And took a deep breath.

No. That definitely could not be right.

The magic smelled like snowflakes, hot chocolate, and snickerdoodles.

All the things that reminded her of Cal.

What was happening?

In the distance she could hear the roar of the Void, its high-pitched howl. She clutched the vial around her neck. Never before had it felt like everything was coming to a frenzied conclusion. And never had Vic felt more uncertain about what the future held.

Closing her eyes, she raised her hand toward the shimmering energy, feeling the waves of warmth wash over her fingers.

Never did she pass through the portal without the accompaniment of a hellhound.

She leaned into the familiar warmth, Cal's energy, and pushed her hand through the barrier, seemingly sinking it into the trunk of the tree. The energy felt thick and syrupy.

Vic continued to push, easing in her shoulder and her head, letting the familiar scent wash over her, envelop her as she did so.

She continued to push herself through until nothing was left of her in the Above World except her footsteps in the snow. The energy shivered and the tree remained dark and lifeless in her wake.

Chapter Twenty- Nine

Cal

Cal wiped the sweat from his brow.

He had never used his magic to this extent before and he was ill-prepared for the exhaustion that ensued.

Hades had summoned the Council. It was clear that barriers had to be established. Ares was tasked with helping Asher to retrieve any further wayward Under Worlders that had gotten into the Above World.

Poseidon, Zeus, and Hades still convened, but it had been Athena's suggestion that she and Cal work to secure the portal from this side. Despite her leather miniskirts and corsets, Athena was a goddess of war. She instructed Cal on the points of weakness surrounding the veil between the worlds. Then as Cal summoned his air element, she quickly showed him how his air was no normal air, it was tangible and could be woven just as Arachne's silk. It wasn't visible, much like the spider's silk, until several strands were woven together. Athena's fingers were deft as she threaded invisible strands of air into links of chainmail. The chains shimmered when combined and Athena began to use it as a curtain between the Above and Below Worlds.

However, Athena had failed to explain just how exhausting it would be to expend his magic in this manner. Then again, she'd been using hers her entire life. What Athena did explain was that his Primordial magic was even stronger and more powerful than that of the Olympians. Even though he wasn't ancient, his magic was. Hades had summoned the Primordials, but Nyx and Uranus had yet to show.

To take his mind off his fatigue, he'd let his mind wander to Nyx and what it would be like to meet her. His biological mother who had given him up eighteen years ago. He'd only ever seen an illustration and the woman had appeared dark and mysterious, with her raven hair and cloak of moons and stars.

Suddenly, Athena's sharp voice broke through his daydream.

"Incoming!"

Incoming? How could there be an incoming? Athena had assured him that the magical chainmail—between his magic and hers—would be impenetrable from either side.

There was a flash of black freefalling from above. Was it a shade? Or had Asher and Ares returned from the Above World?

As the figure tumbled through the air, he caught a glimpse of a braid trailing behind and immediately knew that it was Vic.

Shifting his hands, he redirected his magic toward Vic, using it to catch her and slow her fall. He used the air to cradle her, bringing her to the ground so that she landed gently on her feet.

She looked bewildered for a second before her eyes registered him standing there, sweating and with his t-shirt clinging to his stomach, back, and arms.

His girlfriend ran to him and threw her arms around his neck, planting a kiss on his lips, before shoving him back slightly, a look of concern now on her face.

"Your magic! But you've used too much!" She whirled onto Athena. "He's never used his magic! You've allowed him to use too much! He's practically dead on his feet!"

Athena crossed her arms and huffed.

"We needed his Primordial magic! There was no other choice!" she gestured at the shimmering wall before them.

Vic sniffed. "Snow, hot chocolate, and snickerdoodles. Cal's magic."

"I know. He's been making me want a vacation to the Alps the entire time we've been creating the barrier."

Cal had no idea what Vic and Athena were talking about. He didn't smell anything. Just the familiar smell of sulfur, incense, and maybe something else slightly bitter, like olives. More or less all smells that he associated with the Under World.

Vic noticed the confused look on his face.

"Your magic. Every immortal's magic has a distinct scent. My mother's smells like hyacinths, Athena's like olives…yours smells like snow, hot chocolate, and snickerdoodles." Vic shrugged.

"And yours smells like sugared cream," Athena added. "But really we need to get back to it. You shouldn't have been able to get through the barrier."

"But he's exhausted! If he sleeps for three days, he's not going to be of much further help!" Vic objected.

Both women were talking about him as if he wasn't standing right there. But also, both women were right. Athena was right that they needed to keep at it, and possibly make the chainmail even stronger. And Vic was also right that he felt dead on his feet. He felt he could easily lay down and sleep until at least the Winter Solstice, if not longer.

"Athena is right. Damned souls have somehow been getting through into the Above World. It's dangerous. We have to protect the mortals. My mother and my sisters," he hoped his voice sounded fierce and didn't betray his fatigue.

"But you're of no use to anyone if you deplete your magic!" Vic objected. It wasn't often that he and Vic disagreed, and if he was being truthful, they wouldn't be disagreeing.

Athena crossed her arms and scowled. She was millennia older than Vic, but most of the gods weren't keen on crossing Hades or any member of the Haden family.

"What do you propose, Princess?"

"I propose that River guard the portal. The chainmail will help protect the veil, but the Styx is meant to keep souls from crossing through."

"But the river is at least a mile from here," Athena pointed out.

"Yes, but instead of using Cal's magic to make seemingly endless amounts of chainmail that no one is one-hundred percent certain will work, he could us his air magic to redirect the river."

"And how do you suggest he do that?" Athena looked down at Vic. She was not used to being outsmarted.

"Water vapor."

...

Vic's idea had actually been ingenious and even Athena begrudgingly admitted it. Vic had used her own magic to help him take water from the River Styx—he'd once seen Vic create a serpent out of water using only her magic before—and he had then transformed the water into a mist that now hung around the portal.

The work was less tiring than continuously creating strands of air for Athena to weave. He'd only wished that they had thought of it sooner.

Now they walked back toward the castle, satisfied that the vapor—between Cal's Primordial magic and the power of the River Styx—would keep any demons, shades, or damned souls from escaping.

"What's that?" Vic asked. She kept playing with a vial that hung from around her neck. Her fingers absentmindedly brushing against it.

Once he'd really looked at her, he'd noticed the huge, dark circles beneath her eyes, the scratches that hadn't yet healed themselves, and the strange ring of petrified wood that still wrapped around her finger. She was acquiring an odd assortment of jewelry. But they didn't keep secrets, so he knew that eventually she would tell him everything that had happened to her in the last forty-eight hours. He need only be patient.

"What's what?" Cal asked, redirecting his attention from her face to where she pointed.

She gestured toward his pocket, where the star of Orion emitted a steady white glow.

"Just something I found earlier today. I think it belongs to Artemis," he mused.

Vic's eyes narrowed in thought. "Artemis," she gestured to the vial around her neck. It was small and amber colored with a black lid and black leather cord. "This belongs to Apollo."

Cal wasn't sure he wanted to know what was in the vial if it belonged to Apollo.

The woven spider silk bracelet on Vic's wrist slid slightly up and down her arm as she gesticulated. A constant reminder of Arachne eventually coming to collect, as well as a reminder of the Divine Web. Was it a coincidence that he had something that belonged to Artemis and that Vic now had something that belonged to Apollo?

Everything always seemed to come back to Apollo.

She didn't tell him what the vial contained, but she continued. "I learned something today. Yesterday? Today? Does it even matter anymore?" Cal shook his head. All the days seemed to blend together as they hurtled toward some unknown, unstoppable inevitability. Ever since he'd moved to Olympia time had ceased to hold the same sort of meaning.

"We both know of Apollo's previous incarnations. His attempts at rape, murder, martyrdom. The list goes on and on. But did you know he was like this since birth? His own mother knew that he was set up to destroy. Just as the sun gives life…"

"So too does it taketh," Cal finished. "Artemis and Apollo are opposite in so many ways. And even she, the twin who shared the womb with him, has not been exempt from her brother's savagery."

"The moon and the sun."

"And the stars," Cal breathed.

Vic stopped walking near the rotunda and turned toward him.

"I know how to end this."

Cal did too. They would have to destroy the portal. And they'd either have to stay together in the Above or Below Worlds, or forever stay apart. It was the only way. Cal had caused the imbalance in the Universe and he was going to be the one who stopped it.

The star in his pocket glowed warmer against his skin at the thought. The sun was also a star. And every star eventually burned out.

Vic was about to say something else, when the door to the castle opened and Persephone hurried out, her long skirt dragging across the black gravel.

"Thank goodness you're both here." She hurried to Vic and embraced her then wrapped an arm around Cal's shoulders as she led them both to the castle door. Persephone may look fragile, but her grip on his shoulder was strong and full of vitality.

"We have very important guests." She guided them through the labyrinth of the inner workings of the castle, down into its bowels.

Cal knew what was about to happen and the exhaustion from his work with Athena and Vic, seemed to tenfold as it mixed with his apprehension. He'd wanted this moment for so many days of the past few months, that now that it was about to happen, his stomach twisted in knots and his head swam with uncertainty.

Vic shot him a quizzical look over her mother's shoulders. Where had she been? Her cheeks were sunburnt and the edges of her jawline appeared sharper.

The doors to the War Room slid silently open and the talking on the other side ceased as he, Vic, and Persephone entered.

Smiling softly, her concern momentarily gone, Persephone said. “Cal, I’d like to introduce you to your parents.”

Chapter Thirty

Vic

Vic had never met a Primordial deity before. Aside from Cal, of course.

When the War Room's pneumatic doors opened, she was surprised that they looked so...normal. Nyx and Uranus stood as Persephone, Athena, Vic, and Cal entered the room.

They were seated at the giant table along with Hades, Zeus, Poseidon, and Ares—the rest of the Council of Olympians. Most Olympians enjoyed their quiet lives and wanted to be left alone—the Council helped to make that possible. While Zeus and his sons made up the back bone of the Council, Ares and Athena provided strategic perspective, while Persephone, not technically a member of the Council, provided an alternate, often less violent, view of things.

When Cal entered, Nyx and Uranus glanced at one another nervously. Vic had to give them credit for not running up to their son like it was some sitcom family reunion. Essentially, aside from DNA, they were strangers to one another. Eighteen years was a long time to be apart from someone. A lot could happen in eighteen years. People were made or unmade. Paths followed and diverged. Relationships kindled and ended.

Vic gave Cal's arm a reassuring squeeze. She wanted Nyx and Uranus to see the amazing person that their son had become. The son that Vic herself had fallen in love with. Smart, patient, thoughtful, and steady: Cal. It took someone miraculous to not only love her with her temperamental and dark nature, but to love her father and mother as well. To love the life that she lived.

Finally, Hades stood, brushing a hand through his already neatly slicked back hair. It was one of her father's nervous habits.

"Cal. Callum. You know the Council and these are…" Hades gestured.

"Your parents," Nyx supplied. "Your biological ones."

Nyx was tall with long, dark hair that hung in loose waves past her shoulders and porcelain skin. Her features were angular and her eyes were a piercing dark purple. She had on a long black dress and a dark purple cape that fastened at her collar bone. There was a regal air about her, almost stoic, but the light in her eyes softened when they fell on Cal.

The man next to her was nearly as tall as Zeus, he had a white beard that was neatly trimmed and soft gray eyes. His skin was tanned as if he'd spent a lot of time outdoors. He was dressed in the old ways, not in the modern ways of the Olympians. Uranus wore a simple white tunic that fell to his knees and was belted with a simple brown belt, and on his feet were thick strapped, brown leather gladiator style sandals. He embodied the picture of the gods in Vic's textbooks at school and in any piece of Renaissance art.

"I'm Uranus and this is Nyx," he gestured and for a moment looked as though he wanted to shake Cal's hands, then still unsure, he put his hands behind his back as if that's what he had meant to do all along.

Cal's eyes were wide. "My parents." The words sounded strange and faraway in his mouth. He cleared his throat. "My biological parents."

He stepped forward slowly then tentatively went up to Nyx and wrapped her in a hug. Vic noticed the small "o" of surprise on Nyx's lips, but she didn't hesitate to wrap her arms around her son. Uranus followed suit, wrapping both Nyx and Cal in his arms.

They stood like that, in a small embrace, for nearly a minute, before Cal pulled away. He hesitated as he dropped his arms and Vic knew that he didn't want to let Nyx go. Cal was lucky—he had two mothers who loved him very, very much.

"Thank you for coming," he said.

"Yes, thank you for coming. Please. Cal, Vic, Athena, have a seat," Hades drew his thumb under his eyes wiping away any tears that may have sprung up.

Her father was a sentimental man.

Persephone put her hands on Vic's shoulders and gently guided her toward a seat near her father. She took the seat on Vic's other side and Cal sat in between Nyx and Uranus.

Hades cleared his throat, re-establishing his composure. "Athena, how is the veil between worlds?"

"As protected as can be. Between Cal's and my magical chainmail, and Vic's idea to use the water from the River Styx as vapor for an added layer of protection, it is safe—for now. I must remind you, Hades, these are only temporary solutions."

Vic sat up straighter at the praise—no matter how discreet—from Athena. Athena was millennia old and wise certainly beyond Vic's years, but if Vic had learned anything in recent times it was that sometimes the older gods and goddesses couldn't always see the forest for the trees. While they'd adapted to living amongst the mortals and frequenting the Above World, they sometimes lagged behind in innovation, clinging to old and sometimes outdated or inefficient ways of doing things.

Hades turned toward Nyx and Uranus. "The veil between worlds is crumbling."

"What of Daphne?" Zeus asked. Vic had always thought him a formidable figure, with the jagged scar that ran across his cheek like a lightning bolt and his stormy eyes.

"She was gone," Vic said.

"But how?" Cal asked. "I'd only just seen her in the last day."

Cal had also visited the nymph? That was peculiar.

Vic shrugged. "When I came through just now the tree was dark and empty as if no one was home." Something dawned on Vic. "Do you think she's okay? She isn't in any kind of danger, is she?"

Persephone patted her daughter's hand. "We can send a hound to be sure."

Vic thought about how the entire reason that Daphne was even in that tree in the first place was for protection from Apollo. She'd given up her family, her entire life, to be safe. But if the veil was weakened, what if the tree itself was also weakened? What if the very thing meant to protect her, suddenly made her more vulnerable?

"The time has come then," Nyx said softly. She glanced at Uranus and he put his hand over hers.

"What time?" Vic asked. She looked suspiciously between her father and Nyx.

Her skin was tingling. She and Cal both knew of the prophecy Pythia had made. The one that stated that the air and sword would rise as one.

No, this tingling was different. This was more similar to the dream she'd had where her mother had recognized her. Where she hadn't so much as dreamed, as walked back into time.

The ring on her finger pulsated sending warmth down her knuckle and to her wrist where the bracelet from Arachne echoed in response. Vic knew Arachne would come to collect—but Vic didn't know what or when. Just that the Divine Web was at play.

Vic narrowed her eyes and looked at the shared expression between her parents and Cal's biological parents. There was a familiarity there. This was not their first meeting. The bracelet around her wrist grew warmer.

She studied her father, whose expression was grim. His eyes, usually jovial and mischievous, were downcast and reflected only concern. His mouth was turned down at the corners. Uranus' expression mirrored that of Hades.

The time has come.

And then it all played together in rapid flashes across Vic's mind. Her father sending her to the Above World. Cal seeing her while she was Taking souls. His father being Cronus, a Titan. Apollo aligning with Cronus against the Olympians. Apollo the Destroyer. Aphrodite, also a Titan, trying to destroy Vic and Cal because she thought Cal was creating the imbalance that was causing the Void. Vic coming into her powers. Cal learning that his mother was Nyx and that she had given him to Rachel for safe keeping. Cal coming into his own powers—without Vic who had been sent away only for the Universe to send her to Leto. Cal's fascination with Artemis. Persephone's friendship with Artemis. Apollo's own mother explaining that the twins—not Cal—were causing the imbalance. But could Vic truly destroy Apollo, without somehow also destroying Artemis? In some weird, twisted path it suddenly seemed that everything of the last few months—years even—had somehow led to this moment.

They had known all along.

"For how long?" Vic asked. She realized she'd interrupted a conversation that had been going on, but she hadn't been listening. The table fell silent around her. She repeated herself. "For how long?"

Hades wouldn't look at her. He looked around the table, at everyone but her.

Persephone looked down at her hands folded on the table in front of her.

"Your entire life. We certainly couldn't have predicted that you'd fall in love with one another, but we knew that the first children born of the Primordials and the Olympians in millennia, would certainly be called to fulfill a duty that would impact our world as we knew it," Persephone said softly.

"Pythia had seen it. She had seen the crumbling of the veil, the chaos that would ensue if the two worlds converged. She also saw that it could be stopped," Hades explained.

"This entire time you knew. You knew about Cal's parents! You knew that the veil would crumble! But did you even do anything to stop it?"

Vic's voice had risen in volume with each word. Her blood felt like it was boiling beneath her skin. She hadn't felt this angry in months. Her heart pounded in her chest. As a child and teenager, she'd had bouts of rage, seemingly uncontrollable outbursts where she felt like her fists and feet and words worked asynchronistic from her brain. She hadn't realized that she had jumped to her feet, her hands balled into fists at her sides.

Nyx's eyes grew wide. "It is not something that could be stopped. You wear the silk of the Divine Web. Even you know that destiny cannot be stopped."

Cal looked back and forth between his mother and Vic.

"That's a bunch of crock and you know it! Destiny can be rewritten. Free will matters. We aren't all pawns in some giant chess game."

"So it's all true then? Vic and I are the ones who must close the portal between the worlds. To stop my causing the imbalance. To stop the Void from destroying the Above World," Cal's voice didn't waiver. He seemed to have made up his mind about what needed to be done. Except that he was wrong.

"You aren't the imbalance!" Vic all but shouted. Even Ares, Zeus, and Athena had grown silent, their eyes ping-ponging back and forth between the Hadens and the Bishops—or whatever Cal's Primordial parents called themselves, if anything.

Vic sighed.

"The imbalance is Apollo! Leto told me herself. He is the Destroyer and she told me that he could be stopped. Not only that, she also told me how to do it."

Shock and confusion flashed across Cal's face. This isn't how Vic had wanted to tell him of her findings, of her news. But nothing like this ever went the way she wanted, let alone planned.

"It's not only Apollo," Persephone said softly.

Now it was Vic's turn to be shocked and confused.

"The twins are split from one seed."

"Artemis," Cal breathed.

This time Zeus interjected. His affair with Leto had led to the birth of the twins. It also led to Hera's jealous rage and subsequent banishment of Leto. Apollo and Artemis had been ostracized from before they were even born. Not quite Titans, but not quite Olympians either. Forever creating a rift between the two dynastic deities.

"One cannot survive without the other. But neither can one live without the other's life."

It sounded like something Pythia would say.

The bracelet around her wrist—Arachne's web—burned against her skin.

This was the interconnectivity of which Arachne had spoken. Each one of them was a thread in the Divine Web, overlapping, crisscrossing, starting, and stopping.

"So what do we do?" Vic touched the vial of umbilical cord blood at her neck. Leto had given her permission to kill her son. It was very, very difficult to kill an immortal. However, it could be done. Apollo had almost done it to Persephone, and Vic had wanted to kill him then. Except killing him seemed too easy, she wanted him to suffer in the depths of hell. In the blackness of Tartarus. She had wanted him to pay penance.

"I think you know, Darling. You both do," Persephone nodded toward Cal.

"We kill Apollo," Vic replied fiercely.

"And Artemis," Cal said, but his voice was not an echo of her own ferocity. Instead, it dripped with sadness, and once again Vic wondered what Cal knew that she didn't.

Chapter Thirty-One

Cal

Laying on the fanciest bed he'd ever laid on in his entire life, Cal peered at the locket containing the star.

It glowed through the seams and cracks, warming the metal surrounding it.

His room was on the older, stone masonry part of the castle. His bed was an ornate four poster with thick, velvet curtains around it. The comforter was a deep crimson paisley pattern. A green fire glowed in the fireplace. There was a black velvet armchair positioned near the fireplace, next to it a small table with a tray containing a kettle, teacups, and a decanter of whiskey. He wasn't even old enough to drink. At least in the mortal world. Although, his mother—Rachel—had been known to make him a hot toddy now and then, especially when he'd come down with a cold.

He laid across the bed, rolling the locket between his fingers. Artemis had always seemed a bit sad to him. At first he'd thought her strange, but once he learned her story, he could see the tiredness in her eyes. Vic had told him that long ago Persephone and Artemis were the best of friends. They did not seem close now.

But Cal knew that loss changed people. The aching losses that seemed to gut you from the inside out. The ones that you felt were never meant to happen in the first place. How Vic felt when she had nearly lost Persephone; how Cal had felt at Cronus' betrayal. While, he had lost a father that fall, it had made him angry but stronger. It wasn't a loss that he had grieved. What was revealed to him was not someone worthy of his sadness.

Artemis lost Orion. At her brother's deception, but at her own hand. As an immortal, she had to live with that essentially forever. While it was kind of Nyx to turn Orion into a constellation, it was probably both a blessing and a curse for Artemis. Her lover was gone, but also always there. Always in her sight and just within her reach, but never actually reachable.

What would Artemis want?

He was pretty sure he knew.

There was a knock at the door. When the knob didn't immediately turn, he realized the person on the other side was waiting for his response. This meant that it most likely was not Vic, who he knew had been trying to tell him something very important before Persephone had fetched them during their work with Athena. He had expected her to seek him out once the excitement had died down and they could finally talk without interruption.

"Come in!" he called.

The knob turned and as the door opened he caught a whiff of patchouli and something soft and floral like bergamot. Nyx—his *mother*—entered the room.

She stood awkwardly at the threshold, clearly uncertain if her presence was indeed truly welcome.

In person, his mother looked even more beautiful than the illustration he'd found in a book last month. Her skin was like porcelain and her eyes were striking with long, dark lashes. Her hair was jet black and fell in thick waves past her shoulder. But he knew she was more than just beauty, her eyes held a deep, unwavering wisdom.

"I'm not bothering you?" she asked.

Cal had returned the locket to his pocket when he had heard the knock.

"Of course not…" He was going to say Mom, but it felt weird because Rachel was the one who had raised him. The one who had guided him throughout his first eighteen years of life.

"Nyx. You can call me Nyx," she had sensed his hesitation. Nyx entered the room and closed the door behind her. She was very tall and in a few strides she was across the room, sinking into the velvet armchair.

Cal gestured toward the tea set. "Help yourself."

"I think I will, thank you." She poured herself a cup of tea, decanted the whiskey and poured some into her cup, and took a sip. Her lips curved into a small smile. Satisfied, she held the cup in her lap and looked over at Cal. "I didn't mean to interrupt you. I just felt…I don't know. It's the first time I have seen you in eighteen years. I've lived millennia, and you'd think that eighteen years would pass by quickly, especially since I knew that I would see you again. But I'd be lying if I said they passed by quickly. You look just as I pictured you would." She smiled wider this time, then glanced over at the green flames in the fireplace.

He had so many questions, so many things that he wanted to say to her—to his biological mother, but none of them came to the forefront of his brain, let alone landed on his tongue. There was a lot that he had to figure out on his own in the last couple of months. And he finally felt that he was making progress. That certain things now made more sense—like how his air affinity had made him the best surfer of all his friends. How he felt so free as if he was flying when out alone on the water. With each new revelation, a piece of his life gained new clarity.

But there was one thing that still bothered him.

"You changed her life that day," he said.

Nyx didn't turn her gaze from the fireplace and the green made her porcelain skin glow.

"I hope for the better," she replied quietly.

Cal didn't necessarily know how to respond. His mother (Rachel) would say it had been for the better. That she had his sisters. His sisters who were half-immortal in their own right, and some day he would have to tell them. He would need to be close by until they were at least all teenagers. Even then they would still need him.

But he also knew that when he was given to Rachel in that tailor shop by Nyx that the entire course of her life had altered—and all because of her kindness. That's why Nyx had chosen Rachel in the first place. And if she hadn't been his mother, Cronus wouldn't have sought her out. Maybe Apollo wouldn't have been the one to have released Cronus from his prison in Tartarus.

Somehow all roads led back to Apollo.

"If she were here, she would say it was for the better because that's the type of person that she is," Cal responded.

Nyx turned toward him, her violet eyes were sad. "That is the reason that I chose her to raise my son. It was not easy to give you up. To let you be raised in the mortal world. But the Oracle is never wrong and there were certain things you needed to learn and know. Certain things that I could never possibly teach you."

Cal pushed aside his feelings that he and Vic had somehow been pawns in an immortal scheme. Only because he had faith in the Divine Web and did not feel that destiny made mistakes. Even if Nyx had chosen a different woman, somehow he would have been led to Vic. Somehow they would still be in this exact situation. That was how the web worked. You kept being led to where you needed to be until you got it right.

"I think the gods sometimes ask too much of people," Cal said.

Nyx took a sip of her tea and nodded.

"That is not untrue. Sometimes being immortal, it's easy to think of some things—people—as inconsequential. Of course, we both know that isn't true. Everyone is consequential. I just mean that it jades our thoughts and actions sometimes."

Cal noted this tidbit of wisdom and made a quick, silent vow to himself to not fall into that way of thinking. He never wanted to think of another person as a means to an end. No matter how long he was going to be alive—even if it was forever.

They sat in companionable silence for a few minutes, the only sound the crackling of the fire.

"This wasn't quite how I imagined our first meeting," Nyx smiled and pulled her cloak tighter around herself as if she had a chill.

"Yeah, me neither," Cal admitted.

He'd daydreamed about it enough times. He thought maybe Nyx would contact him—write him a letter or something—asking to finally meet. He didn't exactly think they'd go and grab a cup of coffee or dinner, but that maybe they would meet somewhere like the House of Snakes (Pythia's shop, not the secret society that Apollo had tried to resurrect). His mind hadn't really ever gotten past that point, but the one consistent thing he dreamed about was the look of pride shining in Nyx's eyes. He didn't know why that mattered to him. She was virtually a stranger.

A stranger who had his nose and tall, lean build. A stranger who had his smile. He hadn't had quite as good a study of Uranus and wondered what features he shared with his biological father. Furthermore, what personality traits did he share with either of his parents? Of course, there was the whole nature versus nurture thing, but Cal was of the belief that certain traits were ingrained in your DNA, regardless of how or where you were raised. Did his love of numbers come from his father? His love of art from his mother? Was his propensity for bad jokes from Uranus or Nyx? Did the gods even joke?

Nyx's brow furrowed and she set her teacup back onto the small table.

"You know. Not everything requires so much thinking. Sometimes the best solutions are in the doing."

The comment reminded him of Vic. All his life, Cal had been cautious. Thoughtful. In elemental study, air was equated to the mind and thinking after all. Vic was passionate.

Impulsive. Quick to anger, but also quick to love. Just like fire was represented by sparks and energy.

He pulled the locket from his pocket and slid his fingernail along the seam so that it popped open. The glowing white orb winked from inside the now open locket.

Nyx's eyes drifted closed with recognition.

"I think Artemis gave this to me," he said.

She opened her eyes. "It has been a long time since I've seen the Star of Orion."

Cal knew the modern origins of the star. Clearly, it was from the constellation and clearly it was given by Artemis to Luna for safekeeping. He also knew the story of Orion's murder and how Nyx had helped Artemis 'bury' Orion, but instead of in the ground, placing him into the sky as a grouping of stars in his brilliant warrior form. But he did not know how this particular star had come into Artemis' possession.

Nyx saw the unspoken question on his face. The lift of his eyebrow as he held the small, glowing object. He had shared that Artemis had given it to him. Now it was time for his mother to tell him the rest of the story.

"I could not bring Orion back, of course. He was half mortal. Not only that, he'd been dead half the day before he washed ashore. As you'll learn, there are some things even powerful magic cannot fix or reverse. There are also Universal Laws that must be obeyed. Reanimating the dead being one of them," she smiled wistfully.

"So the best that I could do is place his soul where Artemis would always be able to see him and where he would always be able to watch over his beloved. In the night sky. Where he could reside for eternity. But I don't know if that was necessarily better. Yes, he could watch over and guide

Artemis, but he could not ever intervene. And Artemis could view her Orion in the sky every night, always visible, but never within reach. I wasn't sure if what I had done was a blessing or a curse. She was just so distraught—heartbroken—that I felt I had to do something. Something that would give her some semblance of hope and peace. And yet for many days afterwards, I could not shake the feeling that I'd done Artemis a disservice placing her lover just out of reach.

"Not long after I'd done so, her friend, Persephone, sought me out. Mind you, I am not necessarily easy to summon. But Persephone had gone out, on her wedding night of all nights, and turned her face up toward the night sky. It was a new moon that night. A new moon is when the moon and sun are in conjunction, the side facing the Earth is dark. So my darkness laid across the land with no illumination. The sun—Apollo—hid his sister—the moon—from the Earth once a month. Only the stars can offer guidance during a new moon. She appealed to me that while my intention had been one of kindness, her friend was still distraught and she was concerned that her own marriage and subsequent departure, would be Artemis' unraveling. And so Persephone pleaded with me to help."

Nyx ran a long, slender finger along the edge of the teacup. The repetitive motion transporting her back to that night. That night Persephone appealed to the Primordial god in order to help her friend. In order to save her friend, not only of a broken heart, but of a fate even worse: to tread the Earth with your lover in your sights, but never ever by your side. To see them but never again to feel them, hear their voice, or look into their eyes.

"The Divine Web cannot be undone, of course, as you know. But there had to be something I could do. Some loophole that I could find. Apollo had been most devious, violating the natural order of things for his own nefarious desires. Surely, there was a way for me to help Artemis. As I'm sure you've realized by now, Persephone is very wise. Her idea was to give her friend one of the stars of Orion to warm her heart and guide her while here on Earth. But also to protect her from Apollo.

"And so I decided Persephone was right. On the Winter Solstice—the shortest day of the year—I called down a star from Orion. He gave it up willingly—in death as in life he would do anything for Artemis."

Nyx pulled her cloak more tightly around her.

"You see Artemis is linked to the Winter Solstice and Apollo to the Summer Solstice. It is their correspondence."

"The Winter Solstice is only two days away," Cal replied.

"It is. Artemis' energy will be at its strongest and Apollo's at its weakest," she picked up her tea and took a careful sip.

Cal closed the locket, the glow of the star of Orion escaping through the seams. He looked up at his mother.

"Vic had had something she wanted to tell me, but never got the chance."

Nyx nodded. "Go and talk to her. I am certain what she has to say will be the final puzzle piece in this ordeal."

Chapter Thirty-Two

Vic

Vic felt strange being in her childhood bedroom.

The pinks and purples, soft pastels accented with silver no longer seemed to suit her. It was only about a year since she'd been sent to live in the Above World. And yet so much had changed. She had changed.

That little girl felt faraway and naïve. Vic had been a sweet, curious, and intellectual child. She'd spent her youth with her face buried in her books—history, fairy tales, foreign languages—and her early teens chasing after Asher, trying in vain to win over his affections. But she'd come in second to Asher's desire to serve her father.

Asher had always ignited something in her that brought all her anger and frustrations to the surface. They were like rock and metal: angular and painful, cold. But with Cal he softened something inside her, could calm her fears and insecurities. He was like the water to her rock, slowly smoothing, carefully over time until she was smooth and shiny.

Her experience in the Under World felt confined and suffocating to her now. Having lived in the fresh air and wide open spaces of the Above World, it was hard for her to fathom ever returning permanently.

But wasn't it her duty? She was the Princess of Darkness. She could not undo that which she was. When she was in the Above World, was she simply pretending to be someone else? Perhaps she hadn't really changed all that much. Maybe the Below World was her true self, and no matter what she did or where she went, she could never truly escape it.

She crossed her arms over her stomach, hugging herself, and sank slowly onto the small bed. If they killed Apollo, and it made the Void stop destroying, the veil had still grown too thin. Too much energy had all but caused it to short-circuit was how Athena had described it to her. Energy could not be created nor destroyed, but it could be transferred. Vic surmised it had been transferred to the Void. Which if that was the case, when the Void was stopped, where would that energy then go? She highly doubted everything would just return to normal.

The spider silk bracelet around her wrist grew warm. No, things would certainly not return to normal. Deep in her gut she knew that the portal between the Above World and Below World would be closed. And when it was, where would she go? Which Vic was the real one?

...

A rap on the partially opened door startled her out of her thoughts.

Cal's face appeared in the opening, a lock of his brown hair curled across his forehead. His hair had grown long over the past couple of months. He was beginning the shift from high school boy to college man right before her eyes. College. Would they even go to college? Did they really even need or want to?

"Hey," Vic said. She now sat in her favorite reading chair which was pushed into the far corner, an elaborate, iron reading lamp sat on the nightstand in between the chair and her bed. The chair was placed near a window which looked down over the rotunda and the pomegranate trees of which her mother was so fond. She had a book face down in her lap, unread, trying in vain to distract herself. *Alice in Wonderland* had always been one of her favorites. Everything certainly felt turned upside down and inside out at the moment.

Cal opened the door further and stepped into the room, closing it behind him. His snickerdoodle scent swooshed into the room. As he'd begun using his magic the scent had become stronger, more cloying. It was still pleasant, but no longer subtle.

"I have something that I wanted to show you," he said sitting on the edge of her bed, close enough that their knees barely touched. "And I think that earlier there was something that you wanted to tell me? But maybe didn't get the chance."

Vic nodded. "I've been away. I've learned a lot of things."

Cal nodded. She'd known he'd probably figure as much. It wasn't out of the realm of possibilities that her father sent her places—or summoned her places— and that she'd be gone for several days.

He gestured. "You go first."

Her boyfriend looked as tired as she felt. Vic couldn't even remember the last time she had truly slept—without Dream Walking. They were supposed to be two crazy kids in love. Instead, they were two immortals with the weight of the world on their shoulders.

She closed her book and set it back on the nightstand, then pulled the small vial that was hidden beneath the collar of her t-shirt. As soon as she'd gotten up to her rooms, she'd changed into fresh clothes, the dirty, sweat-laden ones still were in a pile halfway between her bedroom and the attached bathroom.

"My father sent me through time."

Cal's jaw dropped a little. "Through time? As in time travel?"

Vic nodded. "More or less. The Void is essentially a black hole, as we saw with Aphrodite's ship. And since I can Dream Walk…well, I guess it makes it easier to Time Walk too. So you need an object that will take you to the past, and another object that will bring you back to the present. I thought maybe I was going to the time before my mom and dad got married, or maybe just afterward. But instead I landed in the not-too-distant past and met Daphne."

"Me too. I mean, I also met her, but it was in the present."

"She's gone now," Vic shrugged. "Sometime between when we both saw her—because somehow I don't think time necessarily passed in the same way for her—she vanished. The tree looked empty to me."

"She had seemed worried when I saw her," Cal said.

Vic nodded. "Me too. The story of how she got there…became the guardian between the worlds, of the portal…I'm not sure if that was a blessing of protection or a curse in truth."

"The gods always seem to have their personal interests in mind, even when they seem to be doing something kind for someone," Cal offered. Then added, "No offense."

"None taken. But you're a god now too, you know."

"Maybe you and I will be different," he said softly. "Maybe we start something new. A new way."

Vic's heart swelled at his words. How was it that Cal seemed so wise?

"Maybe," she replied letting the hope swell in her chest. Maybe they really could be the start of something different. She still needed to puzzle out her thoughts from before Cal interrupted them.

"So after I met Daphne, I thought the Void would send me home. But apparently it had other plans." She waved the vial.

Cal's eyes narrowed, but she knew it wasn't obvious simply upon looking what the vial contained.

"Where did it take you?"

"To a Greek island. The one that Leto happened to have been banished to by Hera"

"Apollo and Artemis's Titan mother?"

"The very one."

Cal let out a low whistle. "What was she like?"

"Intimidating. But nice enough. If I imagined an Amazonian Warrior Princess, it would probably be Leto. She's unhappy about being banished, of course. I'd never been certain that part of the story was true. She's also unhappy about her son."

"Apollo."

Vic nodded. "Apparently, ever since he was in the womb, Apollo was bent on destroying. He'd nearly sucked the lifeblood from Artemis until they were born. And even as a child, he was oddly possessive and domineering of his twin sister. Leto was concerned even back then."

"Then why didn't she drown him or something? Spare us all the millennia of pain that he's caused and havoc that he's wreaked."

Vic chided him. "I'm not so sure a mother could do that to her child, Cal. No matter how evil."

She thought of her parents and knew with certainty that they would not have done that to her, in fact with her angry outbursts and fiery temper they very well could have. For a time she had been dangerous, more to herself than anyone. Going through puberty in the Under World certainly isn't for the faint of heart.

"But she did do the next best thing," Vic held the vial up so that the red light outside caught it. The contents of the vial glistened inside, moving up the side of the vial in slow, syrupy fashion.

"Is that blood?" Cal was the more squeamish of the two of them.

"Apollo's blood. Better yet, his umbilical cord blood."

"She's kept it all this time?"

Vic nodded. Maybe it was a little weird. "Leto knew that one day he would need to be ended. So she kept it all this time. Then again, I'm not exactly sure what time I met her in. Maybe he hadn't even yet done half the things that we know he's done. Either way. This is the key to destroying Apollo."

"Umbilical cord blood?"

Vic nodded again, tugging the vial back beneath the collar of her shirt. Of course Cal didn't yet know how to kill an immortal. "There are only a handful of ways to kill an immortal. We heal incredibly fast, so the system essentially needs to be completely overwhelmed. It's like we short circuit."

"Poisoning?" Cal suggested, eluding to what had happened to Persephone only several months ago.

"Poisoning at high doses over a long period of time. Fatal, catastrophic accidents that don't give our bodies enough time to heal and repair. Like falling off a mountain, but then being attacked by a grizzly bear. Our body would still be recovering from the fall and unable to fight off the next attack."

Cal nodded. It made sense.

"Another way is with umbilical cord blood. Each goddess keeps the blood of her children. Immortal blood is...different. It's healing to others, but fatal to the one to which it belongs."

"So that's why the concoction with Hades' blood helped save Persephone, but it wouldn't have saved him?"

"Exactly. Our innate healing system is part of our nervous and endocrinology systems, but our blood can be used to heal other immortals, but only by consumption. Unfortunately, consumption of one's own blood is fatal."

"I didn't realize that you planned to minor in biology," Cal said wryly, but he was smiling.

"It's important to know. One drop isn't fatal. It's hard not to get a papercut and immediately shove your finger in your mouth to stanch the bleeding, but this—" she gestured where the vial lay against her chest next to her bat charm—"amount is fatal if consumed. And umbilical blood is the purest of all."

"So how do you plan to get Apollo to consume it?"

Vic bit her bottom lip. "I'm not sure. Leto did say that it needed to happen on the Winter Solstice."

"When Apollo is the weakest. That's what Nyx said. That the Winter Solstice was when Apollo was the weakest, and Artemis was at her strongest." A look of surprise flited across Cal's face. "I have something to show you too."

Vic had known that Cal was not only trying to piece together his own identity—his remade history—but also trying to parse together the story of Artemis and Orion.

He reached into his jeans' pocket and pulled out a small, silver object. Carefully, he took her hand, uncurling her fingers, so that her palm was open, and placed the object in her hand. It was a locket.

Four letters were inscribed on its face: LUNA.

"The moon?" she asked.

"Artemis has a white wolf who goes by the name of Luna," he explained.

This was news to Vic. Long, long ago. Millennia ago, Artemis was a very different person than the waitress at The Rooster that served Vic scrambled eggs, burnt toast, and mediocre coffee. She was the Goddess of the Hunt. A master weaver and archer. The Goddess of the Moon. Ever wonder why wolves howl at the moon? Now you know.

Gently, Vic ran her thumbnail down the seam of the locket, which she'd noticed was warm in her hand. Just like the bracelet at her wrist and the ring on her finger. This immediately told her that it was most likely an enchanted object.

She slowly opened the locket. Brilliant white light spilled out in all directions, multi-faceted like a diamond.

Very cautiously, Vic lifted the tiny object out of the locket. It felt like the smallest pebble, but shimmered in her palm like the most expensive diamond. She knew exactly what this object was. As she leaned toward Cal it grew even brighter, nearly blinding. She leaned away, and it dimmed only slightly. A light to offer protection and guide your way. A compass.

"Orion," Vic whispered holding the star up so that it was eye level.

"And it works too. It led me back to the road after I'd gotten lost in the woods."

"These too," Vic said, lowering her palm and placing the star back inside the locket and carefully snapping it shut again. "This bracelet and this ring, both grow warmer against my skin when I'm not headed in the right direction."

Cal shook his head and grinned. "No, when you're not in alignment with destiny."

Vic smiled. She was fairly certain the Star of Orion had just indicated that Cal was her destiny. Oracle prophecy or not, parental involvement or not, they had found their way to one another. That had to count for something.

"So, if this blood will kill Apollo, what will the star do to Artemis?" Vic's smile quickly faded. She echoed Nyx's words from earlier. "We cannot kill one without also killing the other."

Suddenly, there was a loud crash and a shout. Then Asher's voice rang down the hallway. "Hurry! We don't have much time!"

Chapter Thirty- Three

Cal

Something bad was happening.

That much Cal knew. Being closer to the door, he made it to the hallway before Vic, shoving the locket into his pocket.

Nyx passed him as she ran down the hallway. Servants snapped into presence out of thin air, all running toward the center of the castle.

Vic appeared behind him and together, they jogged after everyone else.

When they reached the entry way Cal skidded to a stop.

Asher was holding a short sword angled above a skeletal body—like the one he'd brought back from the Above World. Blood dripped from the blade. A vase was shattered across the polished floor.

Hades, Persephone, Nyx, Uranus, Zeus, Poseidon, Ares, and Athena stood in a half-circle, looks of bewilderment across their faces.

"What's going on?" Vic asked. "How did that thing get inside?" She turned toward Cal to explain. "They never come inside. There are magical barriers everywhere. To get past River..."

Persephone's face registered alarm. "River!"

She ran out the front door and Vic hurried out behind her casting a worried glance back at Cal before disappearing.

"This is completely unacceptable," Hades said. He had begun pacing, running his hands through his hair so that it was disheveled and stuck out at angles.

"There is no more time," Uranus said.

"The time must be now," Hades agreed.

"But it's not yet the Winter Solstice!" Nyx objected.

Uranus put a hand on her arm. "Isn't it? Remember where we are, my Night Dove."

"Uranus is right," Athena agreed. "Time passes differently in the Under World than in the Above World."

Cal fumbled in his pocket and pulled out his cell phone. He didn't have great reception in the Under World, but his phone screen still displayed the date and time just fine.

"December twenty-first, four a.m.," he read, then held it up to the gathering of gods before him.

"Then it's now," Ares said.

And just like that the gods dispersed, except for Hades.

"Callum, you will need to come with me. We'll pick up Vic and Persephone on the way."

At his words one of the lingering servants disappeared.

"Where are we going?" Cal asked.

"To where this all started."

...

Hades parked the car on the other side of the bone bridge. Normally, River stood at this side of the bridge, as keeper of the Styx. She was born of the River. She *was* the River.

But now she wasn't there.

Persephone stood with an arm around Vic and Vic looked as if she had been crying. It was not often that Cal had ever seen her cry. Vic was usually pretty guarded with her emotions—at least those of the vulnerable variety.

Hades looked at Persephone. "River?"

Persephone glanced over her shoulder toward the river bank, but Cal didn't see anything there.

Hades explained to Cal. "River must have been badly injured. Since she is of the Styx, it has healing properties for her. Her visceral body can morph into water and she can return to the river that birthed her and be restored. It's a different type of immortality."

"That thing attacked her?"

Vic sniffled.

"It would seem that way," her father said. "Uranus is right. There is no more time. This is happening now, before the Void destroys us all."

"But it's not the Winter Solstice," Vic mumbled.

"But it is," Cal said to her, her eyes finally landing on him. They were rimmed with red. "In the Above World, it's the early morning of December twenty-first."

Vic's lips set into a firm line. "Then let's end this."

Persephone led her daughter to the car as Hades said, "Ares, Zeus, and Poseidon have gone to fetch Apollo from Tartarus. Athena has gone to get Artemis. They will meet us in the clearing."

Hades got into the driver's seat and Cal climbed into the backseat beside Vic. He reached for her hand and squeezed her fingers. She squeezed back.

"I will stay behind in case River returns," Persephone said, kissing Vic's cheek then kissing her husband. "Be well, *mon amours.*"

As they drove away Cal noticed that Vic's other hand lay clenched at her side. She was holding something. The bracelet around her right wrist touched his own wrist and it was hot—the Divine Web was now in play.

Chapter Thirty-Four

Vic

Drink and forget.

Those were the last three words River had said to her before she slid back into the Styx to rejuvenate her physical vessel.

The River Styx was intriguing. It cleansed the souls of the damned. That's how strong its healing powers were. Vic had reached River before her mother. River's face was cut and scratched, blood was coming out of her nose and mouth. One arm hung limply, her staff flung to the side. She'd used it to fend off her attacker. One of her legs was bent at an odd angle, and Vic saw bone piercing through the skin. That thing had attacked her like some kind of wild animal, mauling her. Vic's stomach heaved. She was glad that Asher had killed it.

When Persephone approached they carefully gathered the semi-conscious River in their arms and moved her closer to the healing water of the Styx. Vic had never seen it happen, but her father had told her every now and then a demon or a shade went mad, and River would use the Styx to heal herself. He had told her over the millennia River had had many different physical appearances, so that if River ever needed to be rebirthed, Vic should not be scared or surprised when the River she knew looked a bit different.

Still, it had felt as real as any death to Vic.

As Persephone and Vic gently moved River closer, she'd turned her head. Her bottom lip was cut and bleeding, but she'd reached up and cupped Vic's cheek. "Take it," she'd said gesturing at a small wooden container with a cord that was strung from a belt at her waist. Vic hesitated, and River was more insistent. "You must take it."

So they had paused as Vic carefully untied the strange wooden jug from River's belt. It was small enough to fit into the palm of her hand.

River smiled, blood marring her teeth.

"Drink and forget," she said, then closed her eyes.

Vic hadn't been able to stop the tears from streaming down her face as she and her mother slowly eased River into the Styx. It was as if the Styx recognized her—as it should—the water seemed to cradle her body as it slowly pulled her away from them. Away and down until even her face was submerged.

"She'll be back," Persephone assured her. "It just takes a little bit of time. I know it's scary, Darling, but River knows what's she's doing."

Vic had nodded. She knew River would be okay because she trusted her parents and trusted the old magic of the Styx. But what she hadn't admitted to her mother was that River's words had scared her.

Was she willing to forget?

Chapter Thirty- Five

Cal

On a good day, Hades' driving was akin to an elderly gentleman out for a Sunday afternoon drive.

On a bad day, Hades' driving was akin to a bat out of, well…hell. He still wore his leather driving gloves, but that didn't stop him from tearing through the Under World and magically soaring the car up and through the portal.

Vic let out a gasp when she noticed all their work from earlier, with Athena, crumbling down. Silver-white lightning crackled around the portal entrance. Cal noticed Vic's normally olive-toned skin was now pale.

Long ago, well, not all that long ago, but it felt long ago, Vic had told him that she thought sometimes her father asked too much of her. But that didn't stop her from wanting to fulfill his wishes. Cal now felt that himself. When Nyx, Uranus,

Persephone, and Hades had gotten together all those years ago, they'd set something in motion and sometimes it felt life was being done to them, instead of the other way around.

"Hang on," Hades grunted and he floored the gas.

Vic squeezed Cal's fingers. The portal was a swirling mass of energy that normally didn't crackle, but now it sent out those silvery electric streaks. One hit the Cadillac and pinged off with an orange spark.

They soared through the portal which, under normal circumstances, would have them fly out of the trunk of the tree onto the other side and land with wheels spinning in the clearing. The tree being Daphne's tree.

But Vic had said that Daphne was gone and the tree had appeared empty.

Usually, the transition between Below and Above Worlds was quick, a little disorienting, and typically a drastic change in temperature, the Under World residing at an ambient temperature of about ninety-eight degrees Fahrenheit.

This time it was different. Even more different than when he'd driven through with Asher only earlier that day—or a few days—depending on which passage of time you were following.

The car bounced around and Cal noticed that Hades gripped the wheel tightly, his jaw set with the small muscle working along his jawline.

The lightning seemed centralized, emitting from the center of the portal and it shook the car violently as they passed through. It pinged off with a noise sharp enough to let Cal know that the hellhounds would be popping out dents, buffing, and repainting the normally shiny black Cadillac.

Eventually, they pushed through to the other side, emerging from the tree's ancient trunk. When they did so a large branch came along with them, bouncing off one of the car's rear fenders with a metallic thud.

Hades slowed the car down as they hit the snow-covered ground. Snow that immediately melted from the heat of the car's tires. He put the car into park and Vic glanced at Cal.

They all turned around slowly and peered outside the car's rear window.

The sky was dark but with just trickles of pale blue along the horizon. There were no dark clouds threatening snow, just stars fading into what would soon be daylight. The old tree was gnarled and black. It had always looked as though it had been struck by lightning and set ablaze. It was nondescript to mortal human eyes on purpose. A sort of magical: *Nothing to see here!*

Now it looked the same, except Vic was right. It looked…vacant. No, not vacant. Dormant. Cal could hear the howl of the Void in the near distance. It had gotten louder while they were in the Under World.

"What do you think happened to Daphne?" Cal asked turning back around to face Hades.

"I think that her time as the guardian had been served and that she was returned home," Hades said carefully, but Cal understood the things that Hades hadn't said. That Daphne had wanted protection from Apollo, but the cost for that protection was becoming the guardian of the portal between worlds. Now that the portal was crumbling, her guardianship was no longer needed.

He wondered what the wood nymph-like woman would do back in her world. Wherever that was. She'd been alive millennia as a result of her agreement with Zeus. No one she knew would be there.

As if reading his thoughts, Vic asked, "But they didn't send Daphne home, right? Like not her actual home. Because her family and anyone else she knew would be long dead. Her entire city or village could even be gone by now."

Hades nodded. There was a sad look in his eyes as he gazed at the tree and Cal wondered if it was because of the loss of Daphne, or the loss that was about to come. Or both.

"She would have been given a choice. Either to go to Mount Othyrs or to wherever she came from, which I think had been a small Gaelic isle of some kind."

"Did being the guardian make her immortal?" Cal asked.

Hades' near-black eyes reflected the thin light of the horizon. "While she was in Zeus' protection and living inside the tree, yes, she was immortal. But now that she no longer resides there, she would be mortal once more. Resuming at whatever age she'd become the tree."

"So now, the tree is just a tree," Cal said.

"The tree is just a tree," Hades repeated.

"I think Daphne wanted that. I don't think she enjoyed being immortal or stuck living in that tree all alone like that," Vic said. She was still holding his hand, and Cal squeezed her fingers.

Hades' face darkened. "Sometimes we have to do things that we don't enjoy to help others. Or to help ourselves." He turned back around. "Let's go to the manor. The others will have Apollo and Artemis soon. We need to finalize the plan."

"The plan?" Vic asked.

Hades put the car in drive and slowly made his way across the snow-covered clearing and to the main road, their melted tracks disappearing almost instantaneously behind them in their wake.

"I need to call on an old friend."

Chapter Thirty-Six

Vic

Hades had a lot of old friends.

When one was alive for millennia, friends tended to accumulate, especially the immortal ones. But Hades also had his fair sure of mortal comrades. When she was younger, Hades had told Vic stories about Frank Sinatra, Mark Antony and Cleopatra, Da Vinci, Marie Antoinette, Benjamin Franklin, and Joan of Arc. He'd even had a friendship with Bridget Bishop, as in of the Salem Bishops.

And if you think for one moment it was because these souls had sold themselves to the devil for fame, fortune, or infamy, you would be mistaken.

But not all of Hades' mortal friends were historical figures or celebrities, although most tended to reside on the good side of evil. Some of his friends were just good ole-fashion regular folk.

So it may have surprised Cal when the manor's caretaker, Richard and his wife, Anastasia, walked through the kitchen door.

They were bundled up in winter coats, scarves, hats, and gloves. The house was a balmy eighty-degrees because Hades had gotten his hands on the thermostat.

"Blessed child, how you have grown!" Anastasia said shoving a plate of Christmas-tree shaped- peanut butter-chocolate chip cookies into Vic's hands so that she could unwrap from her winter layers.

Richard, who had always been a man of few words, silently removed his coat, hat, and gloves, hanging them on the hooks beside the door.

"It's good to see you both, Richard. Anastasia," her father nodded at Richard and kissed Anastasia's cheek.

Her cat-eye eyeglasses were fogged up from the humidity of the manor. She was a shorter, plump woman who carried her weight in her hips and thighs. She was wearing a sweater and tartan slacks with furry, white winter boots. Her hair looked like she set it in curlers regularly and was a subdued auburn-red. To Vic, who loved all things whimsical, Anastasia looked like a modern version of Mrs. Claus.

Richard, on the other hand, did not look like he would be shaking with laughter like a bowl full of jelly anytime soon. He was only slightly taller than his wife, which made him shorter than Vic, Hades, and Cal. His pants were brown carpenter pants and his turtleneck was navy. He had on an old-style newsboy cap in a brown tweed and sensible winter boots with big treads. His beard was brunette—or at least had been—and now was laced with mostly white and some hints of red. Tufts of faded brown hair stuck out from the sides of his cap. However, his eyes were as clear as the sky on a summer day, a brilliant shade of light blue. So pale, if you only glanced for a second, the irises blended nearly into the whites of his eyes. They also crinkled around the corners, his beard somewhat hiding his mouth, so his eyes often were the only obvious indication of emotions.

Vic and Richard tended to keep different schedules. He was like a ninja—appearing, completing work, and then disappearing with nothing to show that he was even there except a job well done and a plate of his wife's cookies on the kitchen counter.

Anastasia tittered at Hades' greeting and once her glasses adjusted, Vic noticed that her eyes were the same pale blue as her husband's, except her irises were outlined in a darker, midnight blue.

"We came as soon as you summoned."

"We were in bed," Richard added. "This cold hurts the old joints."

"Oh, I'm sorry to have woken you."

Anastasia waved a hand. "We knew if you summoned, it had to be an emergency."

Vic's mind tried to piece this puzzle together. Her father had never told her why Richard was the manor's caretaker. In fact, she didn't even know Richard and Anastasia's connection to her father. Her father trusted them, so Vic had trusted them as well, with no questions asked. Her house was always well taken care of, the garden tended to in summer, the driveway shoveled in winter. Groceries appeared in her refrigerator on a regular basis and she never ran out of toilet paper. There wasn't much else she could ask for.

Hades looked grim. His hair was still positioned every which way and he leaned against the counter, his body in stark contrast to the expression on his face. Both Hades and Vic had a nearly insatiable sweet tooth, and she was certain it was taking her father every ounce of willpower to not plow through the freshly-baked cookies to ease his emotions. Anger, confusion, fear, trepidation—if they were any match for the ones that Vic herself was feeling.

"The time has finally come," he said simply.

Vic and Cal—both sitting at the dinette table—looked from Hades back to Richard and Anastasia.

Anastasia paled slightly and her hand fluttered to her mouth. "Oh dear."

Richard nodded grimly, his mouth a thin, straight line, but his pale eyes held something else. A spark of light.

"You see, Vic and Cal, Richard and I have been friends his entire life. Before I was friends with Richard, I was friends with Richard's father, Benjamin. And before Benjamin, I was friends with his father, Zachariah. And so on and so forth back through time."

"Took you nearly fifteen years to stop calling me Benjamin," Richard grinned.

Anastasia and Hades laughed.

Her father turned to them. "When you live as long as I do, you need friends. Allies. Eyes and ears. But also people who look after, well, everything. We live in the Under World, but the Above World works much differently. Time passes differently, the value of currency changes, leaders pass away and new ones are elected, property deteriorates. As you both know, I can be gone a week in the Under World and nearly double or triple that time has passed in the Above World. Imagine being gone for years.

"So Richard's family—the Malones—have taken care of the Hadens for as long as I can remember. They tend to our Above World affairs, keep me abreast of news and world events, and tend to our properties. You name it, and the Malones take care of it."

Vic had never thought about that. Now, certain memories fell into place. Her father's vast array of daily newspapers from all different cities and countries that he'd spend time each morning perusing. His business trips to the Above World. She's always thought it was immortal-related, but here all the time it was actually mortal-related.

"Wait." Vic pointed at Richard and Anastasia. "You two aren't really husband and wife, are you?"

Anastasia smiled. "No, Honey, we're not. We're twins actually."

Which explained the pale blue eyes and auburn hair, the lack of affection that didn't radiate from them as it did her own parents.

"Typically, the task goes to the eldest born. So in this case, both children received the task of attending to our family."

"But if you're twins, and neither of you are actually married..." Cal said.

"That's right, Sugar."

"So wait, then that means..." A lump formed in Vic's throat. Yes, they'd been talking about this very thing the last few weeks, but now here it was right in front of her. There would be no more Above World for the Hadens.

"That all our affairs will need to be taken care of in the Above World."

"But how do you know...?"

Hades shrugged. "We don't."

Vic fingered the vial against her collarbone. If there was no more Malone line to take care of the Hadens, and there always had been forever and ever back through time, then this really was the end. The portal between worlds was really and truly going to close.

The spider silk bracelet burned hot against her wrist.

Just how much of life was destiny and how much was free will? No matter what choices you made, would you in fact always end up back at the same place? Was the end and the beginning simply two sides of the same coin?

Cal must have been thinking the same thing that she was because he placed his hand over hers. Her stomach did a flip-flop. How on earth was she going to decide which World to stay in? Where did she truly belong?

Drink and forget.

Just then the kitchen door banged open and Asher's looming form took up the entire doorway.

Vic glared at him. "It's called opening the door like a normal human being."

Asher snorted. "I'm no normal human being." His green eyes had taken on a feral look. He'd been on the hunt. He turned to Hades.

"They're here."

Chapter Thirty- Seven —A Story

Vic

Once upon a time there was a princess.

Not just any kind of princess. This was not your typical wide-eyed, smiling, whimsical princess who was maybe trapped in a tower or stuck in a glass coffin until her true love came to rescue her.

Hell no. Emphasis on the hell.

This princess was wide-eyed, but that's where the similarities stop. This particular princess had both a doting father and a doting mother. She was an only child, no evil step- siblings or step-mother. No huntsman left her in the woods as a babe to fend for herself.

She was vivacious and voracious. By the time she was one-year-old, she could talk in complete sentences in English, Latin, Italian, French, and Greek. When she was five she read

A Christmas Carol on her own from beginning to end, and always cried at the end. Thus, Christmas became her favorite holiday, and her father—the King—went out of his way to make each one magical for her, even though they maybe happened to live in a strange world with red and black skies and raining fire and ash.

This princess was not well-behaved. While her manners were mostly excellent, she had a reckless streak and a horribly explosive temper. Her father had her channel that energy into combat, much to her mother's dismay, but also acceptance. Obviously, the princess was more like her father than her mother. At ten, she was training with the other young hellhounds. Grappling, swords, knives. She knew how to fight. And more than once she'd made her friend Asher cry (not like he didn't deserve it—most of the time).

When she was fourteen her father would give her legal contracts to look over, budgets to analyze, and quiz her on Above World current events topics. She learned to read books in over twenty languages, and could also speak fluently in over twelve of them.

This particular princess did not take dance lessons. She did not get fitted for corsets and ball gowns. There were no glass slippers and certainly no pumpkin carriages—although one time, she and her friend, Asher, had tried to pull bones from the bone bridge to make a wagon. But River quickly put a stop to that.

No, this princess was different.

She was not afraid of anything. And sometimes she was overcome with uncontrollable anger. Anger so astute that it would wrack her entire body and quite literally make her blood boil. Over time, the princess had to learn to control these angry outbursts. She would take deep breaths and inhale the scent of lavender and hyacinth that wafted from her mother's rooms. If she did not learn to control them, her father warned, then she could hurt herself or Asher, which she'd already done a couple of times—a bloody nose, but Asher had taken her pomegranates without asking and clearly deserved it.

Her father would take her as accompaniment when he journeyed to the various domains of the Under World. Domains that housed the misguided, the wicked, the evil, and the forsaken. Souls that were so tarnished, some could not even be reincarnated. So malicious that they were forever damned to repent and cleanse their soul, trying to get it back to some semblance of its pure form.

"When a soul is that tarnished, there is no way for the light to get in," her father had once told her. And she had nodded solemnly. "Broken windows can still let the light in, but dirty ones block the sun."

And she was not afraid of these souls. These skeletal figures or black shadows—shades—did not scare her as much as they fascinated her. What must someone do to end up here? How did someone sink to this level? Liars, cheaters, thieves, abusers, and murderers. What caused someone to violate the rules of humanity?

When she was nearing her eighteenth birthday her father summoned her. Her mother had taken ill and being the tight-knit family that they were, they feared they would lose her. She was confined to her bed and every day she grew weaker and sunk deeper into the cushion of her bed, until the princess feared that there would be nothing left of her beloved *Maman*.

She agreed to go to the Above World, to take up residence in a town called Olympia that other immortals frequented, and some even had assimilated. Immortals of myth living among every day, fleeting mortals. The only way to save her mother was to reap the souls of the living. It was asking much of her—to do something such as this—but if it saved her mother, the princess was willing to Take every soul that inhabited the Above World. Taking was a delicate process. It involved slicing someone open—preferably someone near death or freshly dead—and removing the golden, shimmering essence that was their soul, their life force, from their body in order for her mother to consume it. The task required acute attention to detail, meticulous skill with a knife, and most of all, patience. A skill that the princess had worked on tirelessly. She was born for this assignment.

And that's when her thinking had changed from a daughter doing something to save her mother, to a solider with an assignment. No, not a soldier, a knight. She was both the princess and the knight in this story.

Her first soul had belonged to an older woman. She hadn't felt bad when it happened. The woman was driving her car, had a heart attack, and had crashed into a tree off one of the country roads in town. The princess may or may not have caused the crashed into a tree part, but honestly it was better than having the woman crash into oncoming traffic and potentially kill another person. The princess had waited, half-hidden using her heightened sense of hearing to catch the moment that the elderly woman's heart had stopped beating.

She'd carefully stepped out of the shadows of the forest, then used her magic to tumble the lock on the driver's side car door. The woman had looked very alive still, her lips were only slightly tinged blue and her faded gray eyes stared blankly ahead. Uncomfortable, the princess had dragged her fingers over them sliding them closed. Then she had felt around for the breast bone. Her knife would easily cut through both the layers of fabric and skin. Her father had made her practice on dummy torsos made of some gelatin-like substance. She unsheathed her knife from her waistband and dug it in slowly. She heard sirens in the distance. Once she had a big enough cavity, she pushed her fingers into the woman's chest, feeling around for the warm, slippery life force. It was like grasping honey as she pulled the small, glowing orb with its shimmering tendrils from the woman's chest. The golden glow reflected off the woman's face. As she placed the soul into her satchel, she swore she saw the woman's eyes twitch.

Her father had warned her about this. That there were certain body mechanisms that happened as the body shut down, even though the heart stopped, it took the rest of the body time to catch up. Time to realize that it was dead. The mind didn't always understand what the heart already knew.

The Sirens grew louder—closer. The woman had a name badge pinned to her blouse, Marge was her name. Had she been at work? The princess squinted and in smaller type beneath the woman's name it read volunteer.

Marge.

The feeling was similar as when her father had taken her to the Above World and they'd visited a farm. She'd wanted to name the animals, make them her pets. But once he explained what happened to some of those animals, that they would become food, she realized naming them made it that much harder later.

Naming the dead made it that much harder to Take their souls. The princess sniffled. But Marge was dead and Persephone was still alive. She still had a chance to live. At life. But the princess couldn't shake the feeling that she now understood just a little bit better what it meant to violate the rules of humanity.

...

When the Princess was young she did not know that the Oracle had made a prophecy. Or that the prophecy would involve her—the first child born to a pair of Olympians in millennia—or the first child born to Primordial deities in millennia. Two children born near the same time after no new immortal children had been born for centuries upon centuries.

The King and Queen of the Under World met with the Night and the Sky. They were a little rusty on the prophecy, as it had been spoken when the Oracle was enslaved to Apollo on the Mount. But it had been something like:

A girl and a boy will be born
To barren wombs
One of light and one of dark
One of dusk and one of morn
The sword and air will rise as one
When they do it will finally be done
Mortals ye live in peace
Immortals ye be released
From the ties and tethers that bind
Now reside with your own kind.
The web is spun
Destiny is weaved
The worlds are now cleaved.

Come to think of it, it was a bit of an ominous prophecy. It was also rather long, which was rare for Pythia whose prophecies more often leaned to the shorter side. Pythia was the one and the only true Oracle, more out of efficiency's sake than anything.

As the pair of parents sat there, they knew what the prophecy meant. And they knew that this meant they would have to prepare their children for a grave task. As well as protect them from those who could try to stop them or bring them harm.

When the prophecy was first delivered, many wondered if it was about the twins—Apollo and Artemis. One light and one dark. But the sword and air part had never made sense. Until now. Two immortals, one who could take life—cut the soul from the body—and one who could manipulate air. In Tarot, the suit of swords is correlated to the element of air. Together, they represent intellect, clarity, action, and power. Together, they represent change.

...

In the future, that princess will be given a choice. She will be given a choice to embrace her true nature or to forget. There will not be a fairy godmother to grant her a wish. No knight in shining armor will dash in to her save her. And she most definitely will not wake up and realize that it was all a dream. No matter how much she wished that it was.

Some stories end with happily ever after. Some end with your heart left on the page. And some just simply fall somewhere in between.

Chapter Thirty- Eight
Cal

Cal's palms felt sweaty as they drove. He'd assumed that they would head back to the field. But Hades had explained to them that it wasn't as simple as that.

They'd reached the field—the old tree looking dead and innocuous. But Hades had driven the Cadillac off to the left and into the woods, Asher and Brim on their Sportsters flanking the car like a motorcade.

As they drove slowly through the forest, the trees swayed and bent out of the way. Nature sensing the being that was prowling through their forest. Hades was not just a god. He was God of the Under World, an integral part to the cycle of life. To some he represented evil things. To others he represented death. But Cal knew that Hades was all of those things and none of those things. He was kind and compassionate, a loving husband and father. He was smart and strategic, worldly yet modern. Hades was the epitome of dichotomy.

The woods grew darker the deeper they drove, the only light coming from the full moon that had risen in the night sky and coated the snow-covered forest in an eerie glow. He could feel the heat of the star of Orion growing hot inside his pocket.

Vic looked anxiously out the window, absent-mindedly rubbing her wrist. She still had the skull and crossbones brooch pinned near her collar. But she'd left the petrified wood-looking ring on the kitchen counter.

They drove soundlessly, part of the enchantment. Cal felt nervous to see Apollo. It had been several months since the Fall Festival and he'd found out that Apollo and who he thought was his father had formed an alliance. But Cronus had simply been using everyone to get to Cal. He didn't want Cal to know he was a Primordial—a god even more powerful than he was as a Titan. His sisters weren't even related to him. At first, he'd thought he'd only had a different mother. That they still shared a father, and while his sisters were still Halvsies, Cal now knew he was fully immortal. That he would long outlive his sisters. Even if they weren't family by blood, they were still the only family he really knew.

Sometimes it didn't seem fair. It didn't seem fair that he'd been lied to his entire life. Lied to about who and what he was. What about him was even real?

The only time he felt like he knew what was real was when he looked at Vic. He'd felt unmoored as soon as he had laid eyes on her. Vic was different. She not only looked different, but acted differently than any other girl he'd ever known. Heck, differently than most guys he'd ever known too. She was unapologetic about who she was. One minute she could be drinking hot cocoa in her Grinch jammies and the next she could be holding a knife to a shade's throat.

When he looked at her, he realized he could be both who he had been and who he was now, and not have to apologize. Those other parts were still him—the straight "A" student from California and the guy who manipulated air and built a chainmail barrier with the goddess Athena, and who dated the Princess of the Under World, but also who was there to help his adopted mother make bakery deliveries—those were all him.

The star of Orion seemed to pulse in response to his thoughts.

Chapter Thirty- Nine

Vic

Vic's stomach was in a knot.

Arachne's spider silk bracelet burned hot against her skin. Her fingertips grazed over the glass vial at her neck. She watched as the forest bent out of her father's way, the trees bowing as if with sweeping arms as they passed.

Her knife was at her hip, but she was covered in things that were not hers. Talismans. Objects that could lead to decisions. Decisions led to consequences. With Daphne gone, she'd left the beautiful ring on the counter at the manor. It would be there when she returned—a reminder of a tortured soul who had sought out the gods and been both protected and inadvertently punished. Or if she didn't return…it would be a beautiful piece of antique-looking jewelry for Anastasia. Maybe a reminder of the Hadens.

The thought made her stomach turn.

When Asher had burst through her kitchen door—her door, she'd come to think of the manor as her home in the short time that she was there—her father had explained the plan to them. Anastasia and Richard would be ears to the ground. They would gather any necessary paperwork and generate any necessary stories to cover-up the events of the evening, if need be. They were how the townspeople saw no evidence of the events that played out at the Fall Festival. Sure, Zeus had wiped their memories of the two hours that day where it rained pomegranate snow and Apollo nearly killed Persephone. But it was Anastasia and Richard who cleaned up the mess that they had left behind. It was them that paid for the damages with anonymous stashes of cash that appeared in the mailboxes of small businesses located on the square, who paid for a cleanup crew (even though their memories were later wiped). They had access to all of the Haden's mortal wealth—which meant very little to them in the immortal realms.

The part of the plan that mattered the most—the part that involved Vic and Cal—was less cut and dry. If Richard and Anastasia were a well-oiled machine, Vic felt like she and Cal were a rusted out carburetor.

Athena and Nyx would have Artemis and Cal had the star of Orion. Hades confirmed what they already knew, that Artemis would not be the problem. She has known all along and left Cal a crumb trail leading him to the things that he would need.

Zeus and Poseidon would have Apollo, with Ares and Hades as back up in case he tried to escape. As he'd been known to do. Somehow Apollo always avoided penitence for his crimes, but now the price had gotten too high. This time it was irreversible.

Vic would have to take care of Apollo. She fingered the vial again, its glass cool against her skin. She felt bad for Leto, but she couldn't blame her for not killing Apollo herself. No matter how horrible he was, a mother could not kill her child. Hades had looked her square in the eye and told her that this was a case of opposites attract: Cal's light and Artemis' darkness—the moon—and Apollo's light—the sun—and Vic's darkness. No one else but Vic could vanquish Apollo.

The tricky part was that Apollo would have to drink the blood in the vial. There was no good solution for how she was supposed to do that. Once Apollo was dead, then the imbalance would be restored, but the portal would still need to be closed, or the Under World would continue to bleed into the Above World.

It had been too long that the gods had interfered in the lives of mortals—Daphne and Orion were both clear reminders of that.

So Vic's mind reeled. In her dream her mother had whispered to her. Persephone and Artemis had been dear friends at one point in time. Before Vic was even born. And now River's reminder: *Drink and forget* mixed with her mother's words: *The pain is not in the remembering. The pain is in the forgetting.*

The trees opened up in front of the car into a small clearing surrounded with stately pines covered with flocks of snow. But instead of grass there was a circular pad of concrete with concentric circles and a large obelisk in the middle. Even from the car, Vic could see that it was covered in engraved markings.

This was in the middle of Olympia?

She glanced at Cal, whose mouth hung open slightly, his amber eyes wide.

Obelisks were quintessentially Egyptian and Apollo had been the very one to convert the Egyptians to monotheism—to worship him, of course. Upon closer inspection, Vic noticed that the obelisk's markings were not just hieroglyphs, but that it appeared each side had a different set of glyphs marking each of its four sides.

"Energy center," her father explained. He'd stopped the car just beside the concrete pad. "Obelisks, pyramids…anything with a concentrated point gives a place for energy to be directed."

Cal loved world history. Especially ancient civilizations. "Did Apollo invent the obelisk?"

Hades shook his head. "No. They're believed to have been invented in the fourth dynasty and Apollo's reign as Akhenaten wasn't until the eighteenth dynasty. However, that's not to say that he didn't use their power, as they were often considered a tribute to the sun god."

Vic rolled her eyes, then scanned the area. But she didn't see anyone. Asher and Brim had stopped on either side of the pad so that they formed a triangle with the Cadillac.

As if reading her mind, her father said, "They're here. Trust me."

They stepped out of the car. Vic was immediately overcome with a metallic scent. Like blood.

A cloud appeared in front of the obelisk and Zeus took form before their eyes. When he took bodily form his silvery-white hair seemed electrified around his head. He was broad shouldered and tall. His presence was commanding.

"Bring forth the twins," he said. His voice was low, but even Vic could feel its reverberation through the ground beneath her feet.

Around their boots, the snow had melted, but the pine trees still held small piles along their boughs.

Athena and Nyx brought Artemis forward. She was only loosely restrained, a woven thread bound her to one of Athena's forearms and to one of Nyx's. Although Vic knew the fine thread was deceiving. A woven thread from Athena was as strong as any spider silk—neither as indestructible as the bracelet on her wrist was happy to remind her.

But Artemis looked different. Her normally frizzy red hair was long, smooth, and straight. She wore her trademark feathered earrings, but her outfit was less…artistic than usual. Her top was a cream-colored sweater and her leggings looked to be brown suede and she wore matching knee-high brown suede boots. Her green eyes were bright and alert. She looked almost plain Vic thought. But she didn't understand why. Maybe the Artemis who waitressed at the Rooster was just an exaggeration, a costume to put on in one incarnation of her many lives. A role. A part to play.

Vic saw the pulse in her father's jaw when Artemis appeared. Long ago, they had been friends. Were they still? Vic wasn't so sure. She knew what had happened with Orion had fundamentally changed Artemis, and that surely it was bitter sweet to watch her best friend Persephone marry Hades, when she herself had lost her soulmate. Vic wasn't exactly sure what that experience was like, but she had enough knowledge to imagine the confusion and heartache Artemis had probably felt.

On the other side of the circle, Ares and Poseidon brought forth Apollo. Vic's heart stuck in her throat at the sight of him and she felt Cal reach out and grab her elbow, while her father let out a low hiss. To the credit of Tartarus, Apollo did not look well. His normally vibrant strawberry blonde curls were a pale, straw-like yellow and had grown long and tangled in the few months he was imprisoned. They curled around his ears and nearly to his chin. His normally rhubarb cheeks were also pale and his blue eyes looked confused and cloudy. He looked…weak.

Normally, Apollo was a strapping young man. Vibrant like the sun—also egocentric like any star that thought the world should revolve around him. There was usually a youthfulness about him that Vic had always found quite deceptive. Instead of jovial and innocent, Apollo was cunning.

There were iron ore cuffs that bound both Apollo's hands and his feet, made by Hephaestus, the blacksmith, whose fires burned in the Under World, continually stoked by the souls of unforgiveable deeds. Both Ares and Poseidon flanked him. Although to Vic, he looked as though he could barely stand, the bones of his knees and shoulders jutted out, and any jauntiness was gone.

"The time has come," Zeus proclaimed. And a lightning bolt appeared in his right hand, so bright it glowed white hot. "The Circle of Candor has been opened."

So that's *what this place is called,* Vic thought. Had Zeus simply conjured it?

"The Void has come to collect." As if on cue, Vic heard the now familiar howl. "An imbalance needs to be righted. Harmony needs to be restored." Zeus turned to the obelisk so that his back was to Vic, Cal, Hades, and the hellhounds. Artemis and Apollo also turned to face the towering structure.

Zeus yielded his bolt and gestured at the air, as if he were stirring it. Lightning cackled and suddenly the Void appeared above the obelisk's point. Golden light jumped out of the Void and streaked down the sides of the obelisk, hitting and lighting up random hieroglyphs as it travelled down. Over and over as if it was emitting some sort of code.

Apollo fell to his knees, but no one else moved.

Finally, the cycles of golden light stopped, freezing on several symbols, lighting them up golden as if they were backlit.

Vic felt her eyes sharpen. A sun, a moon, a bat, and three wavy lines. Her stomach tightened. She knew what that meant: Apollo, Artemis, herself, and Cal. The three wavy lines represented the movement of air.

Not of their own volition, Vic felt her feet begin to move forward. She let out a grunt and turned toward Cal who was also being unceremoniously glided along the paved stones toward the obelisk. She reached out for his fingers and his grazed hers just before they were separated and planted beside Artemis and Apollo, respectively.

"The Tower of Truth has chosen its candidates." Zeus turned toward them. In the weird glow of his bolt, the scar slicing his left cheek glowed menacingly and his normally pale blue eyes were nearly white, with his pupils merely pinpricks.

Suddenly, her father was behind her, whispering in her ear. "When there is an injustice, the Tower of Truth chooses candidates. The candidates battle in the Circle of Candor. The names are not a coincidence. Only the honest in heart can be victorious."

Clearly, her father knew about this business, and yet he chose now—the very last possible moment—to tell her?

"The Tower will now choose the form," Zeus's voice reverberated through the forest. Once again, the tower lit up with sheaths of gold, like a strobe light moving up and down its length. The golden light danced around, hitting on various glyphs until it reached two. One in the shape of what to Vic looked like a little gingerbread man—a human but with the rounded feet and hands, like a child drew it, and what appeared to be a simplistic representation of a lion.

It went back and forth between the child-like glyphs. Until it settled on the lion.

Arachne's spider silk bracelet grew hotter around her wrist—it was leaving a faint pink line that Vic was beginning to wonder whether or not would go away.

"The Tower of Truth has chosen," Zeus said.

With that, his humanly form dissolved into a gigantic bull, his silvery white hair becoming silk fur and his lightning bolt shifting into elegant golden horns. The bull had pale blue eyes.

And so it had begun.

Chapter Forty

Cal

Cal knew from many lessons in mythology that the gods were anamorphic, but it was another thing to witness it happen right before your own eyes.

He watched as Zeus became a majestic white bull, tossing his horns as though he still had long silver hair.

In rapid succession, he watched as each of the others took their form. As if slipping out of a dress, Artemis shifted gracefully into a small, reddish brown doe with assessing green eyes. The woven thread went from around her neck to the ankle of Athena who now hovered in the air in owl form. She was a beautiful white and brown speckled owl with large, round eyes. Ares snorted and grunted, a black furred-boar with a ring through his nose. He looked like he weighed at least double what Cal weighed in human form. Beside him,

Poseidon had taken his land anamorphic form of a horse, its pale yellow coat clearly marking him as a Palomino. He neighed and placed a warning hoof delicately, but firmly on top of Apollo, who still didn't seem cognizant but who had nonetheless morphed into a shiny black raven, its wings oddly tipped with gold.

Having seen both Vic and her father fly on their own bat-winged appendages, he'd expected Hades to morph into a bat himself, but to his surprise Vic's father took the form of a stoic-looking black ram with a gleaming fur coat and silver horns that curled in on themselves. Following their alpha, the two hellhounds got off their motorcycles and quickly morphed into gigantic, furry hounds—much like the dire wolf that was supposedly extinct. One had light green eyes and the other a pale blue.

Cal looked at Vic and she gave a little shrug. "I guess the Tower has spoken."

And with that she seamlessly morphed into the biggest cobra snake he'd ever seen. She was terrifying and beautiful, which seemed to be the thing when it came to Vic. Her life was one of contradictions. The cobra's scales were an opalescent black-purple that rippled as Vic moved, she'd reared up, her bright hazel eyes expectant as she looked at him. A forked purple tongue flicked in his direction.

What anamorphic form would an ancient deity of air even take? He wondered. How would he even change his form? Everyone, including Vic, had all done it so effortlessly, as if it had required no thought or premeditation.

As soon as Cal had that thought, he had the oddest sensation of his body shifting. It felt as though his cells were collapsing in on themselves, his head throbbed and he noticed the world around him shift and change shape. It grew wider, then narrower. And then became a pinprick, followed by a burst of light and suddenly he was seeing everything in full-on Technicolor. The snow seemed whiter and sharper, as if he could see each individual crystal that made up each flake. The grass beneath Vic's feet was even greener and he was certain he could see each single blade of it.

He felt light and buoyant as if he were hovering in the air. And then he realized that it was because he was. His anamorphic form was that of a bird.

Not just any bird, an eagle, said a voice in his head that sounded very much like Vic. He turned his head, oops too far, there we go, just a little back, toward Vic. Who laughed and continued, "When in anamorphic form telecommunication is the primary means of communication across species. It's kind of like a radio station. You just have to turn to the right frequency for whoever you wish to speak to."

Cal flapped his wings. "An eagle, huh?" He thought. "Eagles represent courage, strength, and truth."

Vic's cobra hood curled forward and back, spreading wide. "And freedom."

He moved so that he was closer to her. Interestingly enough, their human instincts were able to override any of the innate animalistic ones. They were still human souls and minds, just in a different, albeit temporary, form.

"What happens now?"

Vic closed her eyes as if she were thinking, then opened them. The cool hazel had shifted to a cloudy gray indicating that her mood had also shifted.

"My father says the Circle of Candor honors the truthful. So we must battle." She closed her eyes again, as if listening, leaning into some voice that Cal himself could not hear despite his exponentially better bird hearing. Vic opened one eye.

"Hearing and listening are not the same thing," she pointed out.

"How do we battle?" he asked ignoring her comment. In human form he was pretty sure he was an excellent listener. There was just a lot going on at the moment that was all very new to him.

"According to Zeus, the battle is not one of strength, but of wits, bravery, and cleverness. In our animal forms we are on more equal footing than in our immortal human bodies. We must outwit Apollo and Artemis, to show the Circle that we are the virtuous ones."

"But can't it just tell? Like scan our DNA or something? Clearly, it would see just how heinous Apollo is and how much Artemis has suffered as a result."

Vic's laugh reverberated through his white-feathered head.

"You should know by now that nothing is so easy when it comes to the Olympians."

Cal scanned the forest line. Persephone was not present, but he noticed Nyx and Uranus—his mother and father—standing off near the trees. They donned white cloaks. He remembered that technically Persephone was supposed to stay in the Under World during winter. As he took notice of his parents, his keen eyes began to take in additional movements. He noticed a flash of dark hair, purple lipstick, a red jacket. He realized they were people, but none that he recognized. In his human form he hadn't noticed them.

Even now they were just flashes of color, like looking at puzzle pieces before they were assembled into the final picture.

"The other Olympians are here. Pythia. Selene. And others," Vic noted. "They've come to watch."

The vial of Apollo's birth blood still hung around her snake neck. He felt the warmth of the Star of Orion buried deep within his feathers. It felt heavy, like a metaphorical weight for what was about to happen.

The sky was already beginning to shift in color, taking on a gray-violet cast. It was the Winter Solstice. It was the shortest day of the year.

Zeus stomped a foot—hoof—and each of the stones making up the Circle of Candor lit up in the same golden light that had traveled around the glyphs of the Tower of Truth. The concrete now resembled a human chess board.

Zeus stomped a hoof a second time and Cal felt his bird body involuntarily pulled toward the chess board. He flapped but couldn't pull away from the invisible force. He watched as Vic's cobra body slithered to a lit up square on the Circle of Candor. His body stopped, hovering above an unlit square.

All the players—the pieces—were moved to a space.

The game was ready to begin.

Chapter Forty- One—A Story Continued

Vic

"But Daaaaaad, do I have to?" the princess let out a whine, jutting out her lower lip to form a pout.

The king was young and handsome, with hair black as the night, and skin the color of golden sand. "Just one game before dinner."

The princess saw straight through her father's comment. "A single game of Chesstopia can last hours. We could be half-starved by the time we finish."

It was not quite an exaggeration.

Chesstopia was a game with a board and pieces similar to chess, but a game that also involved a fair knowledge of riddles, history, science, and other things. Each piece acted as its own player and the cards would inform a player of its movement—or its detriment.

The playing board was very old, carved from pomegranate tree wood so that it had a mirror-like black finish. Each playing piece was hand-carved of either obsidian or quartz. The princess had been fascinated by the game since she was a young child, wanting to play with its exquisite crystal pieces so carefully shaped into various animals.

There was a cobra, a bat, an eagle, a doe, several other birds, a horse, and even a ram. Her father had carved the pieces himself. The game had always been stored just out of little hands' reach, but when she had turned ten-years-old, her father had finally taken the game down off its high shelf and taught her how to play. It had taken her nearly two weeks to keep all the pieces straight, their strengths, and how they were able to move around the board. Sometimes because of the questions asked, she could convince her father to play Chesstopia in place of her usual school lessons.

But now the princess was twelve, nearing thirteen, and while she loved time with her father, she'd much rather be climbing the pomegranate trees, or throwing their fallen fruit at her hellhound friend. Yet the king regularly insisted she continue to play the game, saying that it instilled wit, strategy, and discipline in her young mind. When she would plead to her mother, the queen. Much to the princess' disappointment, her mother often agreed with her father.

It was a hopeless battle. It was better just to play and get it over with, regardless of how long it took. Then at least her father would be appeased for a little while.

She had to admit though, each time they played the questions somehow got harder. And there was rarely a repeated question despite all the times that they had played. She suspected the game had been enchanted. When she'd asked her father about this, he'd simply replied: "The smarter you get, the harder the game gets." Which to her young mind made little sense.

"Sword or air, my love?" her father asked.

When they'd first started playing, she had always chosen air—unable to resist the transparent, crystal pieces. But as she grew older, she came to admire the opaque, shiny obsidian pieces and preferred to play as the sword.

"Sword," she replied.

Her mother walked through the study and put a gentle hand on her daughter's shoulder.

"You nearly beat him the last time, *ma petite fille.*"

It had been nearly three years of playing, and she had yet to beat her father at Chesstopia. Sure, she'd come close numerous times, but he always seemed to outwit her. She knew she was smart enough to beat her father—her memory was a catalogue of names, dates, places, and events—but it was often in the strategic parts, how the pieces each moved uniquely about the board, that her father would best her.

The princess carefully set her pieces across the board, each corresponding to a unique square. Squares that alternated silver and black.

The king raised an eyebrow. "Perhaps today is the day that our princess finally wins?"

Something caught the princess' eye. One of the obsidian pieces had a blemish. She picked up the player—about the size of her thumb—and held it up. It was an eagle, its beak carved to a sharp point. Both the sword and the air pieces were all made up of the same animals, so there was two of each in the game. She examined it closely, letting it catch the light from the lime green flame that wafted from the wall lanterns. There was something small and white glowing in the eagle's belly.

She squinted. It looked like a star.
Certainly, that had to be a good omen.
Indeed, maybe this time she would finally win after all.

Chapter Forty-Two

Vic

All that time, Vic had thought that it was only a game.

That her father was teaching her to use her brain—to have her wits about her and understand the importance of strategy.

Now she looked across the familiar checkerboard of Chesstopia. But instead of obsidian and crystal animal-shaped playing pieces looking back at her, the board was covered with living and breathing ones. Ones that at their core were also human beings.

In the lithe form of the cobra, she could still feel her human self. She could feel the vial around her neck and the spider silk bracelet tied to her wrist. It was almost as if the animal forms were a projection, like a hologram that simply cloaked their human forms.

She was standing several blocks away from Cal. Her shoulders felt tight so she rolled them, noticing that her cobra body only had the merest ripple in response. She squinted her eyes and curled and uncurled her fingers, then looked down. The faintest outline of a hand rested by her side, its fingers moving in rhythm to her own.

Truth number one.

As if sensing her thoughts, the board moved her two spaces forward and two spaces left so that she was now caddy corner to Poseidon in his horse form.

Chesstopia had cards though. The movement of the pieces—their carefully orchestrated dances—was where the strategy came in. But the cards and their questions was where the true wit and intellect was shown.

Again, as if in response to her thoughts the Tower of Truth lit up, except this time it was the entire obelisk that glowed a brilliant golden light.

The rules for Chesstopia, as her father had taught her, were relatively simple.

Players—or pieces—moved in pre-determined ways. The trick was that when it was your turn, to decide which piece to move based on these pre-determined patterns. The only way to move a player was if you got the question from the card correct. If you got it wrong, you couldn't move a piece, and the other person then got their turn. So in theory, a player could go on continually if their opponent never got a question correct when it was their turn. Vic had experienced this first hand when her father had first taught her how to play.

The way to win Chesstopia was to clear your opponent's players off the board. This was done when two pieces occupied the same square, the incoming piece would "capture" the piece that currently occupied the space. If you continually got the card questions correct, theoretically, a single person could sweep the board without their opponent even standing a chance.

However, there was one caveat.

The single most important piece to either side was the Significator.

The Signficator was a piece that each player deemed representative of his or herself. Sometimes Vic would choose the bat, sometimes the snake, or if she was feeling cheeky the owl or the wolf. Always choosing the shiny, obsidian pieces. It was later why she chose for her dagger to have an obsidian blade. Darkness spoke to her in a way that made her realize she could not have levity without it. Her mother and her father belonged to one another—their duality of opposites both fragile and potentially volatile. The darkness needed to be caressed and subdued—it was a wild, unpredictable animal, but Vic had grown to love it. She loved that part of herself too—even if for a while, she'd thought she'd wanted to be someone else.

Suddenly, her body moved again, two spaces forward and two spaces left, where she was suddenly only one square away from Apollo in his raven form.

Truth number two.

Other players moved about the board slowly and the obelisk continued to glow. That's when Vic realized that the questions were not posed out loud. Much like their animal forms were some kind of elaborate hologram, so to were the questions.

But it was confusing looking across the board and not seeing obsidian and crystal pieces. How did one know who to clear from the board?

Theoretically, Chesstopia could have an infinite number of players, if one had a big enough board. While you could choose which piece to move after answering a question correctly, the decision had to still be carefully made. Only one piece could move any way that it pleased, in any direction, and across the entire board if it so pleased. It was the piece that you wanted to both eliminate immediately and simultaneously protect at all costs.

The Significator.

If this was truly Chesstopia, then were they not all Signifcators?

Suddenly, all the squares across the entire board lit up in golden light.

Vic knew this meant that she could now move around anywhere on the board—no longer limited to two steps forward and two steps left. And she knew exactly where she was going to go.

Truth number three.

Chapter Forty-Three
Gal

Gal pouted as much as an eagle could pout, which was actually rather difficult.

He'd watched as Vic's cobra had moved across the board, followed by Athena's owl moving two squares forward and one to the right.

Obviously, they all knew something that he did not.

The voices in his head had gone silent and he let out a rather dignified sigh. As far as he was concerned, this game seemed rather stupid. How exactly was a game of checkers going to get him to Artemis?

As he thought about the goddess, the star of Orion that had been in his pocket pre-transformation seemed to press hot against his skin. But that was impossible.

He looked up to see Vic move closer to where Apollo rested, his raven head drooped weakly. Cal wondered if it were a rouse, or if Apollo's time in Tartarus had truly been that exhausting.

Artemis's beautiful doe glided across the board, moving three spaces forward.

So far every player—this was a game after all, wasn't it?—had moved from their original space except him and Apollo.

And he'd be damned if he was going to have anything in common with that narcissist.

Artemis turned and looked at him her green eyes sharp. For a single second, he swore that her pupils morphed into the shapes of stars before morphing back to round and black. He blinked. She continued to stare at him, did the pupil thing again, and then flicked her tail before turning around.

She knew. All this time as she'd led Cal closer and closer to answers, Artemis knew. She knew that if Apollo had to be ended, then so did she. One could not exist without the other. Above and below. Heaven and hell. Light and dark. Sun and moon. Unafraid, she had led him not only to his fate, but to her own.

Startled, he felt as though a great gush of wind came and moved his majestic eagle body forward so that he now hovered one space forward and one space to his right.

He had moved!

The star of Orion warmed against his skin. And that's when he noticed, he had skin. He looked down. He had fingers. But when he looked up toward Vic, he still had the vision of an eagle.

Perhaps, if he reached into his pocket…

So he took his hand and dipped his fingers into his jeans' pocket and pulled out the locket that contained the star of

Orion. He could see Luna's name carved into it as clear as he could see anything. Were the animals simply illusions? He felt a gentle tug trying to move him forward, as if nudging him that he was indeed on the right track.

If not illusions…then…

He thought back to his mythology lessons in school. How some creatures, like the fae, could use glamours to disguise their true selves. Not unlike how Daphne was hidden behind the glimmer of the tree. Only when one looked close enough, did they actually see the small nymph-like woman who resided within its core.

The great invisible force thrust Cal forward once again. One space forward and one space to the right. He was now getting closer to Artemis.

He was still unsure of what caused his movements. Maybe something like a revelation. First, he'd had the revelation about Artemis. Then he'd had the revelation about their animal forms being more like thinly veiled disguises.

As he pondered, he caught out of the corner of his eye, Vic in her cobra form, suddenly moving forward. He looked at her and if he squinted, he could actually see her body curled within it, as if her human form had curled up in the place where the cobra's heart would be. An idea dawned on him, these glamours—these were their true essences. Vic had the heart of a cobra—fierce, unrelenting, striking, and strong. Artemis had the heart of a doe—docile, contemplative, gentle. And Hades as the ram—stubborn, stable, and always willing to fight. Did he himself then have the heart of an eagle? Was Cal majestic, intelligent, and free? Could he even begin to live up to those kinds of expectations?

As if in answer to his question, the entire Circle of Candor suddenly lit up in golden light. It was as though it were saying to him: *Yes, you are all these things. Yes, this is the truth.*

But what did it mean if the entire board lit up? Had he won? Despite his revelations, he didn't actually feel all that closer to anything or any nearer to victory.

Athena's owl came screeching past him, heading toward Vic and Apollo. It would seem the others had also come to some kind of revelation as well.

Hades came up beside him. Cal could see his small form, as though sleeping, inside the beast's heart space. "We are all Signifcators," he offered by way of explanation, but it made no sense to Cal.

He watched as the two hellhounds raced across the board, heading in Vic's direction.

Hades began to trot after them, but not before turning around and clarifying for Cal. "A Signifcator can move anywhere across the board!"

So that's why the entire board had lit up. Each piece was able to move in a pre-determined fashion, but only upon each revelation. But once one player realized that they were the Significator—that each animal piece was actually a representation of themselves—the board lit up and any player could move in any which way.

Artemis trotted toward him, morphing as she did, slipping seamlessly from her deer form into her familiar goddess form.

"It is time, Callum."

He didn't rightly know how to shake off his eagle form, so instead he ignored it and replied in what he hoped was a telepathic fashion. "Are you sure?"

She nodded, her feathered earrings bobbing. "Never have I been more certain. Once I am gone, it will make my brother even weaker. Since he is my twin, one of us cannot survive while the other still lives. Please."

He felt the star of Orion grow hotter in his fingers, so hot that he nearly dropped it.

"All you must do is peck me here." Her fingers pointed to an area in her neck where his eagle vision could easily see her pulse. "You must be quick and when you do, my essence will escape from here." She pointed to her mouth. "Then you must toss up the star of Orion that Luna has given you. The star shall catch my essence and take me to be with my beloved."

Cal felt the blood drain from his face. "Is that all?"

Artemis gave a small smile. Gone was the quirky waitress from the Rooster. This was the real Artemis. The huntress of legend. The one who was thousands of years old.

Cal studied her. Her green eyes were tired and sad. He wondered if he himself could possibly face a similar fate. What if something happened to Vic—immortals could die. It wasn't easy, but it could happen. What if he ended up having to spend hundreds or thousands of years completely alone? It was one thing to experience a loss and live for decades, it was another to live forever with that loss.

He took a deep breath. Artemis reached out a hand and gently stroked his beak. But he felt the touch across his human cheek.

"You understand love and you are a compassionate person, Callum. It has been much too long that all of this has gone on. Thank you."

She pulled her hand back and closed her eyes. Cal leaned forward and aimed his hooked beak for the precise spot that she had indicated. The star of Orion grew hotter in his fingers, so hot it burned. But he would not let go.

How could he kill her? Was he killing her? Wasn't it more complicated than that?

Suddenly, Athena's tawny-colored owl swooped in his direction, it's small, sharp beak wide open.

"No!" shouted Hades. "It must be Cal!"

And Cal knew this, so in one awkward movement, he ripped free of what he now realized was the illusion, since Artemis had broken through and touched his cheek so tenderly. He returned the gesture, wrapping his arms around her while simultaneously using his beak to peck the precise spot she'd indicated. Artemis' eyes had opened at Hades' shout and now her mouth formed a small O of surprise.

Syrupy near violet blood spurted from the puncture wound and ran down her neck. She reached up and again stroked Cal's cheek and he realized in that moment he had fully morphed back into himself.

"I'm sorry," he whispered. His eyes filled with tears, but Artemis only looked at him with that small, grateful smile before her eyes closed and her hand fell from his check, dropping to her side. Her chest heaved a giant sigh and Cal suddenly remembered the other part to all of this. He held up the star of Orion, ready. His fingers pink and already beginning to blister from its heat. But he didn't care, because he knew his immortality would quickly heal any wounds.

Artemis released the sigh, and her mouth fell open. A shimmering golden mist escaped from her lips.

Athena flapped nearby. "Now!"

He thumbed open the heart-shaped locket and the white-hot orb flew out. It passed through the golden mist which seemed to wrap around it like a lasso.

It began to ascend but not before there was the sound of something crashing through the forest, snapping tree branches.

A gigantic white wolf—Luna—ran into the Circle of Candor and then leaped into the air breaking through the star and mist. The golden mist grew larger and swirled around her. And to Cal's amazement it began to lift the wolf higher into the air. The brilliant white star was like a locomotive, pulling the golden mist behind it—Artemis' essence acting like a net that carried the wolf up into the sky.

It was the Winter Solstice—the shortest day of the year—and the sky was already growing dark, turning indigo.

The constellation of Orion hovered in the sky and it somehow seemed brighter than Cal had ever noticed before.

The missing star hurtled faster and faster until a sparkling comet-like tail trailed behind it. Luna was growing smaller and smaller and suddenly that star met its destination, crashing into Orion's belt and bursting into a blinding white light.

Cal's ears sounded like he was immersed under water, but he could hear shouts around him. Yet he stood still. Transfixed.

When the brilliant light faded, the sky revealed a new constellation. A woman with long hair and an archery bow in one hand, a large wolf at her heels. One of the woman's hands rested on the shoulder of the hunter. The constellation was a clear outline now of Orion, not just a hodgepodge of stars, and Orion turned his head and looked at his beloved. And in that moment Cal saw the outlines fade and only stars remained—as if he were looking at a connect the dots page waiting to be completed. He choked back tears.

He felt a hand on his own shoulder and turned to see Athena back into her human form standing behind him.

He looked down and a pool of blood was still at his feet but he noticed Artemis' body was no longer there. Yet he hadn't seen her pulled up into the constellation. Only her essence as she had said.

"Immortal bodies are different," Athena said noticing his confusion. "Once our essence is gone, the vessel can no longer survive because it's no longer needed."

"But where did it go?"

Athena shrugged. "It isn't so different from ashes to ashes, dust to dust. Although it's much quicker. And cleaner. One moment you are, and the next one you simply are not."

Cal looked down at his feet once again. Millennia of existence, simply gone in the blink of an eye. He looked up to the sky again. But she was happy. He was sure of that. Finally, Artemis was where she wanted to be.

A gut wrenching scream broke his contemplation bringing him back to the Circle of Candor and the Tower of Truth. And back to the mission at hand. The prophecy. Of only which one half was completed.

"Come on," Athena said. "You have more than proved your worthiness to battle. And now, Vic needs us."

Chapter Forty-Four

Vic

The sky burst into brilliant white light and the world seemed to stand still.

Apollo groaned in between Poseidon and Ares. With the acknowledgement of the illusion, the gods now morphed between animal and human form at random. For Vic, a cobra was not practical unless it was to strike. And a cobra only struck when it was ready to kill.

She used the collective moment of awe struck to make her way closer. She was burning up. The same sensation she would get when she could no longer control her emotions, as if her body was burning from the inside out. It was how she felt when she was furious at Asher or had wanted to kill Apollo for harming Persephone.

Except this time was different. She wasn't mad. She was determined.

The vile around her neck was like a talisman, reminding her of her duty. Her duty to Leto. Her duty to Artemis. To Daphne. Her duty to the town of Olympia. None of them deserved the losses that Apollo had brought to them. It was time to end this.

She knew that without Artemis, Apollo was even weaker. But she also knew a god as ancient as he was also strong. And a god as narcissistic as he was would put up a fight. She also knew that no one else could help her. It had to be her.

Cal had fulfilled his role, now she had to fulfill hers. It was the only way for balance to be restored and for the Void to be closed.

Vic remembered a science lesson with her father in which they'd discussed natural disasters. Her father had explained that it was Mother Nature's way of restoring balance. In the end, nature always won.

Ares had retained his boar form and stood with a tether in his snout. Poseidon was in his human form, his long blonde curls loose around his shoulders, holding the other end of the tether in his fist. Snow fell around the Circle of Candor, but it was as though an invisible dome surrounded them and no snow ever touched them or where they stepped.

Apollo was now doubled over in his human form, but his hair retained hints of raven amongst the blonde curls. Still he sagged from the restraints. Iron rings encircled his ankles.

He lifted his head and his bird eyes dilated at her approach.

"Let's make this easy," Vic said. It was going to be her one and only offer. "End this now."

"You know," he said in her mind. "At one time they thought my sister and I were the ones that were foretold. One of light and one of dark."

"The foretold was about doing something good," Vic replied. "There is not a single good bone in your body. Your mother even told me that you tried to destroy Artemis even from inside the womb." She'd tucked the vial back beneath her shirt. She did not want Apollo to know the power that she weld.

"And had I succeeded she wouldn't be in the predicament of which she now finds herself."

"It's not a predicament. It was a choice she made willingly. That seems to be something that you don't understand. You think that everyone's choices need to revolve around you, and when they don't, you take the choices away. All these millennia, and still you're nothing but a petulant child." Vic was saying the words out loud and Ares snorted.

"Indeed. And a petulant child certainly would not go down without a fight."

Suddenly the lit up squares around them flashed rapidly and Apollo disappeared. Iron cuffs clattered to the ground.

"Shit," Ares grunted at the same time Poseidon said, "What the…?"

She heard Cal call out: "There! Vic, he's turned into a mouse!" His eagle eyes had seen what they all had missed right in front of their faces.

Each god had many animal forms. Her father could become a ram, a serpent, or a screech owl. He too had bat wing appendages, but those came solely with the human form. Apollo's forms included crows, ravens, hawks…and mice. Which seemed fitting given his parasitic, deceptive nature.

Some creatures simply needed to thrive off of others to survive.

Irritated, Vic quickly morphed into her cobra form. It felt seamless now, like slipping easily into another skin.

Her predator eyes quickly spotted her pray, a tawny field mouse at the base of the Tower of Truth.

She hadn't expected Apollo to give in willingly, but part of her had hoped he'd see that this needed to end. That he would see reason. He was weakened without Artemis alive. And even now in her death, he still couldn't allow her the peace that she deserved.

Vic headed toward Apollo, her body moving like an eel through water. First, she needed to catch him. Then she could worry about making him drink the blood that would end his life. End the games. End all of this.

Zeus in his bull form tried to corner the small mouse, but it was futile because there wasn't much anyone else could do. They all knew that it could only be Vic, so the best that they could do was try to help her.

"Turning into a mouse is cowardly, even for you!" Zeus' voice boomed across the circle.

But Apollo didn't care about cowardice, as long as he got whatever it was that he wanted in the end. Or evaded the justice that he so rightfully deserved. The mouse danced in and out of Zeus' hooves, making figure eights until Zeus got frustrated and morphed back into his human form.

Apollo darted away making for the outer rim of the Circle of Candor, but staying along its edge. Vic rounded near the edge and felt a humming against her skin. Indeed, it did seem as if they were trapped inside by some sort of invisible force field. Apollo could not escape, whether he'd realized it or not.

Her cobra vision was nuanced enough to notice the slightest movements of the smallest creatures. It was like hellhound vision times a thousand. Her ears picked up the flapping of wings and Vic knew that one set belonged to Athena and that other belonged to Cal. Bird also hunted mice.

Apollo scurried in and out of quadruped legs, evading capture. But he was slow. Artemis' demise and his months in Tartarus had weakened not only his body, but his mind.

There was a high-pitched squeal as Cal dove down in his beautiful eagle form and grasped Apollo by the tail in his sharp, curved beak. It was stained purple with Artemis' blood.

Vic saw that Apollo shook back and forth and knew that he was trying to morph into a different form. The Olympians had been alive so long that what seemed cumbersome to Vic and Cal, was as natural as breathing to them.

"He's trying to morph!" Vic called out telepathically in warning. And then she had an idea.

She curled up her cobra body so that it formed a ring and called out to Cal once again. "Bring him here!"

Cal didn't ask questions.

Instead he nose-dived straight for Vic who sat with her back half curled up in rings on itself. Apollo squirmed and Vic worried that Cal, unused to his eagle form, would drop the rodent. But he didn't. He landed in the tight ring Vic had formed, and she immediately lunged.

As her poisonous fangs sank into the furry body, Cal morphed into his human form and rolled away from her. Apollo gasped as the bite hit his tiny blood stream and he began to slowly morph into his human form, the process hindered by both the poison of Vic's fangs and his twin's death.

When Vic was back in her human form, she scampered over to Apollo and gripped him by the neck. The other Olympians formed a tight ring—back in their human form—around them. His nose still twitched and there were patches of fur on his face and neck. His eyes were beady and frantic.

She pulled the vial from beneath her collar. Apollo's eyes widened—half blue and half black, his pupils large and fearful.

He shook his head, but Vic's grip was like stone and he barely moved.

Popping the vial with her teeth and spitting out the cork, Zeus stepped into the circle and held his son's head still, using his thumb to open his bottom lip. And before Apollo could react, Vic poured the blood into his mouth. Zeus pressed his son's mouth firmly shut.

"The web is spun. Destiny is weaved," she mumbled.

Apollo let out a gurgling sound. It was pathetic and weak much like he was. Often times, it's the weak ones who leave this world the meekest.

His eyes rolled back into his head and Zeus waited several moments before releasing his son. He took his lightning bolt and waved it over Apollo's body, turning it into stone which then cracked and began to crumble into dust.

Suddenly, a gust of wind came. Whatever force field that had been keeping them all on the board during the twisted game of truth, was gone. Snow and wind rushed in and in a cyclone of winter, the dust and debris of Apollo's body was gone just like that. Millennia of life and destruction. Simply swept away by a cold winter's wind.

"The worlds are now cleaved," a voice said.

They all had been staring in disbelief, and Vic was still kneeling next to where Apollo's body had been her hand suspended in mid-air, the vial empty.

Her father put a hand on her shoulder and she turned. The Circle of Candor and the Tower of Truth had disappeared around them. Now they simply stood in a clearing of snow surrounded by both pine trees and barren trees.

The voice had belonged to a tall, skeletal woman with shaggy black hair.

"Arachne."

Athena scowled and crossed her arms. "I should have known you were up to no good."

"It's not up to no good. It's simply when destiny is involved, I follow."

But Vic was focused on the words that she had said. "The worlds are now cleaved?"

Arachne nodded. She was dressed in a simple white dress despite the cold temperature. She gestured to Vic's wrist. The bracelet she had worn was gone. Instead there was a pink mark around her wrist, like a burn mark except it didn't hurt. She didn't feel anything. Not pain, not happiness, not relief. Nothing. This isn't what she'd thought victory would feel like.

"It never does," Arachne replied as if she had read her mind. She closed her eyes and tilted her head. "Listen."

Vic closed her eyes and so did the other Olympians. The sound of falling snow and snow sliding from tree branches to the forest floor were the only sounds that met their ears. There was no despairing howl from the Void. Olympia was saved. The balance had been restored and for now Chaos would call on another day.

"Now what?" Vic asked.

"And now, you decide," Arachne replied. "The balance may have been restored, but the Olympians do not belong in this world. For too long, they have caused havoc on mortals. And since you are the one light and one dark of the foretold, and have restored the balance of the universe by defeating the light and dark of old, destiny's gift to you is a decision. While the other Olympians will return to the Under World and to Mount Othyrs to reside with the remaining Titans and Primoridals, thanks to your unification of the blood lines, the two of you—generations much separated from the tales of old—get to decide. In which realm will you reside?"

Vic turned and looked at the gods behind them. Hades and Cal stood off to the side. She knew that if she went to the Under World, she could go to Mount Othrys whenever she wanted. If Cal chose that, then she could still see him anytime she wanted. And he could still visit her at home in the Under World. But if he didn't choose that, if he chose to stay behind with Rachel and his sisters, she would never be able to see him again.

Her stomach lurched at the thought.

Could she really never see Cal again? On the other hand, could she really never see her parents ever again?

Her blood hummed in response and she knew her decision. Actually, she had always known. Because you cannot outrun who you truly are. You cannot deny your true nature. The only thing that you can do is own it.

Epilogue

The deer stood still.

Its right ear twitched. It could sense danger was nearby. Snow fell around its feet. It was a late snow—mid-April, so the air had a chill, but the earth had begun to retain a warmth to it. Everything was wet and gray.

The deer did not see the cobra that slithered from the cover of daffodils breaking through the snow until it was too late.

The cobra shifted into a girl with dark hair in a long braid that fell over her left shoulder. This way was quicker. One strike and the deer was felled with minimal blood. The poison from the cobra's fangs took care of most of the work.

Vic slid the motionless deer onto a tarp that she pulled from her back pack and then moved the tarp across the snow.

This time she had been lucky. The deer wasn't all that far from the entrance to Arachne's cave, and this particular deer should last her the remainder of this particularly long winter and well into the rest of spring.

She left the deer on the tarp outside of the entrance to Arachne's cave and turned to head back to where she'd parked her truck closer to the main road.

Her mother had delayed spring, staying in the Under World with Hades much longer than usual much to Demeter's chagrin. She always looked forward to her daughter's return visit, regardless of how short it seemed.

But Persephone had insisted on being sure that Vic was well-adjusted to her new role. Despite both her assurances and even her father's, Persephone had an underlying fear that the events that unfolded in the Circle of Candor were not absolute. That perhaps there was a universal loophole, when in fact, Vic was the one who had found the loophole. Not the other way around.

She'd chosen to stay in the Under World, as much as she loved Olympia and being a normal teenager, she knew that she was anything but normal. And never would be normal. She was the Princess of Darkness and always would be. If Artemis and Apollo had taught her anything, it was that you cannot outrun who you are. And that you could use your life for three things: to do good, to do bad, or to just simply exist. Vic decided she wanted to do the former.

So she'd asked Zeus and her father, if it was possible—now that the veil between worlds was closed and the other Olympians returned to Mount Othrys to reside with the remaining Titans and Primoridals, away from the temptation to interfere in the affairs of mortals—to be an ambassador of sorts.

She could relay messages to those that resided in the Above World. She'd made a promise to Arachne, which she was bound to fulfill. Sure, Richard and Anastasia's family could have been tasked with that for all eternity and each subsequent generation, but why keep them bound to the Hadens? Why not let them be free without the unpredictable burden being friends with the Hadens could sometimes bring? This way, as an ambassador, Vic could also take care of her father's Above World affairs, as well as those of any other god that chose to keep certain ties to the mortal world.

But more importantly this would allow her to see her Cal. And so Zeus and her father had approved of this suggestion. That although the veil between worlds was now closed, Vic would be allowed passage to and from the Above World to fulfill her duty to Arachne and act as a liaison between the gods and mortals that maintained business relationships. It was the perfect scenario to give her exactly what she wanted—and what she sometimes needed. It was hard to un-see the perfect imperfectness of the Above World, after living in just her small realm of darkness for so long. To feel snowflakes on your tongue and the wind whip against your cheeks and to breathe in crisp, fresh winter air. She wasn't sure she could ever again live without it.

Vic reached her truck and climbed inside. The veil may be closed, but there was still a way to enter the Below World. Pythia had returned to Mount Othrys and her shop, the House of Snakes, stood abandoned. As far as a passerby could see it simply was closed indefinitely without rhyme or reason, but people in Olympia weren't exactly the type to go about asking questions.

Inside, the shop was empty, but if no one was looking, Vic could ease her truck up the sidewalk and straight through the front door with its intricate wooden snake carving and come out the other side in the Under World.

The best enchantments always held an element of truth.

Vic cranked the air conditioning as she drove past the various domains. River, looking youthful with flawless skin and a svelte figure, waved as she drove across the bone bridge and over the River Styx.

She meandered up the winding drive and barely had the truck in park before the door opened and someone ran up to greet her.

"You were gone longer than I thought you'd be!"

Vic climbed out of the truck. "Well, you know I had to fell that deer for Arachne, check on my dad's investments, and of course, wanted to drive by the manor and say hello to Richard. I couldn't have been gone more than a few hours."

"Half a day," Cal shrugged.

"Oh, I have something for you!" She reached back into the truck and pulled out a box of apple cinnamon muffins. "Rachel baked these!"

"You stopped at the shop."

"Of course I did. I still have to eat in the Above World." But they both knew that was not the only reason. "She hopes you'll visit soon. She knows you're getting adjusted still. She just misses you."

While Vic had made a decision, so too had Cal.

Cal, inspired by Persephone, had decided to eat six seeds of a pomegranate from one of the many trees that lined the Hadens' driveway. He would stay in the Under World, with Vic and her family for six months of the year—and potentially visit Mount Othrys to see Nyx and Uranus—and then spend another six months in the Above World, helping Rachel and his sisters. He would outlive all of them, Rachel being a mortal, and his sisters being half-immortal. And once he was no longer needed by his adopted family, he would eat another six pomegranate seeds and stay with Vic permanently in the Under World.

"I'll go up soon. Maybe in June and be back in time for Christmas. Who knows maybe I'll even bring you back a Christmas tree!"

Vic reached around his neck and kissed him. "Christmas is my absolute favorite. And now I get to spend them with you!"

He laughed and kissed her back. It had been an easy decision to make. Artemis had lost her love and wanted nothing but to be with him. So much so that she'd become nearly a shade of who she had been—the huntress. The leader of the pack. The bright illumination of the moon's wisdom had reminded him that love was hard to find and even harder to keep—especially for an immortal. He realized while he was air and lightness, and Vic darkness, that they were a perfect complement. He was not afraid to lift her from her darkness when she needed it and encourage her to shine, and she made him realize that despite his own darkness, he could persevere and not let it consume him. That both things could co-exist. That when they weren't distorted and used for personal gains, that the two opposites could in fact exist harmoniously. Artemis had reminded him that love does not bind us to the world, but that it has the ability to set us free.

Cal pulled back and raised an eyebrow. "Should we share these with anyone?"

"Definitely not with the hellhounds. I would have needed to bring at least two dozen," Vic laughed.

"Your parents?"

"Maybe. But my dad is just as bad as the hellhounds."

Cal agreed and slung an arm across Vic's shoulders as they walked back toward the ominous obsidian castle that he now called home half of the year. Over the last few months, he'd learned that cold exteriors could often hide warm interiors.

Laughter met them as they pulled open the large door, a crystal skull knocker smiling at them in greeting. River had told Vic that if she drank from the Styx that she could forget. And her mother had told her the pain wasn't in the remembering, but in the forgetting. Apollo had thought he could inflict pain on Artemis and make her forget Orion. But Vic knew what Apollo had not: that Artemis would not give up her memories of Orion willingly because the pain of forgetting him would supersede the pain of losing him. Apollo had greatly underestimated the strength of his twin.

The laughter of her parents from inside the castle, the smile on Cal's face and the comforting scent of cinnamon and apple wafting up from the box under Cal's arm, the other arm slung across her shoulders. This right here was the very thing she never ever wanted to forget.

...

In the Above World a waif of a girl with dirty blonde hair and a burlap sack of a dress stumbled out of a dead, burnt out tree. Something glinted among the dead root system, catching the early spring sunlight, and it had caught her eye. It was a glass vial.

Not many people left her gifts anymore.

Tiny words were written in black marker on the side of the vial: *Drink and forget.* The girl knew that she had spent hundreds of years working to remember. To never forget. But she was tired. Bone-achingly tired. She wanted to start over. She wanted a new beginning, more importantly, she wanted her life back. With what little physical strength she had left, the girl popped the cork out of the vial and drank from it.

The End

Acknowledgements

As always thank you to my dad for reading (and editing and reading again) all of my books. From book one to now book nineteen!

Thank you to my paternal grandmother (Grandma Bee) who has read ALL of my books and from whom my dad and I inherited our voracious love of reading.

And thank *you*, Dear Reader, if you have been waiting since 2019 for this last book in the House of Snakes trilogy. This manuscript was actually written during NaNoWriMo 2020, but life—pandemics, moving houses and cities, the passing of my fur child, changing jobs not once but twice!—just got in the way. For that I'm sorry to have kept you waiting for 3 years and hope that you can forgive me.

About the Author

Jennifer L. Kelly currently is a digital marketing professional extraordinaire. In a past life, she was a middle school teacher, a production coordinator for a materials science society, and a wizard at making candles. She currently resides in Northeastern Ohio near the shores of Lake Erie.

When she isn't writing, she can be found flying through space time in the TARDIS with the Doctor, hanging out in the Gryffindor Common Room, or tackling her never-ending TBR list.

She is the author of the YA dystopian series The Lucia Chronicles and the YA fantasy sci-fi series The Elementals. Visit her website www.jenniferlkelly.com.

Books by Jennifer L. Kelly

__Young Adult__

House of Snakes Trilogy
House of Snakes
Sword & Air
Princess of Darkness

The Lucia Chronicles Trilogy
The Prophecy
The Dissentient
The Beacon
The Girl Who Wasn't Loved (Novella)

The Elementals Series
Army of Fire
The Earth Key
Genesis of Wood
The Water Queen
Secret of Metal
A Vessel for Darkness (Novella)

__Women's Fiction/Young Adult Fiction__

The Fractured Life of Jenny McClain

__Children's Books__

Lizzy or Liz, Never Elizabeth and the Unbirthday
Lizzy or Liz, Never Elizabeth and the Peanut Kid
The Moon People

__Non- Fiction__

Living Authentically

__Coloring Book__

Mind Power: An A-Z Coloring Book of Positivity

www.ingramcontent.com/pod-product-compliance
Lightning Source LLC
Chambersburg PA
CBHW020600310726
48979CB00008B/1290/J
9780999201763